The Golden

Manuscripts:

A Novel

Between Two Worlds (Book 6)

Evy Journey

Sojourner Books

BERKELEY CALIFORNIA

The Golden Manuscripts /Evy Journey. -- 1st ed.
Editor: David Rose
Book Layout ©2013 BookDesignTemplates.com
ISBN 978-0-9962474-9-8

To Richard Journey
For his love of art and music

I feel like I've never had a home, you know? I feel related to the country, to this country, and yet I don't know exactly where I fit in ... There's always this kind of nostalgia for a place, a place where you can reckon with yourself.

SAM SHEPARD

1979 Pulitzer Prize, Drama

Never make your home in a place. Make a home for yourself inside your own head. You'll find what you need to furnish it – memory, friends you can trust, love of learning, and other such things. That way it will go with you wherever you journey.

TAD WILLIAMS

Table of Contents

April 1945

Spoils of War: East Germany

Everyone knew the end was near. But so much still needed to
be done.

Hands on hips, shoulders stooped, and eyes weary, he
stared at a dozen or so wooden crates. He stood before them,
paralyzed, his body and spirit exhausted. Three years in
training camps and on the battlefields—that was how much
time this senseless war had stolen from his life. But for him, it
was a lifetime of horror no one else could fathom who had not
experienced it. Those years were about to end, and yet he
couldn't say he felt relieved. Another life was waiting for
him—a life of peace his fellow survivors couldn't wait to return
to. But he wasn't ready. He needed a sense of closure for the
life of war he was leaving. But how? Could anyone rise out of
the ashes of hell he had been through?

Had it only been a day or two since his battalion crossed
the border into Germany from Belgium? They had been
among the first to breach enemy territory. They had also been
among the first deployed into the European Theater in 1943,
landing in Sicily to fight the Germans.

In only a matter of days, the Allied Forces expected the
Nazis to surrender.

He was lucky, he was aware of that, having seen too many dead bodies. After a while, it no longer mattered to him what uniforms they wore. They had all perished in service of a mad monster and his cadre of fiendish lackeys.

This morning, the platoon lieutenant told him he was to lead his squad into a cave on Harz, a mountain range that extended down to a few small towns. The battalion commander had been informed of precious objects hidden in the cave by a historic medieval church in one of those towns. His squad had to secure and guard it, and he had been singled out to inspect the condition of the cave, and to inventory its contents. Why him, he wondered, but for a mere second. He was not sent to this war to think. He was here to follow orders. The end was near and that was all he cared about.

His squad had driven to the cave on a road winding through forested hills unspoiled by bombs. They found no one around the cave and no attempt had been made to cover its opening. He posted a couple of his men at the entrance, telling them no one was allowed to enter without his permission.

Inside, he had expected the cave to smell musty and foul. But the air, though it exuded an earthiness he could almost taste, had a lightness to it that made it easy to breathe in. It helped that a cool breeze from the densely forested mountain outside was blowing through the entrance to the cave.

The light in the cave was diffused, not as dark as he had anticipated, and after a few minutes his eyes had adapted enough to see the wooden crates more clearly. He hadn't needed a flashlight to see that each had a number on top and on the side written in white paint.

Dull and wearisome as his task might prove to be, away from the action of wrapping up an unfortunate war, he believed safeguarding this bunch of crates was an important and necessary task, if only to show the enemy that, unlike them, Americans were not pillaging marauders. Rumors of Nazi plunder of cultural treasures from the countries they invaded had been circulating ever since his battalion's deployment in Sicily.

He walked around the crates stacked in five groups. Four had three crates each and one stack had four. Sixteen crates. He needed to know exactly what the cave held. In making a list of objects in the cave, he was ensuring that the contents of crates his squad found when they arrived would be the same when they left.

Each crate held a cardboard box he could see through the wooden slats. What those boxes contained might not be priceless artworks like those the Nazis plundered in the European countries they invaded, especially France. But they were precious to the people to whom they belonged. Why else would they have bothered to hide them in this cave? Left in the church, they would have become spoils of war. Or worse, had Allied bombs hit the church, the contents of these crates would have been lost forever. Shattered to smithereens or burned to dust.

He was sure there could be no paintings in the crates. Those would have been secured singly in their own wooden crates. He estimated the crates to be two feet by two feet at most, inside of which were even smaller boxes.

From history classes as an art major at a state university north of his hometown, he knew that in wars dating as far back as ancient times, victors harvested with impunity treasures from countries they conquered—trophies of war to which triumphant Greeks, Romans, other Europeans, Muslims,

Christians all felt entitled. In more recent times, Napoleon Bonaparte was notorious for ordering the sacking of Italy, stripping it of all the masterpieces his army could find. His subsequent defeat at Waterloo led to the return of about half of his loot, but the rest remained in France, many of them displayed at the Louvre Museum.

In this current war, France could be said to have gotten its comeuppance, as Hitler and his rapacious commanders plundered France's art treasures. An untold number of those treasures, along with so many more from other European countries Hitler invaded, had been hidden in mine shafts and caves in Germany.

Some American soldiers also made off with a few things. Mere souvenirs, though, from dead and captured enemies or in houses and other buildings where occupants had fled or been captured and thrown into concentration camps. Inevitable spoils of war, whose value could never equal the highly prized treasures Napoleon and the Nazis took. To these, the Allied military command turned a blind eye. He himself had pocketed some beautiful silverware and ornaments from a house in what used to be a rich Jewish neighborhood—now desolate and empty—in a small nearby city. The house had been abandoned, and he had no qualms helping himself to a few souvenirs. But he hoped the Jewish family had fled somewhere safe.

It was only mid-morning, and his limbs were already quivering. It puzzled him, these attacks of restlessness amidst his exhaustion. He had no energy to spare. After a couple of years in the battlefield, his body had grown stronger and nimbler, attuned to constant, unpredictable stress. Lately, as the war wound down, inactivity after long periods of high-adrenaline war maneuvers, tired him out more. And yet, while recovering from exhaustion and resting, his muscles could suddenly clench and burn, ready for action.

He looked around for a rock to sit on. Finding none, he eyed the crates, walked towards a corner stack, and eased his butt down to it. A long breath of relief hissed out of his puckered lips. He loosened his hold on the notepad he had been clutching in his right hand and let it drop on the stack of crates next to him.

Staring blankly at the crate on top, his restless fingers brushed against the wooden slats back and forth. Back and forth. A finger poked through the slats. Then he inserted another.

His index and middle fingers touched the box underneath. After the rough surface of the wood, the cardboard box inside was smooth. Soothing almost. What did it hold? Was there a reason it was on top? Something fragile?

Could there be something in these boxes he could take as a souvenir? A token trophy for being on the side that won. A gold-lined silver chalice to hold wine during mass maybe? Something the church could easily replace.

Before he knew what he was doing, he had yanked the top wooden cover and ripped off the tape that secured the cardboard box inside the crate. The uncovering was the work of seconds. The notepad had fallen on the floor.

The contents of the box peeked out of the freed flaps. He thought he saw a flicker of light through the flaps. The glitter of gold maybe? The chalice?

His eager hands swiped the flaps to the side. It wasn't a chalice that emitted the flicker of light, but a rectangular object wrapped in a luminescent orange cloth. Trembling

5

hands lifted the object. The cloth, soft and silky, was neatly wrapped around the object. It was heavier than he thought. He lowered the object on an unopened crate and unwrapped it.

He stared, uncertain what to make of the object. Something gold-plated, tarnished by air, time, and use to a murky green. He could detect streaks of an antique gold color breaking through the tarnish.

But that wasn't all he marveled at: high-relief figures, possibly also gold-plated, were carved inside a rectangular frame in the middle. Red, white, lavender, green, and blue stones of various sizes were embedded in bezels around the frame. Precious stones? Pearls, for sure. Amethyst. Maybe rubies, emeralds, and sapphires. Or colored glass?

He peeked into the box again—another rectangular object wrapped in cloth. Not orange but cerulean blue, and slightly smaller. He picked it up. Soft and silky as well. Gently, he laid it on the first object.

The box wasn't empty yet, and what remained wasn't wrapped in cloth. Inserting his fingers deeper into an edge of the box, he felt what seemed like the spine of books. Two of them. He lifted each one. Bibles, he concluded. No fancy covers, only leather fraying on the edges, and scratched up. Quite old, he was sure. He put the bibles back in the box.

He was certain, then, that the objects wrapped in cloth were also bibles. Maybe rare, centuries-old bibles. Much more precious than the unwrapped ones. Gently, he peeled the blue cloth off the second object. The cover was not as elaborate as that on the first book. Carved figures were set in a frame spanning the height of the book and only six stones were embedded on both sides of the rectangular frame.

He turned the book over on its edges, then on its back. Quite old, he contended, from the patina of age on its cover, its somewhat uneven surface, and wrinkling on the pages' edge. He expected it to stink, but it didn't. Whatever smell it had was subtle. He rewrapped the book and set it down next to the first book.

The first book, larger and thicker with its stone-studded cover, was likely older. Even more carefully than the second book, he rewrapped it in its orange cloth.

For a minute or so, he fixed his gaze on the books, sitting as still as he could to fight an impulse, a temptation seizing his whole body. His chest heaved faster, his jaw clenched, his muscles twitched. He curled and uncurled his fists. He took several long, deep breaths. In, out ... In, out ... In ... But he was powerless to resist. The impulse was too strong.

He lifted the first book, aware but not caring that he lost the battle with himself a little too quickly. Would it fit? He guessed 12 by 9 inches. He was tall and lean, but broad shouldered, and his army jacket had grown too big on him. War had taken a toll on his body.

He slipped the book into the left side of his jacket. The added thickness was hardly noticeable. He picked up the second book, slipped it into the right side and zipped his jacket halfway up. The band at the waist was tight enough to secure the books to his chest.

He pried the wooden cover off another crate and ripped off the tape on the box inside. Again, he stared, incredulous. Another rectangular, intricately decorated object. He inserted a hand to take it out of the box, and found he needed both hands.

Laying the object on top of an unopened crate, he saw that it was much thicker than the books. It was not a book, but a box. A box unlike anything he had ever seen before. On its front, a series of figures were deeply embossed from one end to the other. Like the statues atop the door on the façade of the Paris Notre Dame. He ran his fingers across the figures and realized the box was made of wood. The object was a wooden casket.

Flipping the sculptured latch on the cover, he opened the casket. Inside, an ivory comb glowed in the low light, and several finely chiseled rock crystals set in gold or silver bases emitted rays of color. He picked up one of the rock crystals, brought it close to his face and turned it over. Something was inside. He brought it closer to his eyes, peering into it intently. A tiny piece of cloth. The crystal was a tiny container.

He picked up another rock crystal, then another. Bright, luminous colors reflected out of each one. Peeking into a couple more, he detected fragments of bones or stones in each of them. *Reliquaries*, he thought, the casket and the crystals. He put the crystals back in the casket. Imagining he heard footsteps, he craned his neck towards the entrance. But he saw no one, not even a shadow.

The world outside basked under a brighter sun. The chill inside the cave had dissipated. It must be past noon. He hadn't eaten anything before going into the cave and he was hungry.

As he was about to put the wooden casket back in its box, his eyes drifted to the ivory comb. What was this object of feminine vanity doing among religious objects? Was it also a relic? It did look at home in the casket, like a queen ruling over the crystal reliquaries. Could he take the casket with him? For a moment, he vacillated. No, too obvious. For now. He placed the casket back in its box and secured the top flaps. He closed the flaps on the box of bibles as well.

His gaze swept across the crates around him and caught sight of another light object on the ground. He remembered then—the inventory. The task he was ordered to do.

He bent to retrieve the notepad from the floor. A quick inventory wasn't going to take him a whole afternoon. He only had a few crates to examine and catalog. The inventory could wait. It was more urgent for him to secure his souvenirs deep in his combat pack and send them home by Army Mail as soon as he could.

Before he left the cave, he shoved his hands into the pockets of his leather jacket, pushing his knuckles forward. He looked down on his jacket. No sharp edges or corners were showing through. He flexed the muscles on his face and relaxed them, making sure nothing about him would excite curiosity. As he exited, he instructed the guards not to let anyone in. He would return after lunch to finish his inventory.

*****

Alone in his tent, his mind preoccupied with his recent finds, he chewed the soft chunk of meat from his k-ration longer than was needed to tear it into pieces small enough to swallow. The reliquary casket would be impossible to carry out of the cave without attracting attention. He needed something to hide or camouflage it in. Putting down his can of uneaten k-ration on the ground, he rummaged in his combat bag for a shirt ripped at the shoulder that he had not thrown out.

By two in the afternoon, he returned to the cave, the shirt crunched up into his jacket pocket. Inside the cave, he opened the other crates and listed their contents. When he finished his inventory, he slid the wooden casket and the treasures it held into the opening of the shirt and folded the shirt around the casket. Taking a few objects out of the other boxes, he placed them in the now-empty box that had held the casket.

He found sixteen crates when he first entered the cave and they—the church, most likely—were going to recover sixteen. Eventually, church personnel would realize some items were missing, but that wasn't going to happen for another few weeks, maybe months. The cave was off-limits to all but those permitted by Allied military command.

That night he waited for his tent mates to go to bed before taking his new souvenirs out of his combat pack. He ran the palm of his hand over the books, still in their silky, protective garb. Sending them across the Atlantic in an army mailbag had become safer. Still, he needed to secure them better. There had to be plastic bags, strings, and paper he could salvage somewhere in the towns around the mountain. They had escaped the bombs that devastated the big cities.

The wooden casket would protect the comb and the crystal reliquaries. He wrapped those in the tattered shirt. But the casket needed a bigger package than the books.

Unlike mail he had always addressed to his parents in the past, he would send his spoils of war to his sister. She had always been to him a confidant who could keep secrets. He wrote a short letter to enclose in the package that held the books—he was sending her two packages of war souvenirs precious to him. She must make sure they would be stored in a secluded corner of his closet where he could retrieve them on his return. She could examine the contents, but she should rewrap them once she had satisfied her curiosity. He told her to lock the closet and where he hid the key. He was going to be home soon.

He had no idea how many weeks it would take for his packages to reach his sister, but he was confident their journey would be quicker. They would be on their way, in any case. Safe from prying eyes. Transported by reliable military mail. Waiting for him to reunite with them.

Chapter One

November 2000

Rare Manuscripts

I sometimes wish I was your girl next door. The pretty one who listens to you and sympathizes. Doesn't ask questions you can't or don't want to answer. Comes when you need to talk.

She's sweet, gracious, respectful, and sincere. An open book. Everybody's ideal American girl.

At other times, I wish I was the beautiful girl with creamy skin, come-hither eyes, and curvy lines every guy drools over. The one you can't have, unless you're a hunk of an athlete, or the most popular hunk around. Or you have a hunk of money.

But I'm afraid the image I project is that of a brain with meager social skills. The one you believe can outsmart you in so many ways that you keep out of her way—you know the type. Or at least you think you do. Just as you think you know the other two.

I want to believe I'm smart, though I know I can be dumb. I'm not an expert on anything. So, please wait to pass judgement until you get to know us better—all three of us.

Who am I then?

I'm not quite sure yet. I'm the one who's still searching for where she belongs.

I'm not a typical American girl. Dad is Asian and Mom is white. I was born into two different cultures, neither of which dug their roots into me. But you'll see my heritage imprinted all over me—on beige skin with an olive undertone; big grey eyes, double-lidded but not deep-set; a small nose with a pronounced narrow bridge; thick, dark straight hair like Dad's that glints with bronze under the sun, courtesy of Mom's genes.

I have a family: Mom, Dad, Brother. Sadly, we're no longer one unit. Mom and Dad are about ten thousand miles apart. And my brother and I are somewhere in between.

I have no one I call friend. Except myself, of course. That part of me who perceives my actions for what they are. My inner voice. My constant companion and occasional nemesis. Moving often and developing friendships lasting three years at most, I've learned to turn inward.

And then there's Arthur, my beautiful brother. Though we were raised apart, we've become close. Like me, he was born in the US. But he grew up in my father's home city where his friends call him Tisoy, a diminutive for Mestizo that sometimes hints at admiration, sometimes at mockery. Locals use the label for anyone with an obvious mix of Asian and Caucasian features. We share a few features, but he's inherited a little more from Mom. Arthur has brown wavy hair and green eyes that invite remarks from new acquaintances.

Little Arthur, not so little anymore. Taller than me now, in fact, by two inches. We've always gotten along quite well. Except the few times we were together when we were children and he'd keep trailing me, like a puppy, mimicking what I did until I got annoyed. I'd scowl at him, run away so fast he couldn't catch up. Then I'd close my bedroom door on him. Sometimes I wondered if he annoyed me on purpose so that later he could hug me and say, "I love you" to soften me up. It always worked.

I love Arthur not only because we have some genes in common. He has genuinely lovable qualities—and I'm sure people can't always say that of their siblings. He's caring and loyal, and I trust him to be there through thick and thin. I also believe he's better put together than I am, he whom my parents were too busy to raise.

I am certain of only one thing about myself: I occupy time and space like everyone. My tiny space no one else can claim on this planet, in this new century. But I still do not have a place where I would choose to spend and end my days. I'm a citizen of a country, though. The country where I was born. And yet I can't call that country home. I don't know it much. But worse than that, I do not have much of a history there.

Before today, I trudged around the globe for two decades. Cursed and blessed by having been born to a father who was a career diplomat sent on assignments to different countries, I've lived in different cities since I was born, usually for three to four years at a time.

Those years of inhabiting different cities in Europe and Asia whizzed by. You could say I hardly noticed them because it was the way of life I was born into. But each of those cities must have left some lasting mark on me that goes into the sum of who I am. And yet, I'm still struggling to form a clear idea of the person that is Me. This Me can't be whole until I single out a place to call home.

Everyone has a home they've set roots in. We may not be aware of it, but a significant part of who we think we are—who others think we are—depends on where we've lived. The place we call home. A place I don't have. Not yet. But I will.

I was three when I left this city. Having recently come back as an adult, I can't tell whether, or for how long, I'm going to stay. You may wonder why, having lived in different places, I would choose to seek a home in this city—this country as alien to me as any other town or city I've passed through.

By the end of my last school year at the Sorbonne, I was convinced that if I were to find a home, my birthplace might be my best choice. I was born here. In a country where I can claim citizenship. Where the primary language is English. My choice avoids language problems and pesky legal residency issues. Practical and logical reasons, I think.

*****

Three years ago, my father announced our wandering days were over and we had to settle on a permanent home. After twenty-five years of service, he was exhausted and wanted to retire while he was still relatively young. Used to having his way, he decreed that home would be the Philippines where he was born, and where he has an extended family of near and far relatives. He would request to be posted there for his last assignment. I'd known for a while that Mom's desire and beliefs would not carry any weight in Dad's decision.

Living with my paternal grandparents much of the time, Arthur could call Dad's birthplace home,

Unlike the rest of my family, I had no place I felt I belonged. I was rootless. No deep loyalty to any place I've lived in. I was born in California and though I spent the first three years of my life there, I grew up in at least six other cities. None of which became home to me.

Rambling around new places and plunging into new cultures—sometimes fascinating, sometimes strange in their novelty—was exciting for a while. It didn't bother me that I was always leaving new friends behind. Mom had always been there. Dad, too. They were the constants in my life I was led to believe were all I needed. So, at eighteen, I had no firm ideas of home. But certain that my father's stint in Paris would last for at least another year, I told myself, I still had time to decide.

For now, I occupy space in the art staff office of the university I attend. At the noon hour on a breezy, clear November day, in a city across the bay from San Francisco. Deep in the season when, east of us, rainstorms are pounding towns and cities, we're still hoping for much-needed rain.

Autumn is not how I expected it to be, moving to this area as an adult. I miss the colors fall brings everywhere east of us. Here, Japanese maples, oaks, and gingkoes also shed leaves in shades of yellow, red, and brown. But they are mere accents to the more abundant eternal greens clinging to pine, citrus, and bamboo trees scattered all over the region. Some nights could be foggy or overcast until early morning, leaving damp sidewalks and dewy trees. By midday, the fog usually gives way to sunny and windy afternoons.

Right now, I'm alone, eating leftover pad thai from the takeout dinner I shared with my brother last night. Sitting at a desk at the back of an open area with two rows of desks where graduate assistants park their belongings. Four feet separate the two rows, each desk in a row set apart by enough room to push a chair back and sit.

The professors we work for occupy small offices bathed in eastern sun, their own little havens outfitted with bigger desks, built-in bookshelves, glass windows and glass-topped walls and doors that give them some privacy.

I've closed the door to the whole office. I relish this tranquil hour of solitude when I can chill out as I listen to easy music and eat lunch. Everyone else has left for the mid-day break and won't be back for at least an hour.

I've been working in this office for three months, but I still don't feel I'm in my element. I'm learning it isn't enough to be part of a group with common interests, working in one place. Maybe, I need more time. I'm the newest graduate assistant, and though we're all art practice majors, I want to specialize in what the art world today might consider an obscure or ancient art form—illuminated manuscripts. An art form which flourished in the medieval period, the printing press pushed it into near extinction.

In between slurping long rice noodles pinched between wooden chopsticks, I scan the news on artnews.com on my laptop—the usual way I pass this hour.

A headline catches my attention:

Long Lost Fifteenth-Century Illuminated Manuscript Found?

I put noodles and chopsticks down across the top of the plastic bowl of half-eaten pad thai and lean my body a little closer to the screen.

Art goes missing, too. Like people. Sometimes for a long time. Every piece of art also needs a home, not necessarily its place of origin. Take the famous Mona Lisa. Except for the two years a thief kept it in a suitcase, depriving the public a quick or long view of it, the painting has resided in the Louvre since the early sixteenth century. The king of France had bought it from Italian painter Leonardo da Vinci.

Most readers would be indifferent to this news of a newly recovered illuminated manuscript if it had been reported by general news sources. They may never have heard of medieval manuscripts, nor cared about them if they knew what they were. A few may wonder why or how manuscripts could be illuminated.

Artists might know a thing or two about them from art history classes, but most artists attend college to sharpen their skills and become better painters, sculptors, conceptual artists, performance artists.

But I'm neither one of those artists, nor a reader with a passing interest in art. To me, this is big news.

Among the four of us who work for Professor Adam Fischl, I'm something of an odd fish, not only because I'm rootless. As far as I can tell, no other graduate student in the art department gets excited about medieval illuminated manuscripts. The creation of illuminated manuscripts is a minor genre compared to canvas or panel painting, or sculpture, or conceptual art. You could even argue it's a dead art. But it was a major and thriving genre during medieval times.

I learned about illuminated manuscripts in an art history class, for which I later wrote a paper on the blossoming of this art form under the reign of Charlemagne. In writing my paper, I realized my interest in illustrated manuscripts has been nurtured from the time my mother read to me. No, she didn't read me illuminated manuscripts. She read picture books.

What, after all, are illuminated manuscripts, but picture books? Granted, of a very special kind. How special? They're handwritten, not printed. On parchment—scraped, stretched, and dried animal skin—capable of lasting centuries. An "illumination" is, in fact, a picture or illustration that conveys the meaning of a piece of text. Adorned with gold or silver leaf, these illustrations radiate light. The first letters of accompanying texts, and other decorations on a page, usually also glow with gold or silver. Sometimes, texts are inscribed in gold or silver ink.

I believe illustrated books have been essential to my awakening as a thinking, feeling being. Aren't they, though, for every child whose parents read them stories?

Children's picture books make it easier to understand the meanings of images through the stories that accompany them. The images can tell you more about a story than words alone can. And quite often, we have happy memories of having picture books read to us.

Tap into your memory bank, as I often have of some of my warmest memories of childhood—cradled on my mother's lap, safe between her arms, while she's holding a large book in front of me. Beautiful, colorful pictures adorn each page. A magical story unfolds below those pictures as she's reading it to me. She's drawing me into the story as she adapts her voice to every character. I always imagine myself as one of the characters. The little heroine, of course.

She reads me one book. But it only whets my appetite. So, she reads me another. And another, if she has time. Some books I like more than others—between their pages live the stories I ask her to read to me over and over.

When I turn five, she teaches me how those stories are built up: First, the letters, the basic elements needed to make up, as well as read, a story. Each letter is presented with a picture on a page—an apple with "A," "B" and a ball, "C" and a cat ... Such is how I began my adventure into reading.

The letters grow into words, their meanings illustrated by more images. The words are strung together to form single ideas. Ideas grow into scenarios. Scenarios grow into stories. And stories come alive with narrative images. All absorbed within the warmth of my mother's love. Typical upbringing, wouldn't you say? A lot like yours.

Except, my picture books are different in one way. The picture books Mom reads to me include many about the life and culture of every new city we land in. Picture books that— I realize later—she chose to help alleviate the problems of transitioning from one city and culture to another. Somehow, Mom always seems to find English versions of those books. One such book is *The Little Prince.*

When as an adult, I returned to Paris, I bought *Le Petit Prince,* the French original, illustrated and written by its author Antoine de Saint-Exupéry. It has remained one of my most-loved books. I read it at least once a year, often at Christmas. It keeps me in touch with the child that's in all of us. It reminds me of the unalloyed wisdom in childhood that growing up often buries in the pursuit of reality and knowledge.

My picture books pile up as we move from one place to another. Sometimes, Mom and I visit museums, often city museums exhibiting local artworks. I became aware at age nine that we're both stockpiling experiences and memories of our short lives in a place we may be leaving forever.

After such an introduction, how can I not believe there's magic in pictures? They contain more than what you see, maybe disguise or hide some deeper meaning than what's obvious. You must look longer, probe deeper to see beyond the images your eyes pick up. Maybe that's why, as a child, I loved games instructing you to find a miniscule or camouflaged image or object in a larger picture.

Artists put details in a painting you may see only as part of the background or landscape. But such details may be symbols or icons for the society, time, and culture the artist lived in. Jan van Eyck's famous *Arnolfini Portrait* is frequently cited as full of symbolism, although art historians have not always agreed on the meanings of specific details. The dog at their feet, for instance, has been thought to symbolize loyalty and devotion. But another historian has proposed it portends the death of the woman in the portrait: Dogs have been found on female tombs in ancient Rome.

Apart from my parents' caring, picture books—the artistry they demand and exhibit—may be the only constant in my past gypsy-like existence. Children's picture books planted a seed in me that blossomed into a love of art.

*****

The artnews.com article is brief. An art dealer is selling a medieval manuscript: handwritten on vellum, the finest parchment made from calf skin; gold leaf and tempera; intact and in good condition. It's a fifteenth-century adaptation of *The Utrecht Psalter.*

No images accompany the article. No manuscript cover. No sample page or two from within the manuscript. Odd that those are missing in a news item for an artwork uploaded to an online marketplace for art. No information is given, either, on who owns it, but that's not unusual. And none on how the manuscript was lost—also odd since this fact is emphasized by its inclusion in the headline. And why the question mark?

The article does say the manuscript is a colorful adaptation of *The Utrecht Psalter*, often cited as possibly the best-known, and in some scholars' opinions, the best manuscript illumination produced during Charlemagne's reign in the ninth century. It captivated many medieval artists who copied its lively and expressive figures sketched in brown ink, running across every page.

Faithful reproductions of this psalter still exist, like *The Harley Psalter*, which anyone can access online in the British Library. Other artists infused their adaptation of *The Utrecht Psalter* with their own style, decorating texts, and using color or painted figures rather than sketches. But until this newly discovered manuscript, I wasn't aware *The Utrecht Psalter*'s influence on later manuscripts reached well into the fifteenth century, at least five hundred years from its creation.

The question mark baffles me. What can it mean? Uncertainty about the manuscript's authenticity? Was it produced in the 15th century as claimed?

The art world has had its problems with artists who can create copies of masterpieces good enough to pass off and sell as originals. Forgers, we call them, though they're usually highly skilled artists. And the copies they produce, we call fakes instead of the more neutral term 'reproduction.' Fakes are usually passed off as originals of well-known masterpieces or as previously unknown artworks by old masters like Rembrandt, DaVinci, Michelangelo, Vermeer, and by later ones like Cezanne, Van Gogh, Matisse, Picasso, Gauguin, and Manet—artists whose works are guaranteed to attract big money.

I have no idea how much this particular manuscript would fetch in the art market. Who collects them? Only libraries and museums and rich collectors of rare books? I know an artwork's provenance can make a difference in its sale. Is it in question? Who owns it now? How was it lost? How was it recovered and by whom? Who did it belong to before the current owners? If somewhere in its journey to the present, evidence surfaces of this manuscript having been stolen, then the art dealer and its owner may find it impossible to sell.

This piece of news wouldn't cause a blip in the public radar. But the discovery of original manuscripts as old as the fifteenth century gets art historians and certain art dealers excited. If for no other reason than that an old unique artwork can fetch a lot of money.

What a privilege and an experience it would be not only to see this once lost manuscript underneath its protective glass case. But also, to leaf through its pages. Feast my eyes on its illustrations. It's a psalter so it contains psalms. But who created it and where (that is, which scriptorium)? Was its scribe also the illustrator? Does it have a traceable history from its creation and initial ownership to whoever claims to own it now? Could it be a quest that I can plunge into? That can consume me? Define me?

I sit back on my chair. Pick up my chopsticks. Slurp noodles back into my mouth. Too distracted to taste them. Wondering how I could see this fifteenth-century manuscript for myself. A facsimile, if there is one, might suffice. Given the fragility of these books, only properly credentialed experts could have access to them. And I'm not yet one of those.

How about doing an illuminated manuscript about medieval illuminated manuscripts for my master's thesis? I could analyze this resurrected adaptation of *The Utrecht Psalter*. In choosing to do so, I would be both scribe and illustrator, treading in the footsteps of many medieval artists who copied extant manuscripts or created new ones.

The immediate gut appeal of the idea turns into a frisson of apprehension as I imagine what such a project would entail.

It's an exciting prospect, but would I be up to it? Painting small colorful pictures in egg tempera, a medium I haven't used? Applying gold leaf on pictures and letters, a skill that seems easy enough to learn? Handwriting content on parchment, a material I'm unfamiliar with? Writing with some fancy medieval script I would have to practice? Sewing the pages together to bind the manuscript? Fashioning a wood, leather, metal, or ivory cover, to me the most intimidating task in the whole process?

I would have wanted to spend more time indulging my fantasies and confronting my trepidation, but my reverie is abruptly cut short by someone opening the door to the office from the outside.

Lena, the office secretary, strides in, glancing at me as she passes by on her way to her office. I acknowledge her with a nod. She waves to me in response. She's on her way to her office at the southern end of the row of professors' offices, one larger than those of faculty. But it has neither windows nor a door. Its space accommodates the office machines by her desk and the deep filing cabinets lining her walls.

Don, the assistant to the professors of color, composition, and painting classes, saunters in a minute later. Two other assistants trickle back from lunch.

The trickling in of my office mates signals me it is time to leave. I have a painting class the rest of the afternoon. I pick up my backpack off the floor, gather my empty lunch box and chopsticks, shove both into my backpack, and rush out of the office, backpack slung on my shoulder.

Three and a half hours later, I leave the painting class a little early and hurry back to the office to catch Professor Fischl, hoping this isn't one of those infrequent days when he

25

doesn't return to his office after his afternoon classes, and wondering if it might be premature to talk to him about my thesis. I'm only in the first semester of graduate school.

But I'm too fired up to control my impulse.

How often does a medieval illuminated manuscript resurface after it has been missing—maybe for a long time? It should draw even more attention if the art world had not known of its existence. Am I not being thrown an unexpected opportunity? A rare challenge staring me in the face that I have no choice but to seize? A foray into a form of art meaningful to me, helping sustain me through the many transitions I've had to endure?

Chapter Two

Seizing the Moment

Professor Fischl is alone when I arrive. His other assistants are either attending classes or working on his mural. He waves me into his office when he sees me. His door is always slightly ajar when he's around.

Professor Fischl is a busy man, an expert on Italian and Greek renaissance art before the 17th century and consultant to artists and art institutions involved in artwork conservation from those periods. He's also a painter of grand narrative pictures, who lists 16th-century Flemish painter Peter Brueghel among his top favorites. His current project is a huge mural of an event in American history commissioned by a bank.

I stop at the entrance to his office, hesitating for a moment. Maybe I'm being hasty and haven't given this idea enough thought. But I can't help myself. I march into Professor Fischl's office.

He motions for me to sit on the chair across the desk from him, and without a word, lays a folder on the desk in front of me. I know what's in it. He teaches an introductory art history class two days a week and an all-afternoon upper-division art history class covering ancient times to the early modern period. I work as his graduate teaching assistant for the introductory class.

Once a week, he gives pop quizzes of twenty multiple-choice questions before he starts his lectures. My job is to run answer sheets through a scanner and record the results. I also attend one of his lectures every week so I can track the progress of his classes and answer questions on content from his students. An easy two hours counted toward my daily four-hour worktime. My assistantship slashes my tuition fees and helps me pay my graduate-student apartment on campus, my meals, and an occasional dinner out with Arthur.

Professor Fischl is in his late forties, with thinning, graying hair smothering clumps of blonde hair underneath, a roundish face, and squinty blue eyes. He's a big man, and though he's probably not overweight, he has a pronounced paunch. Randall, the assistant who's assisted him with his painting projects for three years—longer than the rest of us—says he works out, but he likes his wine and deep, dark chocolate muffins.

He waits until I release my hold on my backpack and it drops to the floor with a thud.

"So, Ms. Clarissa. What's new with you? You and I haven't had the chance to talk much." Professor Fischl calls us by our first name, but precedes it with a Ms. or a Mr. I suppose it's a throwback to an older world.

"Well, Professor, there could be an easy explanation. Your other assistants spend more time with you working on your mural. You have more time to chat."

He chuckles. "True. But I also think you're not into small talk. That's what we do as we paint. I put a ban on politics and religion. Also, weather talk. Painting with a group should be a fun community experience."

I search my brain for something banal to say outside of a remark about the weather—something he can count as small talk—but all I can come up with is, "I'll try to do better next time."

He has a keen eye, as artists should have. He's right about me being uncomfortable with small talk. Maybe it's what happens when you grow up with adults, listening to them talk about serious adult topics. As his newest assistant and the only one helping him with his teaching duties, I'm often alone in the office—a setup offering too few chances to practice small-talk skills, even in the open atmosphere of an office that gets quite lively when more of us are around. But I have other problems. Some people have an easy way about them. They can draw people into their orbits with a look or a smile. I'm not one of those. I suspect first impressions of me tag me as being aloof.

After my lame attempt at small talk, the professor points to the folder of answer sheets. I pick it up. Usually, this is the moment I get up to leave, but this time I stay seated.

Professor Fischl says, "Anything you're dying to tell me?"

"Yes, there is, actually. Have you seen the item in artnews.com about a once-lost illuminated manuscript someone is trying to sell?"

"This isn't small talk, then," he teases. "I don't think I have. Which manuscript is it?"

"Possibly, a 15th-century adaptation of *The Utrecht Psalter.*"

He raises an eyebrow. "Possibly? Don't they know for sure?"

"The article is vague and brief. It doesn't show any images. I'm curious because, in researching the term paper I did for your class, I learned the Psalter was copied or adapted for about two hundred years since the original was finished in the ninth century. This one in the news would have been done about five centuries later."

"Might it be a fake? Or is someone attempting to sensationalize and attract attention to their work?"

"It could be. The headline ends with a question mark."

Professor Fisch stares at me for a few moments, a steady gaze that's not seeing me, but is probing inward. The first time he looked at me like this, I became uncomfortable at his protracted silence, and started to say something. He raised a hand to signal me to be quiet. So, now I wait. "Let me guess: this news item interests you because you'd like to do a follow-up to the paper on illuminated manuscripts you wrote for my class. What exactly are you thinking of?"

"Maybe, to make an illuminated manuscript."

"Is this the work you're submitting for your first-year project?"

"No, it's for my thesis."

"I see. What artwork are you submitting this year?"

"An oil painting about my experience living as a transient in different places."

He nods, pleased. "That sounds like an interesting subject for a painting. Why not expand on that for your thesis? Consider the various angles you could examine for that theme. Experiment with the possible ways you might present it. When you're ready, we can talk about your two or three top choices."

I hesitate. "Um ... I'd like to try something I've never done before. Is that okay? Maybe, I'll try establishing a connection between medieval illuminated manuscripts and the picture books of today." I chose my first-year project, knowing he'd like it because it meshed with his own interests.

Crunching his brow and biting his upper lip, Professor Fischl eyes me for a long minute. "You're allowed to explore different art forms, of course. But do you know exactly what it is about illuminated manuscripts you want to explore?"

I'm not prepared to answer the professor. And the look on his face is far from encouraging. I knew it's a question he would ask, that I should have thought through before talking to him. "Vaguely, at this point. I don't want to do a psalter. I'm more interested in an extensive and deeper analysis of illuminated manuscripts."

I pause, momentarily distracted as he picks up a ballpen on his desk. "Maybe I'll focus on the manuscript featured in Art News, if I can get a facsimile of it."

He twirls the ballpen between his fingers, watching it. He says, "A secular manuscript, then—not a religious one. You're also aware you need access to at least a facsimile in order to write about a specific manuscript." Still twirling the ballpen, he looks up at me. "Good start but narrow your focus. Decide on what you hope to accomplish. Do you have a message? Then submit a thesis proposal."

He releases the ballpen and as it clatters against the hard surface, he slaps the desk with his palm. "No need to hurry. You have the rest of this year to draft and present it for my approval. Plus at least another year to write content and paint pictures to accompany the text. You're choosing an ambitious project, and you'll have a lot to think about. And make sure you work on that first-year painting as well."

"Thank you," I say, aware only then that my body is tense and rigid. I shifted in my seat. I can see he's disappointed, but he's giving me time to explore and not discouraging me from a topic in which he only has a superficial interest.

"As you know, it's not my area of expertise so you can't expect much guidance from me. But I assure you my support. I wish there was someone in this department I could recommend as your thesis adviser. Unfortunately, I know no one here even remotely interested in manuscript illuminations."

"Does my adviser have to be knowledgeable about manuscript illuminations?"

"Obviously preferable, but no, not absolutely necessary. We, teachers, always learn something from a student's work."

"I can do all the research I'd need."

He picks up the ballpen again, but to my relief, he doesn't twirl it. "I don't doubt it. The paper you submitted for my upper-division art history class this summer was clear and cited all the necessary references." He gives me that probing but not-seeing look again.

Moments later, his eyes brighten, and I relax a little. "Hmm. I might have someone who can help. He might say no. I've never asked him about something like this. But it's worth a try."

He takes out his cellphone from his jacket pocket, dials a number and waits for someone to answer.

"As far as I know, he's studied old manuscripts and followed the trail of a couple of them with questionable

provenance. He won't be your thesis adviser, though, if he agrees to help. He's not faculty."

Seconds later, he talks into his cellphone, his face animated. "Nathan! Adam. How have you been, my friend?" He pauses, smiling, averting his gaze away from me and swiveling his chair a little to one side. "Yes, it's been a while, but I'm sure you've been at least as busy as I've been. How's the writing going?"

I'm caught in a private conversation between friends that I shouldn't be listening to. I grab the arms of my chair to rise and leave, but I suppress the urge to do so. Leaving would be rude and disruptive. Despite the professor's lack of enthusiasm, he's making the call on my account. Besides, I'm tingling with curiosity. If the professor's friend has a burning interest in old manuscripts, like I do, then he might be a kindred spirit who I could talk to and who would understand. But would he agree to help?

I sit back again, so I wouldn't appear intrusive. I turn my head towards the outside window to the professor's left. We're on the third floor and all I see are clouds, thick long rows of white clouds slowly floating westward against a light blue sky. I try to relax my limbs as I stare at them, but intent on catching the professor's words, I fail.

After listening for a while, the professor speaks again. "Still working on my mural. Maybe a few more months, but you know we tend to be a bit too optimistic about such dates. I do have a little more help. Three instead of only one assistant to prepare surfaces, do the underpainting, and clean-up after every session."

Eventually, he says, "I wanted to ask you a favor. Can I refer one of my graduate students to you?"

My ears prick up, and I shift my gaze back to the professor, hands clasped tighter on my lap.

He glances at me. "She wants to do a master's thesis, producing an illuminated manuscript on a topic related to the illuminated manuscript cited in Art News and currently seeking a buyer." A slight pause. "Yes, fifteenth century."

"Super," he says, flashing me an okay sign, his forefinger and thumb touching each other. He also unleashes a wide grin that, to me, renders the wall, built only minutes ago, more scalable. He thanks his friend, and bids him goodbye, "Let's have dinner sometime soon."

He lays the phone on his desk and writes a phone number and a name on a post-it. I scoot closer to the desk and rest my clasped hands on its edge.

He hands me the post-it. "Well. You lucked out. It's just a 'hobby' for him—his words—but he's the only one I know who might be able to guide you on content and can critique both your draft and your final version. He's writing a book that I learned is on looting of old manuscripts. He's had a special interest in them for a long time. Call him soon."

I glance at the name. "Nathan Adler? Is that a fairly common name? I know someone by that name. But he was studying medicine and should be a doctor by now."

"Common enough name, I suppose. Nathan is a journalist, but his parents are doctors. His father's name is also Nathan. He bought two of my paintings. That's how I met them. Now, it seems I've become a family friend. His mother wants me to paint their family portrait. Not the usual thing I do, but it'll be a nice challenge. One of these days, I hope, when I finish my mural."

"The Nathan I knew was only a few years older than me." I shrug. "Anyway, I don't think it matters. I'm sure this will help. And if he's too busy, he might at least agree to talk to me and help me focus on a specific topic."

The professor chuckles. "Believe me, he can do more than that if he decides to work with you. Nathan is driven and thorough once he sets his mind on doing something."

I stick the post-it inside the folder of pop quiz answer sheets and rise from my chair.

Chapter Three

Reaching Out

It's half an hour to midnight and my mind still refuses to succumb to sleep. I lie on my right side, and a minute later, I roll over to my left. My body can't find a comfortable position to settle into.

I've done relaxing yoga stretches, read a boring book that I endured for only five minutes, drunk a glass of milk, and imagined a long row of lambs skipping across a meadow of lavender, red poppies, and dandelions. Nothing has helped.

I switch on my bedside lamp to its lowest setting and push my body up against the wall behind me. I sigh, and my inner voice sighs with me, reproachful: *That meeting with Professor Fischl discombobulated you. Your problem is you do too many important things on impulse and expect immediate answers. Confront your problem head-on, but learn to delay gratification. Talk to someone. It always helps to seek a new perspective.*

I push my inner voice deep into my brain and swing my legs down to the floor. Maybe I can tire myself out walking around the apartment until sleep comes. But it takes only one turn—around the short path from the bedroom to the living area and back—for my brain to start churning again, looping back to my conversation with Professor Fischl. I'm watching him spill his disinterest and impatience on the ballpen twirling between his fingers. He would have preferred for me to submit a large painting for my master's thesis, and I'm letting his disappointment bother me—maybe more than it should.

It's my choice, though, isn't it? The ideas and labor that will go into the project will be mine.

Only this morning, I still had no inkling what to do for my graduate thesis until Art News announced the reappearance of a once-lost manuscript. To me, that manuscript was a rare and precious gift dropped onto my lap at the opportune moment. Whether it's fate at work or merely chance, I have made a weighty, spur-of-the-moment decision. Not well thought out, I admit, and I haven't much of a clue what I'd want or could accomplish, and how I would proceed. But as the professor pointed out: I have time. And maybe his friend would agree to guide me, to share his expertise and critique the content of my illuminated manuscript.

After tottering around the apartment several times, my muscles are still twitchy. At least, my brain has wound down from full speed. Frustrated, I plunk down on the couch in the living area. Maybe another glass of milk or plodding through that boring book again would help.

But maybe, my inner voice is right—I need another perspective. But whose? Not Arthur's. Like a lot of people, he might not understand why anyone would care about old and musty handwritten books with texts you can't even read. He may like the colorful and vibrant drawings or small paintings ("miniatures" in art parlance). But will he still be curious when he discovers they're usually of saints and religious rituals? He might be familiar with modern picture books, though—graphic novels and manga comic strips, for instance.

Mom. She would understand. She might know little about medieval illuminated manuscripts, but she would listen to me, try to learn more, and share her thoughts. Having immersed both of us in picture books, she'll see what I find so special about old manuscripts enriched with images.

Before I could get carried away with everything I want to tell and ask mom, I remind myself that she requested to be left alone until she contacts us.

When Dad declared he would retire in the big house his great grandparents had built in his home city in the Philippines, Mom was uncertain. She agreed to accompany Dad on his last assignment until he retired. When the assignment was over, she returned to her Illinois hometown to reunite with her parents and a brother and his family—all of whom had been lifelong Illinois residents. Blood relatives neither I nor my brother have ever met.

My white American mother had cut ties with her family when she married my father. For reasons my parents have never bothered to explain. And Arthur and I never thought to ask.

Our parents were finally divorcing. It had been brewing for at least the last five years. When mom finally left dad, she asked to sever all communications with us until she felt ready to see us again. She needed to be unshackled to do what she thought was best for her. I could understand her reason, but I was deeply hurt.

In the bedroom, I pick up a photo of her and gaze at it until my tears blur her image. What's the harm in writing her? Though I cannot send it, writing her will be like talking to her. I can conjure up an image of her sitting next to me at the kitchen counter. It wouldn't be the first time.

Out of the night table drawer, I pull out a nearly forgotten pad of special stationery I bought in Florence, along with a Zecchi sketch notebook as highly prized as the Moleskin is in the US. I take it to the kitchen counter, the all-purpose surface where I eat, write, work, and do art.

Before I begin, I pour myself another glass of milk, fill another glass with water for Mom, and place them on the counter next to the stationery.

Past Midnight, November 2000
Across San Francisco Bay

Dearest Mom,

I miss you and can hardly wait to be with you again.

I hope you are well and enjoying your freedom. I won't ask you where you've been or what you've been doing. Those will be more satisfying to share when we meet again. But I admit it would reassure me immensely if I knew whether you've received the emails I've sent you.

Me—I'm still in the Bay Area working on my graduate degree.

Do you remember how we used to talk about the things I learned in school? You were as inquisitive as any eager schoolgirl, opening my mind to possibilities I didn't consider. Well, for my master's thesis, I'm planning to make a medieval illuminated manuscript. Do you know what it is?

It's an illustrated, handwritten picture book on parchment. It's illuminated by gilding, usually with gold leaf. In medieval times, they were produced to inspire religious devotion in the populace, the majority of whom couldn't read. Literacy was not a priority in ancient times, even for the ruling class. So, institutions resorted to illustrations to inform and teach.

Scholars speculate that Charlemagne—Holy Roman Emperor, Father of Europe, and the medieval alpha male who fueled the cultural revival (a renaissance) that resulted in the prolific production of these manuscripts—might not have learned to read in his youth. Can you picture him a grown man, his beard hanging down his chest, sitting on his mother's lap learning his ABCs (Ha, ha! Forced laughter okay, too)?

After years of reading me picture books and teaching me how to read, I don't need to tell you how useful illustrations are. I owe my love of art to you and those picture books.

Medieval illuminated manuscripts are uniquely valuable. They can connect our present to our past in a way paintings on canvases can't. Partly because of textual content. Our past experiences, mood of the moment, peer influences and things of that sort can shape how we see canvas paintings. Words make images less subject to idiosyncratic interpretations, so an illuminated manuscript is weightier and more objective as historical evidence. As cultural artifacts of the period, they help us understand our evolution into a civilized world.

As you can see, I'm quite excited about my proposed thesis project, but I have a lot more learning to do. If you were here, I'd share with you every stage of my progress. And you can tell me what you think. Who knows, maybe I can develop enough expertise in illuminated manuscripts to carve a niche for myself in it. Would that be as good as finding a permanent home?

I love you, Mom. Please don't stay away too long.

Hugs and kisses,
Issy

P.S. What do you think of a campaign to make illustrations standard in fiction books for adults? Like a publisher did for 19th century editions of Jane Austen's books and probably more that I didn't know about.

It's two o'clock in the morning by the time I conclude and sign my letter. I read it to myself before I fold it carefully and insert it in an envelope that came with the stationery. I don't seal it, but I put a stamp on it. Unsealed, I can reread the letter when I lose confidence in what I'm doing. It will reassure me and keep me going.

I kiss it once before I tuck it under a couple of seldom-used cashmere sweaters in a small cedar chest I keep in the closet. One day, I'll put this letter, sealed, in mom's hands.

Chapter Four

A Second Found Manuscript

The next morning, eating a breakfast sandwich at my desk, I go online to see if more has been written about the once-lost fifteenth century manuscript. Nothing. Instead, another news item glares at me, not from the middle of the page but at the top:

Ninth-Century Lost Manuscript Found

No question mark like yesterday's headline. This manuscript is older. Likely to be more valuable. This can't be mere coincidence. Two very old manuscripts coming to light in two consecutive days.

I read on. As in the first news item, there's no information on provenance. No details to help identify the manuscript. No images shown either of the cover or a page. It does describe the cover as studded in precious stones. And it's being offered by the same art dealer of the 15th-century manuscript.

My impulse, after reading this news item, is to pick up the phone on my desk. Each graduate assistant has one with the same phone number and a unique extension. I'm more determined now to discover the mystery behind these manuscripts. I dial the number Professor Fischl gave me for his friend, Nathan Adler.

The phone at the other end rings once, a second time, a third. By the fourth ring, I tighten my hold on the phone, frustrated, afraid Mr. Adler won't answer. A tad annoyed at myself for my impatience, I'm about to give up after the eighth ring when a person at the other end of the line picks up the phone. But no one answers right away. Only silence for a few seconds.

I say, "Hello, my name is Clarissa. I'm a graduate student working with Professor Fischl. Adam Fischl. He told you he has a student who wants to do a thesis on illuminated manuscripts. It's me."

"Clarissa? Clarissa Martinez? Arthur's sister?" A familiar voice says. "Is that you?"

I'm dumbfounded for a few moments. "Yes, it's me. I'm the graduate student referred to you by Professor Fischl."

"He didn't give me your name and I didn't ask. Students hardly ever knock on my door to ask about old manuscripts. I figured if someone calls and mentions Adam's name ..."

"This is unbelievable. I told him I once knew a Nathan Adler, but he's a doctor. So, I was sure it wasn't you. This is certainly a big surprise. And I'm amazed you recognized my voice over the phone. It's been two years."

"Yeah, long story—the doctor thing. But that's for another time. Adam says you want to do a thesis on manuscript illuminations."

He is eager to move on. I remember him being ill at ease those few times we talked in the past. But he was always direct and told you what he thought.

I tell him why I'm calling him—the news items on artnews.com; my early and enduring fascination with picture books; my interest in studying manuscript illuminations—the label sometimes used for illuminated manuscripts—and trying my hand at producing an illuminated manuscript about some aspect of illuminated manuscripts.

"Wow. Are you sure? That's practically doing two master's theses, an artwork and a study of some subject matter or existing artwork."

I ignore the touch of skepticism in his voice.

Nathan goes on to say he has read both artnews.com articles, and like me, they intrigued him. Something is amiss about the reporting of the "lost manuscripts" that, to him, raises questions. He's currently writing a short piece on those questions. He intends to submit it to the online publication as an opinion piece, or at least as a long comment to the articles.

So, yes, if I also have questions about these once-lost manuscripts that beg for answers, and I have a genuine interest in medieval illuminated manuscripts, we could work together to search for answers to questions and issues related to them.

We agree to meet at a Peet's Coffee in Emeryville, not too far from campus. The area has ample parking, and the place doesn't buzz with conversation. Its habitués are often alone, absorbed in reading while slowly imbibing their daily dose of caffeine. It's an ideal place for long hushed-up conversations.

I don't have a car, but the coffeeshop, for me, is a walkable distance. Having lived in European cities, particularly Paris, I'm used to walking. If I'm pressed for time, I can take a bus to the coffeeshop.

Nathan says he'll bring a bibliography, a couple of books and some copies of articles he's extracted from art journals.

"See you on Saturday," he says.

"I'll be there, and thanks for helping me."

I'm about to hang up, but I can still hear Nathan breathing. Does he have something more he wants to say? It takes him a few seconds before he speaks. "I'm writing a book on old manuscripts and rare old books lost in World War II. There are books out there on Nazi war loot, but usually they're about paintings or jewelry or gold bullions. I need thorough research because there might be some sensitive stuff I'll discover and reveal that could rile certain people. I'll need facts to back me up. Would you be interested in helping me?"

"Umm ...," I say, my voice trailing off. What could I say? "No" might make him change his mind about helping me, and "Yes" would require a commitment I'm not ready for. When I called him on impulse, I had no idea how it would turn out. It's disconcerting enough to find this Nathan Adler is indeed Arthur's friend, the guy who traveled with us for nearly three months across Europe. Being enmeshed in researching and maybe writing his book never crossed my realm of possibilities. The end of our tour, to me, was the last time we'd ever see each other.

Nathan spares me from having to answer. He says, "I'm sorry. I know this is too soon and too much to ask. We don't know yet if we can work together. But think about it, anyway."

Chapter Five

Summer 1998

Family

Earlier this year, my parents and I had moved to Rome for my father's last assignment in a foreign country.

I was a few months short of my twentieth birthday, of legal age to decide for myself. But all I was certain of was I didn't want to settle in either of my parents' choices. And yet, I couldn't think of a place where I could declare, as firmly as my parents did, that my heart is in it.

Having finished a year of college at a university in the Philippines, my brother had joined us in Rome weeks before my parents' flight to Manila.

Arthur was excited to go on his first tour of Europe and anticipated a travel adventure lasting a few months.

Dad was taken aback. "A few months! You're flying back with us when we go home. Two weeks—that's the time you have left to sightsee. Many guided tours don't even run that long. Besides, you're only seventeen and this is your first trip away from home. No, I can't allow you to go off on your own to strange places."

Arthur protested, ranting and shaking his head vehemently. "Not fair. You all have lived in Europe and this is only my first time visiting. I'd like to experience it, too. I'll skip a semester if I have to. I can take care of myself. I read about kids my age dropping out to travel by themselves for a year or two before going to university. Why can't I do that, too?"

Dad wiggled a finger, glaring at Arthur. "Uh, uh, no! You're going back with us."

"But I'm not sure I want to live there."

"I decide where you live."

Arthur tried pleading. "Dad, please. I flew here on my own. Why can't I go back by myself?"

But Dad didn't budge. He strode towards the door, shoulders squared and scowling.

Mom and I had been watching the exchange—mom sitting, still and tight-lipped, gripping her hands together on her lap.

I stood by, vexed at my father. Was he worried his naïve and precious son would be devoured by European wolves? I empathized with Arthur. Dad needed to loosen up.

I'd dealt with dad's pig-headedness in the past and believed I could allay his qualms about Arthur by suggesting a solution. One that would also let me postpone declaring my intention to break away—rejecting Mom and Dad's chosen homes.

Before he reached the door, I called out to him. "Dad, wait. Can I please say something?"

He executed a military about-face and stood where he was, waiting for me to speak.

"How about I stay and serve as Arthur's guide? I'll map out our trip, take him to places we've been to. I was planning on continuing school here, anyway. You told me that was okay, remember?"

He didn't answer right away. Glancing at Arthur, then at me, he dragged his feet back to the couch, and sat next to mom. He stared ahead, body erect and his face revealing nothing.

We waited—Mom staring at her hands, and Arthur biting his lower lip, fidgeting as he leaned on a wall a few paces away.

I caught Arthur's eye and crossed my fingers. He laid a palm on his chest in response.

It took dad a few minutes to speak, and all he said was, "All right," his voice soft and weary. We might have worn him out; or maybe his anger did. He gave my mother's hand a squeeze and walked quietly out of the room.

Mom, Arthur, and I looked at each other, incredulous. Arthur raised his fist, uttering a soundless "Yes."

He hugged me and kissed me on both cheeks. With a surreptitious gesture of my head towards Mom, I hinted for him to kiss her as well. He crinkled his nose at me before he gave her a peck on the cheek.

I was happy when Arthur arrived. I had often wondered whether he and I would ever have a chance to open our psyches for each other's scrutiny and knot our sibling ties tighter and longer. Traipsing together minus parental rules and anxiety seemed a good way to start doing so.

For the first time, I would also have a person in my generation with whom to plunge into adventures and harvest memories. And I would have the luxury of reflecting on my future minus my mother's anxious gaze and my father's barely restrained urge to interfere.

*****

On Tour: At A Paris Café

We met Nathan at a café in Paris. A serendipitous acquaintance, driven by Arthur's recent obsession with Parisian café culture.

Before going to Paris, Arthur and I spent a month in Italy after Mom and Dad left, going on short trips to different cities and returning each time to an apartment in Rome Dad had paid for to the end of the month. On the long train ride from Rome to Paris, Arthur immersed himself in the *Lonely Planet* guide to France. It contained a section on cafés.

We had booked an apartment a week earlier, choosing one the rental agency assured us was equipped with a modem. The moment we arrived, Arthur spotted the modem. He dumped our luggage on the floor, hooked up his laptop to it, and scoured the internet to find out more about the history of cafés. I could see his obsession developing before my eyes.

In the morning, we stepped out of our cramped apartment, down a flight of stairs, through a dark, dank shaft of a hallway lighted by dim bulbs at both ends. We opened the apartment building door onto a narrow street smack in the middle of a Latin Quarter commercial section, where tourists, restaurants and other food shops reign. Located within the innards of an old building, our pied-à-terre overlooked an inner courtyard where it was insulated from the noise and hustle of life in the neighborhood.

At a quarter before nine, the street wasn't as busy as when we checked in the evening before. Some business establishments hadn't yet opened. Having lived three years in this metropolis before moving to Rome, I knew it didn't start hopping until about ten in the morning.

Our last full meal was lunch on the train, and having subsisted on chips and chocolate the night before, we were both in dire need of coffee and croissants. We found a café one block from the apartment. At this hour, customers tended to be tourists and several tables were empty. Unless a café was busy, you could usually sit yourself without waiting for the waiter.

Only one waiter appeared to be around to serve customers, a wiry man, thirtyish, with a swarthy face, plastered dark hair and a plastered smirk. Before we could sit down, he was already standing by our table, waiting to take our order.

It was Arthur's first Parisian café, and he was thrilled. Over coffee and croissant, he asked me what topics or issues I thought a stranger might find interesting enough to keep him talking.

Nonchalantly, I said, "It has to be about something you know and like. You've been reading a lot about café culture. People in cafés would find that interesting to talk about."

"I don't know nearly enough about café culture. The internet doesn't tell you much about its history. Can you take me to that famous English bookstore, *Shakespeare & Company*? They might have a book or two on the subject."

"Sure. It's a few blocks from here on the quay along the Seine."

On the way to the bookstore, past two other narrow streets of meat, cheese, and bread shops, we emerged on Quai St Michel, bustling from two-lane traffic and people rushing to the Notre Dame. Arthur pointed to the cathedral across the river on Ile de la Cite. "So, that's what a gothic church looks like. Nice. I love the gargoyles."

I rolled my eyes skyward. What a philistine my brother was. Aloud, I said, "Show some reverence, little brother. You're looking at close to a thousand years of history."

At the bookstore, he found *Paris Cafés*, written by a French author and translated into English. It was thin but twice as large as the usual size of a paperback.

Arthur read it that evening, finishing it before he went to bed.

In the morning, he dragged us back to the café. As we waited for our coffee and croissants, he said, "Guess when the first cafés were opened for business in Paris."

"Early nineteenth century, maybe," I said breezily. My stomach rumbled and all I cared about at that moment was café au lait.

He smirked. "Nah! You're more than a century off. Late 1600s. In fact, one of those first cafés is still around, Le Procope. Do you know it?"

"Yes. Quite famous. A tourist attraction."

"Can we go there sometime?"

"Not sure. I recall reading it's been turned into a restaurant, and maybe we can't afford it."

To my relief, the waiter—the same man from the morning before—had finally come with a tray bearing our breakfast.

Arthur snatched a croissant off the plate and took a big bite. "Too bad, but there are others. Like Café Guerbois."

"That's long gone, too. A favorite hangout for Edouard Manet and his crowd."

"It doesn't matter. What matters is it had history it can boast of. Artists and writers, whose names and works live on, flocked to those places. Struggling young men with no money but rich in ideas, zeal, and ambition, discussing and arguing over art, politics, and revolutions. How cool is that!"

He looked through me into a world imagined and long gone. I waited until he was back to this century and this café to say something to keep him talking. "I know about an art revolution in the late 1800s."

"You mean impressionism? The book talked about that."

"How about a real war in which a few artists died?"

"The Franco-Prussian war? That's in the book, too."

"You sure have learned a lot in a couple of days, little brother."

He thrust his chin out and raised his espresso cup to me. "Thank you, big sister. I found café culture so fascinating, I wanted to learn as much as I can. Cafés were vital to the lives of artists and writers—Manet, Monet, Degas, Zola, Baudelaire. But they weren't the only ones. Before them, philosophers like Voltaire, Rousseau and Diderot congregated in cafés."

The waiter, who interpreted his raised cup as a summon, came back to our table. "More café express, monsieur?"

"Huh?" Arthur said, startled, glancing sideways up at him. "Yes, yes, *s'il vous plait.*"

Arthur continued as if he wasn't interrupted. The waiter walked away. He didn't bring Arthur a second cup of espresso, and Arthur forgot having asked for a refill.

Arthur's wonder increased with every nugget of information he rattled off to me. These artists and philosophers were starving "bohemians" who later became famous. He hadn't read or seen their works, but he had encountered their names, in his Western Thought and Culture class, dealing with European philosophy and art at the university he attended in the Philippines.

He said, tilting his head towards me, his voice rising above the din of the growing café crowd, "What's a bohemian? I get that they're usually poor and into art. Is there a place called Bohemia?"

"There is I think, in the Czech Republic. But I doubt that's the origin of 'bohemian' in the sense we often use the word."

"So, what makes one bohemian?"

"Not sure. Could be a term that stuck when one of those poor artistic souls wrote maybe a book or a play, later turned into an opera. You know, *La Bohème*."

"Have you seen it?"

"No, I like classical music including arias from popular operas, but I've never watched an opera. But Mom took me once to an art exhibit that focused on bohemian artists. The artist/writer of *la vie bohème* might have been inspired by gypsies—how free they were to move from place to place, and how they made music, sang, and danced with abandon."

Dreamy-eyed again, Arthur said, "I wonder what it was like living in the era of café culture. Young men, strangers to each other at first, forming cliques and debating hot issues of their day. The social media of olden days. I wonder if it's still possible to live it for the short time we're here. How I'd love to be able to say I've lived the Parisian café life. Shall we stay longer?"

Arthur's obsession with experiencing 19th-century café culture amused me. But I thought it awesome as well. He was only seventeen, and yet he was already driven, as zealous as those café habitués of long ago. For him, going to the spots where cafés thrived was not enough. He had to experience what it had been like for those bohemians.

Unfortunately, Arthur had a problem. He learned only a smattering of French words that guidebooks dictated tourists must know to have a good time in France. And what little he picked up from those books didn't solve the trouble he had getting his English-accented French understood by the French. His imagined verbal sparring friend couldn't be a Frenchman, unless he spoke English.

*****

On our third morning, I steered him to Le Départ, on the corner of Boulevard St. Michel across the Seine from the Notre Dame Cathedral. I told him he would have more luck connecting with someone there.

"It's popular, right on the beaten path of a few tourist haunts. Many would think it the quintessential Parisian café. Red awning jutting out to the street. Outside tables behind chained iron bars a foot from the sidewalk. People wearing cultivated bored looks, lingering over small cups of espresso. If it isn't too crowded, we can choose a table on the Seine side. The café has glass walls, and you can sit facing the Notre Dame and stare at the gargoyles. But better than all that, this café has history. A hangout for young writers when it opened in the early 1900s as Le Caveau du Soleil. I'm sure you'll love it."

"How do you know so much about this place?" he said.

"I went to the Sorbonne before Dad was assigned to Rome. Le Départ is a mere ten-minute walk from the university. When someone told me how old it was, I was intrigued so I did a bit of research."

Le Départ was close to full, and all the tables in the open air by the sidewalk were taken. A waiter led us to one of two empty tables deep inside the café.

Arthur didn't seem to care where he sat. He was in a famous café that was a hundred years old. "This is great. I swear I can feel the vibes from those philosophers and artists."

We ordered coffee and croissants. The café was a little too noisy and busy for me. Neighborhood cafés off the beaten path were more my thing. Cafés where the clientèle were mostly area residents. Where servers anticipated your order and faces became familiar.

But Arthur was all smiles as he looked around. And I was content to see him happy with my suggestion.

It didn't take long before a man walked in, and Arthur nudged my arm with his elbow.

"See the guy who came in a moment ago? Definitely American. Tall, and good-looking, eh? Sure of himself but not cocky. Uneasy, though. Must be his first time in Paris."

I chuckled but said nothing. It was only his third full day in Paris, and Arthur was already feeling superior to someone he guessed had just arrived.

I glanced at the man—clean-shaven, dark haired, lean and athletic, skin a bit lighter than Arthur's. Sporting a haircut shorn close on the side of his head and two inches long at the top, a creaseless blue shirt tucked into black denims, its standing collar open at the neck, and long sleeves folded neatly up his elbows, he struck me as ... antiseptic.

His gaze darted around the room. The café was packed— every table I could see flanked by customers whiling away their hours over their cups of coffee. He could have spotted an empty chair or two that kept him scanning the crowd. But he did seem unsure what to do next.

The guy's gaze soon landed on us, and Arthur unleashed his bright smile on him. He smiled back and sauntered towards our table.

"May I join you?" he said, glancing at Arthur, then at me.

I turned to Arthur, leaving the decision up to him. He said, "Oh yes, yes. Please do."

The guy plucked an empty chair from a table behind us and before he sat down, he introduced himself. "Nathan Adler, from California."

Arthur extended a hand which Nathan grasped. "Arthur Martinez and my sister Clarissa. I came from the Philippines, but we're both born in California."

"Small world," Nathan said, shifting his gaze to me. A quick tilting of my head backward passed for my welcoming nod. I kept a hand on my lap and the other around my coffee cup. He didn't put out his hand to shake mine.

"Can I offer you refills?" He raised his forefinger for the waiter in a gesture I'd seen in paintings of Jesus blessing his followers. I was curious to see if his nails were manicured. They were not, but they were trimmed,

"I'm good, thanks," I said.

"Me, too," Arthur said, though his espresso cup was empty.

Nathan addressed me. "Did you also come from the Philippines?"

"I've been here and there. I was in Rome for a few months."

Arthur introjected. "My sister's home is the planet earth."

"He's exaggerating." I averted my eyes from both of them. I was uneasy.

They took the hint and the usual tête à tête followed between Arthur and Nathan—how long we'd been in Paris, where we'd been. What we liked—to which Arthur enthused, "The cafés, for sure."

Fortified by cups of espresso and the freedom to speak unencumbered by a French/English dictionary, Arthur spent two hours regaling Nathan all he'd gleaned about café culture from the book he bought and the two days he'd spent in a café. To his credit, Nathan listened patiently, sometimes asking questions. Arthur was inspired.

On our fourth morning, Nathan joined us again, having taken a hint from Arthur that he'd find us at Le Départ the following morning. From then on, the three of us met at various cafés. The two guys nursed a few cups of espresso or café américain, and I slowly sipped a cup of café au lait. Around noon, we ordered sandwiches.

*****

We had booked our short-stay apartment for two weeks and would have extended it, had it not been reserved through the end of fall. Arthur was disappointed. He wanted to complete a whole month in Paris. I reminded him that we had already reserved hotels at our next three destinations in Brussels, Bruges, and Amsterdam. We should move on. He had his whole life ahead of him for travel adventures.

I suspected he was having too much fun with Nathan. Having lived in the city before, I begged off going to the usual tourist spots and chose to do some sketching elsewhere by myself. So, the two went off on their own.

Two days before leaving Paris, Arthur told me Nathan asked to tag along for the rest of our trip.

"How did that happen?" I wasn't enthusiastic about the prospect, but Arthur was too thrilled to notice I was miffed. Nathan's presence was a distraction to my efforts to deepen the bond between Arthur and me. But this was Arthur's first European tour, and though I fancied myself savvier and more experienced, I let him plan our trip despite my promise to our parents to do it myself. I also deferred to his decisions in most unforeseen events we encountered.

"He's on his own, you know, and doesn't have an itinerary like we do. Many times, he waited until he arrived at a place to find lodgings. He said he often found hostels that could accommodate him. If not, he hopped back on the train to a nearby town."

"Hmm," I said. I hadn't expected Mr. Antiseptic to be that adventurous.

In retrospect, Arthur's decision had been good for him. I could see he enjoyed our tour. Probably more than he would have had I been his only companion. He and Nathan related to each other in a way they might not have with me. Or women, in general.

Women entertain such friendships as well. We share little secrets we're convinced are beyond men's understanding or caring. For me, sharing little secrets with a friend (like Mom) can be gratifying, helpful, naughty, dangerous; a source of relief, guilt, or power.

We ended our European sojourn in Florence, the city both Nathan and Arthur professed wanting to see again. They might have met a couple more times after they flew on the same plane to California. Nathan was finishing his final year of medical school, while Arthur had to stay for a day on layover before taking another flight to the Philippines to resume his undergraduate studies.

I stayed in Florence a couple of months longer, revisiting works of art, sketching, sampling gelatos from the many gelaterias in the city. Relegating the future to the back of my mind, I returned to Paris to enroll in more art classes, biding my time, percolating ideas on where to set roots.

After one final semester of art classes, the Sorbonne granted me a "licence," the equivalent of a bachelor's degree from an American university.

Chapter Six

Chapter Six

Getting Down to Business

Peet's Coffee, in the gentrifying city of Emeryville, sprawls along the edge of a commodious structure that was once a warehouse recently renovated and converted into an open market of food stalls and restaurants. The market hall has morphed into a lively go-to place for quick bites and socializing.

Set apart by a wall from the noisy open market hall, Peet's cave-like space exudes tranquility. An undulating banquette lining a long solid wall, equipped by a dozen or so small round tables dominates the space. No music streams from overhead speakers and conversations, when they occur, are subdued. The builders of the coffeehouse have taken account of the demographics of its surrounding neighborhood—college-educated solitary souls—students, graduates, and residents of modern one-bedroom condominiums and upscale apartments.

Nathan is already at the coffeehouse when I arrive, sitting on one end of the banquette far away from other occupied tables. He gets up as I approach, casual but business-like in black pants, gray shirt open at the neck, and a slightly rumpled navy linen blazer. In contrast, I'm wearing a black turtleneck, topped by a black long-sleeved shirt that hangs loose over my denim jeans. I've wound my long thick hair into a bun and clamped it with a barrette at the nape of my neck to keep it from blowing on my face. The two-mile walk to the coffeehouse is often breezy.

He extends his hand to shake mine as if it's only been a few days since we last met. "Good to see you again, Clarissa," he says, letting loose a genuine smile. One lasting impression I had of Nathan in Paris was his smile. If his mouth stretched and curved, but his eyes didn't light up and crinkle, it was a forced, polite smile. His palm is rather warm, maybe from cradling his cup of hot drink.

"Good to see you, too, Nathan. How are you?" I say, smiling back.

I sit on a thinly padded wooden chair across the table from him. The banquette has a thicker, more comfortable cushion, but I prefer facing Nathan than sitting next to him and craning my neck as we talk.

"Okay. Busy. Can I get you something to drink?"

"I'll get it myself. Thank you for offering. Need a refill?"

"No thanks, I'm still good."

Minutes later, we regard each other from across the table. Nathan is sipping his coffee drink. And I, my café latte. I'm searching for how Nathan has changed from two years ago and I'm sure he's sizing me up, too.

He doesn't seem older, and he hasn't added heft to his lean frame. "Six feet, one inch," Arthur informed me a while back. "Half a foot taller than me." Arthur was impressed. In the Philippines, he stood taller than his friends.

Nathan has let his dark hair, once neatly trimmed into an Ivy League cut, grow longer. A couple of wavy locks fall over his right brow. It has made a difference in the personality he projects.

I remember him being tense and uptight, reluctant to talk about himself though he seemed to have no trouble getting others to talk about themselves.

He seems more relaxed now. More casual. The smile he greeted me with was natural, rather than forced. What has brought about his transformation? Not only in the first impressions he elicits but also in his drastic change of careers. A medical doctor to a journalist/writer interested in a nearly obscure art? From Mr. Antiseptic to—well, Mr. Rumpled.

Moments later, he puts his empty cup down and says, "Let's first clarify a few things: I cannot help you, nor provide you any kind of guidance on your art project. That's Adam's purview. If I work with you, I'll do what I can to help you, guide you on content."

"I understand."

"Good. How much do you know about medieval illuminated manuscripts?"

It seems we're not wasting any time catching up. Fine by me.

I stare straight into Nathan's dark eyes, hoping to project my earnest interest in illuminated manuscripts. I assume he knows a lot more than I do, and I'm trying to compensate for what I believe to be my want of knowledge.

I say, "Not much really. I took Professor Fischl's upper-division art history class as an elective. For the most part, it covered architecture, sculpture, and painting until the modern period. Illuminated manuscripts were mentioned in paintings in the medieval period, but that was it. He did let me write a term paper on the subject from the time of Charlemagne, to the fifteenth-century when the Limbourg brothers produced some now-famous books of hours. I have a printed copy of Duke de Berry's *Très Belles Heures* translated into English. And a digital copy of *The Utrecht Psalter.*"

"Impressive, actually," he says, his eyes lighting up. "More than most artists might know about this genre of art. Anything else?"

I didn't expect his reaction. Encouraged, I ramble through a few factoids. "I learned a lot writing my paper. *The Utrecht Psalter* was done at monastic scriptoria in Rheims or Hautvillers in Northern France maybe between the years 820 and 830, during the reign of Charlemagne."

"Ah, yes. Places we now associate with champagne rather than rare old manuscripts."

I note a hint of sarcasm in his remark. Afraid I might be distracted, I ignore it and continue. "What's most interesting about *The Utrecht Psalter* is its illustrations. The content was nothing new. They were psalms, followed by some canticles. But the artist, also the scribe, broke from the tradition of previous manuscripts in which the few illustrations of figures were more static, frozen. Instead, he chose passages in the psalms denoting action and did quick, well-executed, sketches of animated figures infused with energy. He adapted an expressionistic style you'd see in first-century Roman frescoes and stuccos in Southern Italy." I stop, self-conscious. I'm sounding like I'm giving a lecture. Or too eager to impress.

Nathan's unwavering gaze is inscrutable. "Uh-huh," he says, his tone revealing nothing about what he thought of my recitation. "You're saying *The Utrecht Psalter* is unique. But in what way? Its illustrations were copied."

"He did copy images from existing picture cycles. By Charlemagne's time, those images had been around for centuries, preserved from one manuscript to subsequent reproductions. But he did line drawings—sketches instead of book-size paintings—using brown ink rather than various colors of tempera which were typically used in the early Middle Ages. He didn't frame his illustrations either. His figures ran across a page with no frames, borders or spaces."

Nathan nods. "Copying other manuscripts was not only accepted; it was standard practice in ancient and medieval times. Without typewriters, copy machines, printing, and photography, how else could one reproduce a book? Medieval artists suffered no qualms copying. In fact, a lot of them would list the works of other scribes they copied. Nowadays, being creative means being original. But is anything truly original? I've never seen an art piece you can't relate to something that's already been done."

"I agree. When I first saw *The Utrecht Psalter* sketches, they reminded me of a running frieze at the base of an altar in Pergamon I saw in my teens when my dad was stationed in Germany. The Pergamon frieze was created eight centuries before *The Utrecht Psalter.* No psalms, of course. It's the frenetic action of carved figures projecting from the wall of the frieze that's so like those in *The Utrecht Psalter.* And they ran continuously across the width of the altar."

Nathan says with a touch of impatience, "Tell me again in a nutshell how *The Utrecht Psalter* is unique?"

A bit mortified, I can't respond right away. Does he think I'm showing off telling him about the Pergamon frieze? I guess I might have been—a little—though I really did connect these two works of art. But I also realize I might have gone off-topic mentioning the frieze.

"Well, images were copied, yes. But the artist was also inventive, fusing forms and styles into something fresh and uniquely his own."

Nathan nods. "You're saying it's unique because the artist created something new from the stuff he borrowed. Okay. Here's the last thing I want to know: What do you hope to accomplish doing a thesis in this form of art? Manuscript illumination has often been viewed as a minor art except during Charlemagne's Carolingian renaissance and the international gothic period in Europe. No famous artist I know of practices it anymore. And using modern technology, we've moved on with book illustrations."

His remark deflates my enthusiasm all over again. Am I making too much of those recently found manuscripts? Somewhat defensively, I say, "I believe we haven't given manuscript illuminations their proper due. They're an artifact of a certain period of human history, and not only art history. Sometimes, they may be the only source of information we have about the society and culture of ancient times. From them, we could trace how we've arrived to where we are now. And don't you think they live on in some modern form, reincarnated as modern-day picture books and graphic novels?"

"Yes, images and words enriching each other will live on. They have served certain purposes that have evolved with the growth of civilization and depending on available technology and the needs of their patrons. The early ones dealt with matters of worship that churches used to teach and inspire faith in a population where few could read. But medieval manuscript illuminations were costly to produce. By the gothic period, they often took the form of gilded prayer books, reproduced for the rich and powerful who could afford them. Maybe, their quality and the people who owned them helped them survive. More than a thousand years since Charlemagne's renaissance, the marriage of images and words has lived on. I find that quite remarkable."

"Are you agreeing with at least some of what I've said?"

"It doesn't matter whether I agree with you or not. I'm trying to be a devil's advocate, giving you a taste of what you'd face in front of a thesis committee and others you might meet whose sincere interest in this subject can make them critical. I also wanted to see how much you already know."

I'm relieved he's not discouraging me, but again, I wonder why I'm stirring all this fuss about medieval manuscripts. I don't even know where I'm going with it. "You think I should continue?"

Nathan sizes me up again. He smiles, hesitantly. And doesn't give me a direct answer. "I'm impressed by your enthusiasm and how much you already know. I promised to bring you a few things to move you further along on the topic."

He picks up a messenger bag from under the table and pulls a folder out of it. He hands it to me. "No need to return those. I have copies. You may already know a good deal of the stuff in the folder."

He takes out a couple of books. "I'm lending you these books. If you decide to help write my book, they're yours to keep."

"Thank you," I say. "I'm interested, but to be honest, I don't know if I'm up to it or if I'll even have the time."

"It's a start—interest. But read the materials I gave you. When you're ready to talk some more, call me. You do need to find a focus for your thesis. Ask yourself what resonated with you in the news on those lost manuscripts. The manuscripts themselves or the fact that they were lost and found. They'll lead you to quite different paths. Okay to meet here again? Two weeks?"

"I think so. Yes. I'll read as much as I can before then," I say, stacking the folder on top of the books.

He pulls a wallet out of his blazer, takes out a business card, and hands it to me. In return, I pull out a pad of post-its from my purse and write my office phone number and extension.

He glances at it, then at me, and says, "How about a cellphone number? More direct."

"I'm sorry. I don't have one. Can't afford it. I had to buy a laptop first. I'm saving up for a cellphone, though."

"How about an email address? I don't use my email much, but it helps to have it."

I write my email address under the phone number and give him the post-it.

He puts my post-it in his wallet with his business cards, zips up his messenger bag, picks up his empty cup and throws me a glance.

I take it to mean our meeting is over. I yank my bag off the back of my chair, swipe up my cup and rise. My bottom has gone a bit numb.

Nathan pushes the table far enough to give him room to rise and slings his messenger bag across his chest.

Without a word, we walk towards the door together. Outside the door, he stops. And I stop. He says, "Don't sweat it. If the materials I gave you help you focus, then they've done their job."

As I'm about to walk away, he says, "Can I drop you off somewhere?"

"Thanks. I prefer to walk. I live only a couple of miles from here."

He nods, hesitates for a second, and says, "Say 'hello' to Arthur for me. We used to text, but it's been a while, and we haven't seen each other since the plane trip from Florence."

"I will," I say, suppressing an urge to ask him why he left medicine. It's a rather major decision. Why does someone do something foolish, reckless, audacious, or out of character to change his life radically? But why should I care? Because there might be a lesson or two I can cull from those major changes. To help me understand me better, push me in a direction I've never considered, and which might prove rewarding.

But I sense Nathan is hesitant to talk about himself. So, I stay on the topic of Arthur. "He's grown two inches since you last saw him. And he's doing bodybuilding in his spare time."

He chuckles. "Good for him. You've grown, too, and I don't just mean physically."

He waves his goodbye and walks towards the parking lot. I stand a few seconds, watching his receding figure, wondering what he meant by his last remark.

Chapter Seven

On the Trail of Found Manuscripts: I

A week later, Nathan calls me. "Can you take a few days off from work and school?"

"I might be able to. I'll have to talk to the professor. How long is a few?"

"Two or three days. I'm going to track down the history of those manuscripts. I'm always curious if there's something fishy about priceless artworks that seem to suddenly pop up. Who knows? This could turn out to be big news. These are rather rare manuscripts."

Later that afternoon, I call Nathan back to tell him I can go with him. Professor Fischl has given me as long as a full week.

He says, "I've made an appointment with the art dealer selling the illuminated manuscripts. He's our best source of information for now. You might learn something to direct your research for your thesis."

I say, "And you might discover material relevant to the book you're writing."

"That goes without saying. Have you thought more about what I proposed?"

I'm still not sure about his book. But going to a source that can tell us more about these manuscripts? Unexpected. And exciting. A rare and precious opportunity thrown into my lap.

I must have paused too long for him to wait for an answer. He says, "We're flying early morning, day after tomorrow, from San Francisco International. I'll email you the details." Then, he hangs up.

*****

Two mornings later, we're on the plane to Switzerland. Nathan bought plane tickets and reserved rooms for us at a modest hotel. He paid for them from the advance he received on the book he's writing.

On the plane, after we settled in our seats, I sense some awkwardness between us. A subtle underlayer of discomfort since the time Arthur introduced us at the café in Paris. It persisted while he tagged along with Arthur and me as we toured Europe.

I take my headphones out of my carry-on, ready to retreat into my music, but Nathan touches the back of my hand and says, "So, you took Adam's art history class."

"I was enrolled in his summer upper-division course. I also work for him as a teaching assistant."

"How was it? The class."

"A lot of it wasn't new to me. I already had a couple of art history classes at the Sorbonne. But Adam is an energetic teacher. Funny, but incisive and inspiring."

For the next hour or so, we talk about Professor Fischl and short anecdotes about what Nathan says are "the many hats Adam wears." I'm surprised he doesn't ask about Arthur. The two of them seemed to like each other well enough to want to continue to keep in touch. But maybe, that was Arthur talking.

We manage to keep a conversation going until the stewardesses wheel out carts of food and beverages to start lunch service.

Somehow, through lunch, the airline movie of the day, and talking about Adam Fischl and art in general, we survive the long flight. By early evening when we check into the hotel, we've whittled away enough of the awkwardness between us. Though the lost manuscripts are likely to dominate our conversation, I feel less constrained to talk about other things. And try small talk à la Professor Fischl.

I've set foot only once in Switzerland when we were on our way to Dad's new assignment. He took us on a cable ride up Mt. Pilatus in Lucerne. I was a child and all I can remember now is the endless stretch of snow and me shivering from the cold, unable to appreciate the "spectacular landscape" Mom kept drawing my attention to.

Zurich, for me, is a new destination. We arrive at night, my brain still swirling from the long plain ride. The next morning, we meet at the hotel dining room for a continental breakfast we consume in a half hour. From there, we proceed to our appointment with the art dealer.

A burly man in a tan suit—an administrative assistant, according to the nameplate on his desk—ushers us into an overheated office where everything seems large: the high-ceilinged space, the desk, the chairs, the paintings on two walls, and the man behind the desk. He gets up as we enter. He has a mask-like white face that seems whiter from the reflected light of his white dress shirt and the contrast with his artificially darkened hair. I place him between fifty-five and sixty and two hundred and fifty pounds.

Only when he introduces us to the art dealer do I learn that Nathan is passing himself off as an interested buyer and me as his assistant who knows a lot about medieval manuscripts.

Seated across the desk from the art dealer, Mr. Rochat, I steal a glimpse of the wall paintings—maybe eighteenth-century Italian—and Nathan asks if he has the manuscripts and whether he has received offers to buy them. I keep my silence. I'm a novice at sleuthing, and assessing the monetary value of artworks is totally beyond me. Plus, I don't want to interfere with whatever Nathan is up to.

His voice hoarse and low-pitched, possibly from smoking, Mr. Rochat says, "Let me just say that for someone offering rare medieval manuscripts for the first time, I've been busy receiving interested collectors."

"Can you tell us more about the manuscripts? Better yet, can we see them?"

"The manuscripts are in safekeeping at a bank. But I have pictures I can show you. They'll do a better job than me describing them to you."

"Which bank?"

"I can't disclose that."

"No, of course not. Can you tell us if each book is complete? No missing pages? Intact covers?" Nathan says.

The dealer says, "Yes, each book is complete." He takes what appears to be a photo album out of his drawer and hands it to Nathan.

Nathan says, amused, "A photograph album. Aren't these photos saved in your computer?"

"The owners prefer photographs. They don't keep digital copies." He sits back on his chair.

"You must have had some expert—an art historian, perhaps—who examined these manuscripts and who was able to tell you when these were produced and could vouch for their authenticity," Nathan says as he repositions the album for both of us to examine.

The art dealer says, "Of course. But like you, he only saw these photographs and he said he would bet they're most likely from the ninth and fifteenth centuries."

"Is he an expert on old manuscripts?"

"On rare books, yes."

"Do you have documentation from your expert you can share with us?"

Mr. Rochat takes a moment or two to answer. I suspect he's getting defensive. Nathan is firing questions at him he has been reluctant to answer. "The family has it. They showed it to me, but I don't have a copy. They'll provide a copy to the highest bidders."

Nathan says, "I'd insist on a copy before the sale can be finalized. How much did you say the sellers are asking?"

"Three million for both, but I wouldn't be surprised if they sell for more."

"I see. Well, let's see what three-million-dollar manuscripts look like." Nathan flips the album cover.

He and I go through the photographs together.

The first two pictures are large, each covering a whole page. They're the covers of the two manuscripts, inevitably darkened to a dirty green by exposure to elements and handling across the centuries they have survived. The first thing that strikes me is how elaborate the covers are. They have high-relief figures in the middle, and stones embedded on the top, bottom and sides surround the figures on the ninth-century manuscript.

Nathan says, addressing me. "Treasure binding. These were commissioned by royalty." To Mr. Rochat, he says, "These covers must be made of metal. Gold?"

"The ninth-century one, yes. I'm not sure about the other one."

"Are these precious stones?" I ask, unable to rein in my amazement at the extravagance of the covers.

"Semiprecious, at least. These are very old, so the colors don't show well. The owners tried to clean them, but I told them to leave them alone."

"That's wise," Nathan says. "Cleaning amounts to conservation and only professionals should do that."

"Yes, I told them buyers like the patina of age."

"The owners, who are they?" Nathan says.

"These are part of a family legacy. The current owners can't say how far back their acquisition could be traced. Some relative had acquired them a while back in France."

The owners, it's clear to me, don't want to disclose their identity or when they gained possession of the manuscripts, and the art dealer has complied to keep them anonymous. Nathan doesn't press for more precise information.

The rest of the photographs consist of pages from the manuscripts.

As we're leaving, Nathan says he's definitely interested in bidding, but he'll have to consult with an expert about a bidding price. He will have his lawyer set up his offer and send it via secure file sharing. They exchange business cards, including one for Nathan's lawyer. Our meeting lasted a little over an hour. We're taking an early evening flight back home.

From the dealer's office, we go to a nearby café for a light lunch. We have three hours to spare before going to the airport for our flight. As we wait for our sandwiches, glasses of white wine, and French fries for Nathan, I say, "Did this meeting tell you what you wanted to know?"

"The manuscripts are authentic, which is the first big question I needed an answer to. But the art dealer was evasive, and the whole business smells fishy to me." Nathan pauses and is thoughtful for a moment. "Something about the sale doesn't sit right with me. We must find out who owns these manuscripts, and if possible, why they're selling them."

I recall the questions that crossed my mind reading the Art News articles, and I'm curious about what Nathan found suspicious.

He spreads the table napkin on his lap and sits back. "First, let me disclose that much of what I know about collectors, I've learned from journal articles and a book or two. I've only come in contact with a few collectors at an art auction. Collectors like artworks they can show off. Famous paintings like those of old masters—Van Gogh, Cezanne, da Vinci, Rembrandt, Vermeer. They signal money, maybe good taste, and they are usually profitable investments.

"Very few people own complete illuminated manuscripts, especially those before the twelfth century. Mostly they're in museums or national libraries. The Getty in Los Angeles has quite a collection. Private individuals interested in old manuscripts are usually high-profile collectors known and respected in the art world."

"Are you saying there's something suspicious about the art dealer's reluctance to disclose who's selling these manuscripts?"

"It's healthy to be suspicious of art dealers. Anyway, if the sellers came by them honestly, I doubt Mr. Rochat would keep their identities a secret. He'd have an easier time selling them. My guess is these manuscripts were stolen during World War II. Precious items like these worth millions of dollars wouldn't have been easily accessible at any other time. They would have been in museums or libraries or securely stored by a private owner. But the war made it easy to seize and steal artworks and other precious possessions left by Jewish families and others who fled the war or were sent to concentration camps. Too many were probably also thrown out to the elements when buildings like museums and churches were destroyed by bombs."

Like me, Nathan apparently wonders how these manuscripts were lost and when they were found. "So, you think these manuscripts weren't Nazi loot?"

"Hitler had some art background and apparently knew about priceless classical artworks. The famous ones, mostly. Helping himself to those was a big part of his war agenda and he might have had lists of artworks he wanted for a museum he planned on building. A paean to his deluded ego. If he ever laid eyes on these manuscripts, I think he would have ignored them for the showier pieces."

"Who could have stolen them, then?"

"That's what I mean to find out. They could have been items left behind while German soldiers were pillaging the better known artworks, and some soldier or officer took them as souvenirs."

"They're relatively small and would have been so easy to steal."

The waiter has brought our order and we stop our conversation as he lays them on the table. He wishes us "Bon Appetit," and leaves.

Nathan sits up, takes a sip of wine, and smiles. "You're catching on. Yes, they could be tucked inside a jacket or an army uniform. If the thief had no idea what they were—quite likely, I think—they might have been tempted by the covers, particularly that of the ninth-century manuscript with its wide borders set in precious stones."

For a few minutes, we focus on eating. Our continental breakfast was not enough to sustain us through our exciting fact-finding session with Mr. Rochat. But we've been talking about a topic too interesting for me to set aside for too long. I ask, "How do we find out if your suspicions are correct? Where do we go from here?"

Nathan shrugs, "Forward, I hope." He chews thoughtfully on a couple of French fries, staring at his half-eaten chicken sandwich.

I sip my glass of white wine, reluctant to intrude into his thoughts.

Moments later, he looks up at me and says, "Maybe you can do some online research on war looting by British and American soldiers."

"British and American soldiers?" I say, perplexed.

"Many people may be aware of the Nazi plunder of European art treasures. What's not so well-known is Allied soldiers did their own looting. Nothing like Hitler's massive thievery nor those of his commanders, but I wouldn't be surprised if taken together, Allied looting amounts to millions

79

of dollars. And I'm not including in that number the untold value of art the Russians, our allies in that war, appropriated from the Nazi loot.

"It could have been worse. Most people who stumble on artworks that could fetch a lot of money would be too tempted to pass them up. Art that's there for the taking in the chaos of a world war? Jackpot. How many could resist?

"The American military command didn't. They sent more than two hundred artworks to the United States allegedly for safekeeping. But some honest, committed officers of the Monuments, Fine Arts and Archives organization suspected the military command didn't mean to return them. They wrote a manifesto—Wiesbaden Manifesto, they called it—asserting those artworks constitute cultural property and should be returned to the countries which owned them. If the military high command was tempted, why not individual soldiers?"

"Were they returned?" I ask, admitting to myself Nathan does have some impressive knowledge about art. And when it pertains to art looting in the second world war, it's much more than I know.

A frown flits across his brow, an expression he does a lot of. Another impression I'll remember if years from now, I look back to these days. He says, "The two hundred artworks? Fortunately, yes, eventually. After they were exhibited here."

As we're finishing lunch, I say, "Are you serious about buying these manuscripts?"

He shakes his head. "No. I'm assuming they were stolen. That means they can't legally be sold although it won't stop certain collectors and even some museums."

"But what if no one else makes an offer and they accept yours?"

"I'm confident it won't come to that. I'm bidding below the asking price and pretty sure the dealer will receive higher offers. For further protection, my terms of sale will include a clause requiring sellers to provide proof of ownership."

"But can't that be faked as well? I mean if there are forgers who can reproduce coveted masterpieces, surely, it's simpler to fake a document of ownership."

His eyes light up. "You are catching on. Yes, it can be faked." He pauses, frowns for a moment. "In which case, I'll be faced with a dilemma if no one else submits a bid or mine turns out the highest figure. Honestly, I'm not sure what I'll do in that case. This is the first time I'm bidding on an artwork. We're here because I wanted us to see these manuscripts, judge for myself whether they're authentic. I bet on being outbid."

He pauses, knitting his brow again. This time, I detect worry. Is he regretting having posed as a buyer? He says, "This was the only way we could have seen them. I admit I didn't dwell too much on whether I'd be taking a risk. I also ignored ethical questions."

I watch him, but I stay silent.

He averts his gaze and says, talking more to himself than to me, "But I'm confident some institution will want them in their collection and make a higher offer. And if they're buyers who insist on above-board transactions, they'd ask for a legal proof of ownership."

We are among the last to leave the restaurant before it closes and prepares for dinner service. Our lunch lasted nearly two hours and we only have an hour to retrieve our luggage the hotel is holding for us while we went about our business.

On the way to the airport, Nathan picks up the thread of our restaurant conversation. "There's something else that bothers me about this sale. Why did the sellers pick Mr. Rochat, who admits he hasn't offered rare manuscripts before? Art dealers often specialize in one or two forms of art and sometimes in specific time periods. That way, they could gain some expertise in their chosen genres, earn respect, and establish a steady clientele. I would have expected the seller to entrust this deal to a specialist on rare old books."

Chapter Eight

On the Trail of Found Manuscripts: II

Nathan took a risk pursuing the truth about the manuscripts. I never expected that of him. Despite his tactics, we still hadn't seen the manuscripts. We had to be satisfied with photographs. To Nathan, though, they were enough. He concluded they're authentic, not fake. I'm new at this sleuthing game, but I believe he's right. In the photographs, I saw book covers so unusual they have to be real. And those precious stones—would someone from medieval times embed fake stones? Did fake stones even exist in the ninth century?

Paintings can be reproduced and copies passed off as original. Skillful and unscrupulous painters and conniving art dealers have done so for a long time. But a medieval manuscript would need varied skills and may require more than one artist or craftsman to fake. Plus, the parchment has to date back to several hundred years. Technologies now exist to test the age of artworks, from the canvas (or paper, wood, etc.) to the paints and how they're applied.

Now that we know the manuscripts are most likely not fake, Nathan says he can't wait for the outcome of his offer. We need to trace their provenance. People who claim to be their owners don't want their identity disclosed and it makes them suspect. So, who do these manuscripts legally belong to? Where, when, and how did they acquire these manuscripts? And from whom?

For my own interests, I would like to go as far back as the origins of these manuscripts—the monastic scriptoria that created them and for whom. But Nathan may not need that kind of information for his book.

I decide to call the reporter who posted the news items on the manuscripts. Though they aren't bylined, the managing editor of artnews.com does not hesitate sharing the name and cellphone number of the reporter.

He doesn't answer my first call, so I try again. On the third try, I leave my name, number and reason for my call. And I begin to wonder: Will he bother to answer my call? If not, is he in on some shady deal with the owners and the art dealer?

The next moment, my rational inner me asserts herself: Stop being paranoid. You're seeing a conspiracy where there may only be coincidence. Events happening by chance. The reporter is probably busy chasing stories.

There is intrigue in tracing provenance. It's like doing detective work.

Early the next morning, the reporter returns my call.

I introduce myself as a graduate student who needs information for a thesis I'm writing on medieval manuscripts. I don't mention Nathan who Professor Fischl says made something of a name for himself writing articles for an art magazine investigating the provenance of some lost manuscripts. Professional rivalry exists in journalism at least as much as it does in other professions, and I worry the reporter would withhold information if I let it slip I'm working with Nathan.

He listens to my intro, then says, "So, what do you want to know?"

"I was curious—why does the headline on your first article—the one about the fifteenth-century manuscript—end with a question mark? You don't do the same thing for the second article."

"The information for those rather short articles comes from the art dealer. He's selling so he wants some publicity, but he wasn't exactly forthcoming with details." Mr. Reporter sounds annoyed. "My experience in such cases is something shady might be going on."

"So, the question mark is your way of communicating your suspicion?"

He chuckles. "Brilliant, don't you think? A punctuation that implies a lot. As to the brief content, I gave him as little as he gave me."

"Did you follow up on your suspicions?"

"No, the dealer was stingy with facts and the story was a waste of my time. I freelance for a few publications and am quite busy. Besides I know nada about illuminated manuscripts. If I write about art thievery, it will be about some sensational art pieces like the ones stolen and still missing from the Isabella Gardner Museum in Boston. That one is well-publicized and there's a reward worth millions for verifiable information about the heist."

I stifle a retort at the tip of my tongue: who cares about musty old handwritten books compared to such treasures?"

His remark stung me in a way I didn't expect, but he was kind enough to return my call. Instead, I say, "Why no question mark on the second headline?"

"The second is a repeat of the first except it's about another manuscript. I lost interest and had better stories to report on."

"Any opinions of the lost manuscripts."

"I haven't seen them. Not that I care to. I'm more into paintings. I was curious, though, about the price those ancient things would fetch. Some reporter with an art history background thinks they're worth millions so they must be quite precious. He also thinks they were taken by a soldier, possibly American, at the end of World War II."

"Do you know who this reporter is?"

"No, sorry. I hear rumors through the grapevine. I didn't check this one so I couldn't put it in my report."

"Okay. It helps to know someone suspected the manuscripts were stolen during World War II. That might prove to be useful information in the future."

Before I can thank the reporter, he says, "I take it you study illuminated manuscripts."

"Yes, I'm doing graduate work in art history focusing on those 'ancient things.'"

"Do you mean to be an art historian in a few years?"

"Maybe. Que sera, sera."

"When you finish your thesis, can you share it with me? You've made me curious about old manuscripts. Maybe, I can mine something interesting from your thesis. I'll share authorship with you. That would give you some exposure. In the art community at least."

"I'll think about it. Call me in two-years. And thank you so much for your help." I'm amused. Does this reporter keep an inventory of information to use in articles for publication? Or is he flirting with me?

Chapter Nine

Nathan Weighs In

I put off telling Nathan about my conversation with the reporter until I've done some internet research on the looting of artworks during World War II by Allied armies.

My search words, "American soldiers looting art WW II", yield more entries of Nazi war looting and the efforts of the men in the Monuments, Fine Arts, and Archives (MFAA) Section created by the Allied forces to find, recover, and return this loot. I find bits of factual information about individual Allied soldiers, but often they're about war booty such as military weapons, money and items taken from dead enemies—all purportedly taken as souvenirs. Spoils of war the military command tended to ignore or accept as inevitable consequence to a long destructive war. Looting by vanquishers is a historical fact.

Sometimes, though, the chaos following the war years allowed stolen objects worth thousands of dollars to slip under the radar. Unless someone or some group came searching for them.

That's what happened in one case, well-publicized I believe because it involved an old German royal family, whose heiress, a princess no less, reported the loss of precious family heirlooms. Jewelry she needed to wear for her wedding.

The theft was traced to three American officers, one of them a woman. They were tried and sentenced, one of the men to twenty years in prison.

*****

A couple of days later, I call Nathan to tell him about my progress and he suggests meeting again at Peet's Coffee in Emeryville.

I arrive at Peet's a few minutes ahead of Nathan. I've marked out a table for us with a book on a chair. I'm at the service bar deep within the coffee shop waiting for my café au lait when he approaches me from behind. I didn't see him come in through the door sixty feet away.

"Hello again, Clarissa."

"Oh, hi! I got us a table by the banquette. Close to the one where we sat last time."

I hear the barista call my name, and she hands me my coffee drink ensconced in a cardboard insulating sleeve. Nathan orders an espresso.

"I'll see you there, okay?" I tell Nathan, pointing my thumb towards the banquette.

Minutes later, while he's sipping his espresso, I update him on what I've found from my internet search. He scowls when I finish my recounting. "Nothing on stolen manuscripts?"

"Nothing, I'm afraid. Mostly reports of lost paintings, jewelry, gold bullions, stuff like that. There was mention of rare books in a couple of places, but they were Nazi loot that were returned to owners. You're right, though. Our soldiers weren't saints. Abandoned homes, especially those of rich Jews, had valuable things they could take. So, they took them.

Maybe everyone did. Spoils of war soldiers might have felt entitled to."

"I expected that. I lent you my copy of *The Rape of Europa*. Have you read it?"

"I'm still reading it. It's fascinating, but depressing, too."

"For now, that's the definitive book on Hitler's plunder and it recounts the burning of thousands upon thousands of books by the Nazis. It mentions surviving medieval manuscripts only once when a monuments man found a barge full of them on the Rhine."

"I can see why you want to focus on medieval manuscripts."

"There are too many untold stories in history, and many told only from a certain favored perspective." He shakes his head, lamenting the flaws of historical accounts.

I give him time to stew a little. I've reserved for last the conversation I had with the reporter. But, I hesitate, wondering if Nathan will resent me talking to this reporter without informing him first. "I talked to the reporter who posted about the lost manuscripts."

He assumes his low-key, matter-of-fact tone. "What did he say?"

"He suspects, like you do—the manuscripts were stolen at the end of World War II and has heard rumors the perpetrator is an American soldier."

"Do you know where this information comes from?"

"He says from a reporter with an art history background. He doesn't know for sure."

"I should be reassured, I guess. Another person out there believes as I do. Still, it's hearsay until we dig up some proof."

Why did I not see that last remark coming? He must get excited sometime. Aloud, I say. "I think you're on to something, Nathan. We need to dig deeper."

"No doubt," he says and lapses into his usual thoughtful silence.

I try to prod him again. "Are you curious what kind of person might have taken these manuscripts? Seems to me they must have known what they were doing."

"I'm curious about the deeper motivation for taking these particular manuscripts. If we know the motive, it might help narrow down our search."

"I think the person who took them was someone who could appreciate these art pieces. Like you said, they're not the usual objects of art thefts. Maybe it's a person who has some kind of art background."

He concurs, though he's frowning. "I would say so, too. But why have we come to know about these manuscripts only now? If these manuscripts were lost in World War II, whoever took them kept them for more than half a century. If he knew what they were, he would have guessed he could sell them for a fortune. So, why didn't he sell? Did he develop a special attachment to them or did they have some personal meaning for him?"

"It's also possible he was afraid of being caught."

"True. These are such rare treasures that if they change hands, they're sure to attract press coverage. If the seller can prove he's the legitimate owner, he has nothing to worry about. If not, no museums or honest collectors and art dealers will buy them."

"What about hushed-up transactions between less-than-honest people?"

He shakes his head again. "Risky, but, unfortunately, it happens more than it should. More than we can guess. And some museums, including a few big ones, have acquired artworks that were part of the Nazi loot."

"Oh, yeah. I vaguely remember a few years ago reading about some people who disclosed that the Hermitage and Pushkin museums have kept and refused to return artworks the Soviet army took from the looted art collection of Hitler and Goering."

Nathan nods, absentmindedly. "Yeah. We have to dig farther and deeper to find out everything we can about these manuscripts."

I sigh. "We're looking for needles in a haystack."

"Needles worth millions."

"Maybe we should take a detour. See if we can find out who owned the manuscripts before they were stolen."

Nathan's eyes brighten. "Great idea. You're getting the hang of this whole process. So, will you help me research my book? Officially, that is. You've already started, anyway— Switzerland, some internet research, talking to the reporter."

"Information I can also use in my thesis."

"Does that mean you've decided to write your thesis on the loss of these manuscripts?"

I shrug. "Still undecided. The fifteenth-century manuscript fascinates me."

"Not the pricier ninth-century one?"

"Fascinates me, too, but somehow, not as much."

"Well, the two are tied together so going after the facts of their loss, and provenance is the same process. Anyway, I'll offer more than that reporter: co-authorship. And a share of the royalties."

This time, I stare straight into his eyes and shake my head. "You can't mean that. You're, in effect, my thesis adviser and Professor Fischl only takes credit for it. He gets paid and you don't. I owe you."

"I'll be paid in royalties for the book. If you help me, it seems fair to give you a part of it."

This is the Nathan with his uncompromising sense of what's just and fair. But maybe I would have done the same thing. "Okay, I'm officially in."

Nathan says, "I'm glad. Here's what we do next. There's an organization putting together a database of stolen or lost artworks. Complete with a history of ownership of a piece— the provenance—when such data are available. I've contacted them before about lost old books. They're not too organized at the moment, but they're computerizing their vast lists of art treasures that have been reported missing or lost. They include books and manuscripts lost in various countries during World War II. Going through their lists will be tedious and time-consuming. Fancy a trip to London?"

"Not my favorite city but I can go to do research. How long will it take?"

"I hope no more than a couple of days. I can give you the names of two helpful ladies who believe in what they're doing. Tell them we're doing research together for some manuscripts on sale I'm considering buying and I want to make sure it's not in their list of artworks reported looted by the Nazis."

"Can't I tell them we're doing research for a book and a thesis?"

"I'm not sure if they'll be as helpful. This organization exists mainly to facilitate restitution or repatriation of lost or stolen art and other objects. Anyway, why not use an angle that's worked for us before?"

He has a point and it's easier to acquiesce. "Okay, I'll do as you say."

"You'll be on your own. Don't worry about plane tickets and hotel accommodations. I'll take care of those."

"But Professor Fischl ... Will he let me go? It's only been a couple of weeks since my last trip."

"I'll talk to him. He's a family friend and my parents are clients of his. But you're right, there are rules. We're okay for now, though."

"When do I go?"

"As soon as possible."

Before we part, Nathan says, "I'm glad you're on board, Clarissa, but, please, next time you contact someone or do something other than internet search, give me a heads up. We don't want to jeopardize our inquiries and we'll have to make sure what we do doesn't hurt either of us. There are some dangerous characters who get involved in art theft."

I heard the gentle reproach in Nathan's words. But I can't help wondering: If we have different reasons for pursuing the truth about these manuscripts, can we be partners?

My main interest is in the manuscripts themselves, and if I follow their trail, I would start from where they were produced. What I intend to do might be of academic interest only. Valuable to the university professors and experts who'll read and analyze what I write.

Nathan is pursuing a more recent path—how they were lost before the current offer to sell them by someone who wants to keep their identity secret. Who's this individual and how did they acquire these manuscripts? Why sell them now? These are potentially sensational, news-worthy issues.

I say, "I'm sorry. I'll tell you next time."

"Remember also: We're partners. You play my assistant only when it helps us obtain information that will throw some light on how and why these manuscripts disappeared and how they were found. And we should be open with each other in everything we do for this project."

Chapter Ten

The Tedious Pursuit of Truth

Late afternoon on Friday, Nathan calls me at the office to ask if he could come by my place on Saturday morning to drop off my plane tickets.

Saturday is my laziest day and I don't get up before nine in the morning. "Can you come at ten?"

"No problem."

On Saturday, I hurry to make myself coffee, and change into blue jeans and a red pullover printed with the name and logo of Université de Paris. "Sorbonne" in big letters runs below the logo. I've owned it for five years though I seldom wear it. I want to keep it until it begins to fall apart. I comb my hair and let it hang below my shoulders.

The doorbell rings at ten on the dot. Nathan stands at the door in blue jeans, a white shirt, and a black leather jacket, his ubiquitous messenger bag slung across his chest. I stare at the slick leather jacket. It seems he's not above going à la mode once in a while.

He eyes me for a couple of moments before his gaze roams down to my chest. "Sorbonne," he intones.

I suppress a smile of amusement at his reaction. "Come in. Make yourself comfortable. Would you like a cup of coffee? I'm having some myself."

"That would be nice. I hoped you'd offer me a cup. I brought breakfast sandwiches."

My apartment is like all other graduate student apartments. I have a tiny kitchen with a stove and no oven, a small sink, a few shelves, and the kitchen counter where I eat, write, and often leave my books and my laptop. At its end, next to the wall, sits my Moka pot when it's not in use. An old fashioned stovetop coffee maker, Dad bought two of them in Italy—one for me and the other for himself and Mom. I keep mine clean and ready for my morning ritual.

I dump the used coffee grounds in the Moka pot into a metal bowl half-full of grounds from previous mornings. I rinse the pot to make Nathan fresh coffee.

Nathan scans the living area. Though economical of space, the living area is comparatively luxurious, outfitted with an armchair, a couch, and a rectangular coffee table—all generously bought for me by my father. The large window at the end of the room keeps it from feeling too confining, and I close the light-filtering drapes on the window only when Arthur stays the night.

Nathan chooses to sit on a stool at the kitchen counter across from where I'm standing, waiting for his coffee to brew. He puts his bag on the counter and takes out the breakfast sandwiches and paper napkins. He watches me.

"Sugar, milk? I don't have cream."

"I take it black."

I knew that, but I don't often blurt out my impressions of people. I pour coffee into an espresso cup and place the pot, perched on a trivet, on the counter.

"There's more in the pot for at least another cup."

"Thanks," he says, offering me a sandwich.

We eat, facing each other in silence, and to my surprise and relief, the silence doesn't feel awkward. There's serenity in shared silences like this that reawakens my memory of a Zen passage I read once, a calming passage teeming with implications:

"Sitting quietly, doing nothing,

Spring comes, and the grass grows by itself."

I look up from my sandwich and find Nathan still watching me as he chews his sandwich.

I turn my attention back to my sandwich, perplexed— something in his eyes unsettled me a little. Neither of us utters a word.

When he finishes his sandwich, Nathan pours himself more coffee, sipping it slowly, looking away as if he's embarrassed I caught him staring.

Soon after I crumple my empty sandwich wrapper, he takes out an envelope from his bag and passes it on to me across the counter. In it, are round-trip plane tickets, hotel booking information, and a booklet of traveler's checks.

Before I can thank him, he raises a hand and pulls out a stuffed unicorn from his messenger bag. He wiggles it, squishes it, and hands it to me. He says, "For good luck. Cushy, too. Better than airline pillows."

This gesture is a lighthearted touch I never expected of him. I relax. And I laugh. I like this side of him.

He doesn't laugh. But he smiles.

Later, he helps me clean up, wiping the kitchen counter with paper towels.

"I have an appointment at half past noon," he says as he adjusts his messenger bag on his shoulder. "Thanks for sharing a late breakfast with me. "

I follow him to the door where he stops and turns to me. "Shall we do this again?"

I nod, more to acknowledge than to agree.

He waves goodbye and walks away.

I lean my back on the door after I close it and mutter: what just happened? He was only supposed to give me my plane tickets. We hardly talked. And we didn't exchange a single word about the lost manuscripts. But something passed between us in the hour or so he was here. Something that didn't need words.

*****

I fly to London on Sunday. Wide-awake at the start of a nine-hour overnight flight, I dig into my carry-on for my headphones. To my dismay, they're not in the bag. I have forgotten them in the rush to pack for this trip. Out of the seat pocket in front of me, I retrieve the headphones the airlines provided me. I put them on and connect to a station that pipes music into my ears. The old guy in a suit next to me inclines his chair soon after takeoff and covers his eyes with the airline-supplied mask. He must be a weary, frequent traveler.

It's hard to feel peacefully alone in a claustrophobic airborne cabin. A slight movement of your arm and you can elbow the person sitting next to you. Pick up your carry-on bag on the floor and you bump your head on the occupied chair in front of you. As if that's not enough of an annoyance, the playlist of adagios and andantes programmed by some airline staff to entertain or lull me into shallow tranquility for a stress-free flight fails its duty after a while. I yank off the headphones.

With the unicorn under my head, I close my eyes and let my mind wander. So many things have happened in the last three weeks. Unexpected things. Things I couldn't breeze through. Things leading to actions with clear objectives.

Some people think I've led an exciting life, going from one country to another, experiencing different cultures, meeting diverse groups of people. But, in fact, not staying long enough in a place to set roots in it has left me aimless. Wondering as I wander: What is it like having a place I go back to after each foreign adventure? A place of my own in one specific town or city I can call home?

Yes, my wandering life was exciting, but the excitement wore out sometime in my teens. Now that I'm involved in a quest for truth about manuscripts shrouded in mystery—manuscripts no ordinary person can read—has my life become exciting again?

Maybe not in the usual way people define exciting. An adrenaline rush that quickens your heart and your breathing. Flushes your skin. Primes you for action. Even gives you a sense of floating off the ground. But the quest for these illuminated manuscripts has meaning I can understand and embrace. A pursuit I can't say no to. About a fascinating subject matter rooted in my childhood.

With those thoughts, I slumber off to several hours of disconnected dreams. And wake up as soon as lights are turned on in the cabin, the pilot announces our approach to Heathrow, and I hear window shades being rolled up.

Four hours later, after a quick check-in at the hotel where I leave my luggage and freshen up a little, a cab drops me off in front of one of a row of old narrow five-story brick buildings. The entrance to it is a white door nearly as wide as the building and topped by an arched white transom. It looks a bit incongruous with the old brick façade and must be of relatively recent construction.

Inside the small lobby, a directory tells me the office of the registry for looted art is on the third floor. This particular building houses several other unrelated offices, a few of them commercial.

The lady at the desk in the registry office greets me with a smile. Behind her are rows of tall shelves. She has been told of my coming. Nathan called her yesterday. She leads me to a table behind the shelves and on which lays a thick folder. "Our list of old books and manuscripts lost, stolen, or found but not yet claimed. Here and there, you'll find other objects listed if they were taken at the same time and from the same place as the lost books. Good luck." She pats the folder and returns to her desk.

The table is one of two on each side of a French door leading to a small balcony. On the other side is a larger desk, folders filed up on top. I assume it is used by the lady I see working between the tall shelves. Next to her desk is a table with office machines.

I start combing through a list of rare books that disappeared from World War II repositories and private homes. This is one time I lament not having a Walkman I'd have equipped with a lively playlist of current pop songs and songs my parents loved to play when I lived with them. I may need that playlist to stay awake. I did remember to stuff a few small packages of M&Ms in my bag. But food, I learn upon entry, isn't allowed in the registry office. I can take them out to the balcony, though. They're a good excuse to take short breaks and rest my eyes.

I've persevered at my tedious task. But by the time the office closes in late afternoon, I still haven't come across what I'm searching for. I'm tired. My bottom prickles from a thousand tiny pins, sitting for hours on a wooden chair. But I'm not discouraged. Instead, I'm impatient for the next day. Tomorrow, I'll find what I am looking for.

I've gone through the worst part—listings that aren't the target of my search. Surely, something will turn up in the remaining dozen or so pages. The Germans were noted for having kept better records than the Allies of art in their possession, whether they were stolen or bought at vastly reduced prices from Jewish art dealers and collectors.

*****

I arrive at the art registry office at a quarter past nine the following morning, fortified by two cups of hot tea, a scone, scrambled eggs and sausage—a huge breakfast I'm not accustomed to. But I have a long day of work. Tedious jobs can be as stressful and exhausting as strenuous work.

The lady at the front desk and I exchange morning greetings. She says, "You haven't found what you're looking for yet?"

"No, but something tells me, I'll get lucky today."

I pass between tall shelves to the desk where I was working the day before. The lady organizing files yesterday is at her desk this morning. We greet each other. She adds, "May Lady Luck smile at you today."

I place an open palm on my heart, a gesture I picked up from Arthur.

The folder containing the lists of lost art lies where I left it yesterday. Before I open it, I knock lightly on the desk.

I go through three pages of lost books and manuscripts with no success. But towards the bottom of the fourth page, I stop. I blink and bend my head a little closer to the page. Am I really reading the words "illuminated manuscript, 9th century?" The words send an electric jolt through my body that makes me shudder.

I lower my gaze to the next line with some trepidation, like someone who's afraid that the round ball of chocolate in her mouth would turn out to be marble. But there it is— "illuminated manuscript, 15th century!"

The ancient ancestors of my picture books. The manuscripts that could give purpose to my life.

Eight other items—reliquaries—follow. All reported missing, along with the manuscripts, in June, 1945 by a church in the Harz Mountain area in the Saxony-Anhalt region of Germany.

I go back to those two lines on the manuscripts, unable to tear my eyes away from them. Transfixed for a few minutes with a mix of excitement and relief, I feel like a child who gets the birthday gift she fervently wished for, but never expected because her parents can't afford it.

After minutes of staring and marveling at my luck, I ask the lady organizing the lists if I can make a copy of the page.

My next thought is to call Nathan, but it's past three in the morning in California. He'll have to wait for the good news.

To make sure I haven't missed anything, I go through the rest of the list. A little faster this time.

We are making progress. And for the first time, I know how exhilarating it feels when sleuthing for truth is rewarded. Now, we're certain someone had taken the manuscripts before the last world war ended in Europe. But even more remarkable—proof exists that the thief was an American soldier. The church reporting their loss was in the zone occupied by the American military after Germany surrendered. But how did he (or they) do it? And how could this deed escape the notice not only of the military command, but also the monuments men responsible for tracking and accounting for objects reported lost?

Chasing the trail of these valuable medieval artworks becomes even more seductive when, in the afternoon, I talk to the lady who's back to working between the shelves.

"Do you have more information on old manuscripts listed in your registry? I'm researching two reported lost by a church in a town east of the now torn-down Berlin wall."

"So Lady Luck did shine on you today," she says brightly.

With a wave of her hand, she beckons me to follow her. She stops in front of a shelf, and like the other shelves, it's crammed with filing boxes of documents. "We keep information reported to us or we've been able to find on the hundreds of thousands of lost or stolen artworks in these boxes. And we're proud of how we've organized them."

"Do you plan to computerize all the data in these documents?"

"Of course, but it will take time. We're a non-profit group. We rely on grants and donations. We've been lucky so far and hope that we can start soon. When that database is finally online, there would be little need for the effort and expense of a trip to London."

She seems to know exactly where the information I'm asking for is stored. She pulls out a box from the third shelf, and extracts a folder about an inch thick out of it. "If we have any more details, you'll find them in this folder, and if you're lucky, there may even be pictures. All artworks reported lost from centuries-old towns in the Harz region are in there."

The folder is nowhere near as thick as the one containing the lists of lost rare books and manuscripts. This search will not be as laborious. Anxious not to miss anything, I go through them with the proverbial fine-tooth comb.

My luck is holding up. The claim by a Stiftskirche, a church in a well-preserved medieval town includes pictures of the covers. The pictures are smaller, but they match those the dealer showed us. The church provides an abbreviated history of the manuscripts. It has owned both manuscripts, not just decades, but centuries since they were bequeathed to the church. They were produced at scriptoria in the Saxony region of Germany, a former duchy in the Holy Roman Empire. The ninth-century manuscript is a gospel inscribed in gold ink. A fact likely to increase its value. To keep the manuscripts safe during the second world war, they were stored in a cave from which they went missing.

This is all heady stuff—of the adrenaline rush type. And because the mystery concerns something I'm passionate about, my brain runs amok with possible scenarios. The look, smell, and feel of the manuscripts in my hands. The sound of the pages as I turn them—carefully, of course. The marvelous art I've been longing to see directly in front of my eyes.

Sadly, though, I'll probably have to be satisfied gazing at these manuscripts under a protective and secure glass case. I may see the covers and a few pages from each one, but that may be all. So, I hope whoever owns them will make facsimiles of both manuscripts that anyone who wants to study them can access.

The adrenaline rush is short-lived. We're still left with many questions. The facts provided by the church strongly suggest these manuscripts were stolen. But we still don't know how the American family that's selling these manuscripts came to possess them. And what fate awaits these manuscripts?

To Nathan, whose interest is in drawing attention to Allied theft of art, particularly old books and manuscripts, these facts will help him describe these manuscripts, but they won't tell him who stole them and why the thief kept them for more than half a century. To the church which owns them, whose primary concern is getting the treasures repatriated, it's essential to know who took them, where they are now (the art dealer in Zurich knows) and what they have to do for them to be restored.

The angle Nathan is taking may be a sensation in the making, not only in the art world, but also among those interested in the events of the second world war. Too many lives were being lost, but many countries were also losing their cultural patrimony—a fact that has the potential to pose moral issues about greed and deception.

*****

I can't wait to tell Nathan the success of my solo detective work. My adrenaline rush has left my muscles a little shaky and I hear my heart drumming in my ears faster than usual. Instead of taking a cab, I decide to walk the three miles back to the hotel to tire me out and calm down.

It's almost dark by the time I cross the short lobby of the hotel, tired and eager for a relaxing shower. I greet the lady in a colorful sari behind the reception counter. She was talking to the man at the counter when I arrived to check in yesterday, but she left when she saw me, disappearing into a room behind a wall of small cubbyholes. Today, she smiles and waves her hand in greeting.

I trudge up the stairs to my room. It's dark and reeks of cleaning fluid and room freshener. I draw the drapes and open the window, but the air is cold and damp, and I close the window minutes later.

It's mid-day in the Bay Area when I dial Nathan's number. He answers by the third ring.

"We've got him," I say.

"The thief?"

"Well, not his name, but we can be more than fifty per cent sure he was an American soldier."

"Now, we're fairly confident the manuscripts were stolen, most likely by an American soldier. But who exactly might it be? And why did he wait fifty years to sell the manuscripts? We're closer, but we're not there yet."

I can tell, across the several thousand miles of cable that Nathan is pleased. But he will never overflow with enthusiasm. Or is he a master at keeping his emotions to himself? Anyway, we should be saving our hallelujahs for when we discover the thief's identity.

Tonight, I do feel bleary-eyed and spent. I've taken a shower, and dressed down to my underwear. All I want now is to watch television until I fall asleep. I'm also famished, so I call a nearby Indian restaurant I passed on the way to the hotel and order takeaway curry.

*****

The following morning, I fly back to California.

The plane lands at the San Francisco International Airport in late afternoon. Minutes after it comes to a full stop, I rise from my seat, the stuffed unicorn in one hand and the carry-on bag in the other. I blend in with the passengers already standing on the aisle. We disembark and exit the jetway into the gatehouse. There, to my surprise, I see my brother Arthur standing among a group welcoming arrivals. He's waving at me vigorously.

I come close enough for him to put his arms around me for a moment. "How did you know I was going to be here?"

"Nathan texted me. I had to come, dying of curiosity. What have you two been up to?"

"But why come to the airport? How did you get here?"

"With a friend and his car. I want you two to meet. He's in his car waiting for us."

He snatches the unicorn from my hand, scrutinizes it. "Cute. Is this a souvenir from London? For me?"

"No, sorry. It's a pillow."

"Hahn. Whimsical. I like it." He wiggles it like Nathan did and says, "I'll meet you when you come out of baggage pick-up."

He takes my carry-on bag and walks away with it and the unicorn.

Chapter Eleven

Arthur Gets Curious

Outside baggage pick-up, Arthur pulls me close, this time for a French greeting—a couple of alternating kisses on each cheek. "Hello again, Sis," he says, "Long time no see."

"It's only been a month. Besides, you didn't call or email me, either. So, not all my fault."

"Well, you know what it's like. The busy life of a student. I brought dinner for the three of us. Baguette sandwiches from The Cheeseboard. Ham and cheese on buttered bread, *bien sur. Très Francis, eh!*"

Arthur became a real francophone on our European tour, so when he found out about The Cheeseboard in Berkeley, he was ecstatic. A combination bakery and cheese shop, it offers artisan breads including baguettes, baked on the premises and a selection of cheeses to rival many cheese shops in France.

He hands me back the unicorn, hooks the strap of the carry-on bag on the handle of the rolling luggage, and says, "*On y va*"

At the loading zone outside the terminal, he doesn't find his friend's car and we wait a few minutes until he sees an old blue Volvo cruising along in a line of cars waiting to pick up arrivals. He waves and the Volvo stops at the empty space closest to us.

He opens the back passenger door and pushes my luggage and carry-on next to a backpack. He says, "You sit in the front with us, Sis."

We both climb into the front seat, with me wedged between Arthur and his friend. As he buckles himself to his seat, he says, "Sis, my very good friend Jeffrey, also a student at the university. Jeff, my sister, Clarissa."

Jeffrey glances at me with a wide smile that crinkles his eyes. He has a tanned complexion, a tousle of curly brown hair, deep-set brown eyes, and a budding beard.

He says, "Arthur talks about you a lot. All good things, of course. So, I told him I wanted to meet you."

We talk all the way to my apartment. The usual getting-to-know-you stuff: how did the two meet? Where's Jeffrey originally from? How much time before they graduate? Jeffrey's plans to go to law school, like Arthur.

Jeffrey drops us off in front of my apartment and Arthur tells him my apartment number. My brother collects everything from the back seat, and hands me the bag of sandwiches and the unicorn. We take the elevator to my fourth-floor apartment.

Arthur deposits my baggage into my tiny bedroom, a separate space with a door, though it's not much larger than a closet. It's wide enough for a night table on each side of the single bed and long enough for a bed, a narrow clothes closet, and some three feet of space between closet and bed that leads towards the door.

Arthur dumps his backpack and the bag of sandwiches on the kitchen counter. I toss the unicorn onto the armchair in the living area.

For the moment, the walls of the apartment are bare. I plan to hang a couple of paintings when I've painted a few more. Mom took the ones I've done.

I don't mind the cramped space. Though temporary, I own it and can pretend it's home.

Arthur pulls a bottle of red wine out of his backpack when he joins me at the counter. He presents it to me, cradled on his hands like a baby. "Making up for the one month. Also *pour dune fête modeste* to celebrate my new job as kitchen help at the campus cafeteria."

"But I thought Dad was taking care of all your schooling expenses." Dad is making sure Arthur gets into law school.

"He's generous enough and I only work two hours, three days a week. Pin money, that's all. For the occasional bottle of wine and take-out dinners with you."

He takes three wine glasses out of one of the wall cabinets on each side of the kitchen sink. Places them on the counter and pours out less than half a glass of wine in each.

He sits one bar stool away from me at the counter and takes a sip of wine. "Do you know if their divorce is final?"

"No idea. They'll never talk about it with us. In my mind, our parents parted years ago."

"Was it tough living with them?"

"Not really. I guess they succeeded in keeping their problems to themselves. One thing they shared is the art of saving face and shielding me from their disagreements."

"Someday, I'll sit down with you, ask you to tell me what it was like growing up with them. You and me, no one else. I'm sure you have stories to tell. Today, I want to hear about this new project with Nathan. But let's wait until Jeff gets here."

"I doubt Jeffrey would be interested. He may not care about art, and he doesn't know Nathan."

"Jeffrey paints and he took art classes. He's into art. More than I am. You're the reason he offered to drive me to the airport and pick you up. He's curious about lost or stolen art. Plus, I did say my sister is very pretty."

"So—Nathan texted you about our project."

"Yeah. A real surprise. I hadn't heard from him in a year at least."

"I don't understand. You were good friends and now you both live in the Bay Area, but you haven't met up again? Not even texted each other?"

"We're both busy, I guess."

At a knock on the door, Arthur jumps off the bar stool to let Jeffrey in. He continues as if he hasn't been interrupted. "I don't even see you as much as I want to. Besides, I have made new friends who're more my age. And here's my best buddy."

"Hello Jeffrey, welcome," I say, distractedly, wondering what Arthur means by "my age." Is he comparing himself to me or Nathan?

Jeffrey says, bowing to me, "Nice to meet you, Clarissa." He sits on the stool next to mine.

I continue to address Arthur. "Yeah, I suppose age has something to do with it. Interests, responsibilities change with age. How much did Nathan tell you about our work?"

Jeffrey takes a sip of wine and pretends to ignore us.

Arthur picks up a sandwich, takes a bite and with his mouth full, says, "That you're writing a book with him. I couldn't believe it, but I tell myself Nathan never lies. I know you didn't exactly get along well. How can you endure writing a book together?"

"I guess we'll have to see about the endurance part. For now, we share a strong interest in some old manuscripts. My thesis adviser turns out to be a friend of Nathan's family and he recommended him as a resource for my thesis project. Did you know he switched careers?"

"No, not until the cryptic text he sent me. I had to text him back to find out what's going on with you. I was more curious about that than his career switch. I knew his heart wasn't in medicine. He went into it in college to please his parents so I can kind of understand why he got out of it. But come on now, talk to us about your new project. Nathan said you were in London doing some research."

Jeffrey perks up. "What are you researching? Is it related to your book?"

"It's not my book. Right now, I'm helping him research. If I do some of the writing, I'll be a co-author but we're not there yet. My priority is writing my thesis."

Arthur says, "Are they related? Your thesis and his book?"

"Yes, there's an overlap. Maybe a big one."

Jeffrey says, "So, you can both use the research you're doing. You haven't told us anything about it yet."

"It's about some lost medieval illuminated manuscripts that have resurfaced in the last few days."

Arthur and Jeffrey exclaim in unison, "What are illuminated manuscripts?"

"They're manuscripts so they're not printed, but handwritten. And they're illustrated. But they're also adorned with gold leaf, gold or silver ink, and sometimes some other luminous paint colors."

Arthur says, "So, they shine."

"I get it. That's how they're illuminated," Jeffrey says, grinning and enlightened.

Giving Jeffrey a gentle slap on the shoulder, Arthur says, "Yeah! Thanks again, man, for illuminating me on art." They both laugh and Jeffrey returns the slap.

Amused by their camaraderie. I say, " *Tu melon, mon petit* Arthur. Art wasn't your thing."

"The French are big on art, so I thought I should cultivate an interest in it. Besides, I'm finding out it can be a lot of fun."

"Even old manuscripts?"

"I'm not sure about old books in general. But the ones you're studying are artsy, right? With pictures? So, I'm curious. Anything that fascinates you, Issy, I check out. So, what's it about them that makes you want to study them?"

I ponder his question for a moment. "I think it's because in my mind, you can trace the evolution of children's picture books back to illuminated manuscripts. They were initially created for people who couldn't read the psalms, gospels, etc. Like we do now with picture books for little kids. It's like what Nathan said—more than a thousand years since those early illuminated manuscripts, we're still using illustrations, images to make the meanings of words clearer, more vivid, more accessible. Illuminating words, you could say. And we'll keep doing so, but how we illustrate words has evolved with the technology we have at our disposal."

Jeffrey says, "Do they have titles, these manuscripts?"

"Not titles like we think of them now. They're often named for their current owners or those who originally commissioned them to be produced."

"I know what scriptoria are, from an art history book. They're like an office for scribes—writers, you know."

"I think the word 'scriptoria', as often used by experts, only refers to monastic places for scribes. Those writers or copiers of religious texts also did illustrations for the manuscripts."

Jeffrey says, incredulous, "That's all? Bibles and books of that sort? No literature for the masses?"

"I don't know in the earlier years of manuscript production, to tell you the truth. I know there were secular or nonreligious manuscripts centuries later, maybe from the thirteenth century onward."

Arthur says, "Do you have a copy of one of those old books?"

"I do, in fact. Anyone can download a copy of an old, old illuminated manuscript from the ninth-century, *The Utrecht Psalter*. I have a copy in my laptop. The university library in the Netherlands now owns it. They scanned the whole manuscript, made it available to anyone with internet access. It's free to download as a PDF file."

Jeffrey takes a big bite of his half-eaten sandwich. "Have you read it?"

"No. It's in Latin and written in an old script only a few scholars can read. The library might have been thinking of scholars and students who do research when they opened up access to the manuscript. But you can download it, too, if you're curious about what makes it a work of art, or you want to understand why it's a unique part of art history. Me—I love the illustrations. I'm never bored or tired looking at them. *The Utrecht Psalter* is my favorite of the ones I've studied or seen in museums. I love looking at the small, animated figures drawn in brown ink. I always discover something I haven't seen before."

"Sounds amazing. Like comic strips. Maybe I'll check it out," Jeffrey says.

Arthur says, "Issy, I can believe you going for this sort of thing—artsy rare books. But Nathan?"

"It surprised me, too, frankly."

"I'd like to see him again," Arthur says, frowning at Jeffrey who's noisily chewing his sandwich, "I guess I miss him. Maybe, the three of us—Nathan, you, and me—can go to some museum and you can both teach me about illuminated manuscripts."

I say wryly, "Like old times."

"Why not? We three had fun."

"You two had fun together. I sometimes felt like I was intruding."

"I'm sorry. I thought you enjoyed our European tour as much as I did."

"I did, but on my own terms. Nothing like what you and Nathan seemed to have shared."

Jeffrey drums his fingers on the counter. "Invite me. Then the third person doesn't have to feel left out. I'm more into art than Arthur is. And if there's any pairing, it can be you and Nathan since you're writing a book together. And me and Arthur. I can teach him a little more about art."

Arthur throws Jeffrey a glance. One that seems to say, "Keep out of this."

To me, he says, "Well, we did meet Nathan because of my interest in café culture. Nathan and I visited many places you didn't care to see again because you've lived in Paris." He wiggles his shoulders in gentle mockery. "You preferred to go sketching. So, of course, we became close and had this thing between us. Nothing romantic, you understand. A guy thing, that's all."

"I know. Don't worry about it. I assure you I had fun and it might be nice to go again."

"Okay," Arthur says, but I can see in his eyes that he's still concerned.

"*N'inquiete pas, petit* Arthur. Believe me, I enjoyed our tour."

He nods, and turns to Jeffrey. A little contrite, he puts an arm on Jeffrey's shoulder and pulls him close. "You can come, but we'll have to ask Nathan if he's okay with it."

Back to chomping on our sandwiches, I talk about the trip to Switzerland, where Nathan and I hoped to see the newly found manuscripts. I don't mention Nathan making an offer. I also tell them about the art loss registry, sparing them the details of my search. Since Nathan's rant—subdued, I grant him that—about the unspoken rules of a work partnership, I've resolved not to talk to anyone about the outcomes of my research until I've informed Nathan of them and he's okay with sharing them.

As I eat, I watch the easy interaction between my brother and Jeffrey, glad he's found a new friend. They obviously like each other.

Little Arthur. Who gets huffy when anyone calls him Art. Who, even now, pulls my hair to get my attention. The older sister he didn't grow up with, whom he's anxious to please. The one who went with our parents to all the different cities our father was sent to. And yet, he seems to have taken what he's been dealt with in stride. If he ever resented it, he's kept it hidden.

Now, only the two of us have to put up with each other. Only three years separate us, but I wonder if sometimes he regards me like a mother. Counting our European tour and his coming to California to join me, we've spent more time in each other's company than he has with our mother. Does Mom regret not bringing up her son? Is she curious about how Arthur feels being the one left out?

We've become a team, both of us trusting that, in this city, or any other city we may inhabit together or apart in the future, we'll always have each other.

I look up from my sandwich and he interrupts his banter with Jeffrey and meets my gaze. Those few seconds are enough to reassure us that neither of us is alone.

Before they leave that evening, he says, "I mean it. We should go on another trip, the three of us." He glances at Jeffrey. "Or four of us. It can be short. Maybe we should do California. We're just getting acquainted with it."

Jeffrey butts in. "Me, too. I'm from Arizona, born and raised."

I say, "We should plan it, then. But we'll have to wait until the school year ends. Who'll tell Nathan?"

"You seem chummier now and you talk to him."

"I wouldn't say we're chummy. You two were. We get along better. We have to, I guess, working together on a project."

Chapter Twelve

Summer 2000

Family

My father's family is rich. For generations, they have owned coconut and rice plantations in the Philippines and invested their profits in stocks and business ventures that have increased their wealth. As the oldest and only son, Dad will inherit more than half of the family fortune and continue managing family properties. By tradition, his two sisters will divide the remaining inheritance between them. As I grew older, I began to think this tradition unfair. And sexist.

I was in my early teens when I slowly awakened to the fact that as loving and generous as my father was, he had a sexist streak. He showered Mom and me with gifts, took us to places for fun, presented us with pride to his friends and colleagues, and never said or did anything abusive. When he got angry, he walked away, went somewhere by himself, and returned hours later in his usual persona of loving and generous husband and father. I was happy and didn't find a reason to complain. Until months before he and Mom left Rome on his final assignment in his birthplace two years ago.

Mom, I noticed, had become unusually quiet and more distracted. She didn't answer when I talked to her, and when I called her name louder, she'd say, "Huh" with a faraway look in her eyes. Sometimes she sat still, staring at nothing in particular. More than once, I heard her sobbing in the bathroom while she took a shower. Once, in the middle of preparing dinner, she heaved a long sigh and murmured, "Nobody listens to me."

Mom was unhappy at yet another move in which she had no say. Whenever important decisions had to be made, Dad made it, no discussion or consultation necessary.

A few weeks before they left Rome, I couldn't help myself. I confronted Dad. "Why do you treat Mom like that? We're way passed Victorian times, you know."

He had been reading a newspaper, which he put down on his lap. "What are you talking about? Treat her how?"

"Like she's incapable of making decisions."

"She makes all the decisions at home. But as 'head of household'—by IRS definition—my word is sacrosanct."

"But that's sexist. And old-fashioned."

He scowled at me. "Live with it." He returned to his paper.

As if that wasn't enough, I dredged up the Martinez family tradition on distributing his parents' legacy. He lowered his newspaper again and glared at me. The muscles on his face quivered. "How dare you? How dare you call a long tradition sexist? That tradition was adopted for good reasons. The men in this family have worked and managed the plantations and kept them profitable. Why should we not have a greater part of the fortune amassed through our efforts? Generations of Martinez men have made sure we lived not only in comfort, but in enviable luxury. The women have been pampered, given all they wanted, from trinkets to education. How could you, who know nothing of this tradition's history, call it sexist?"

I stepped back: why did he become more incensed over my accusations against the family tradition. Why not his Victorian treatment of my mother?

A few days later, he apologized for his angry outburst. "I'm aware I have a short fuse. That's why I trained myself to walk away."

This summer, I had another confrontation with my father, an incident I'd remember for a long time: he accused me of unduly influencing Arthur's decision to live in California. An offense for which he might never forgive me.

Following family tradition, Dad had paid for all my undergraduate education expenses—tuition, housing, food, other necessities. When I graduated, we tacitly agreed I'd be on my own. On the last week of the lease on the Paris studio I was living in, he telephoned me.

He congratulated me on getting my degree, and followed it up with "But I'm disappointed in you. In fact, I'm angry."

It had been a while since I accused him of sexism, and I couldn't recall another offense that might have angered him.

"You've influenced Arthur to leave. He's packing up to join you in California. Has he contacted you?"

"We exchange emails, but he's never mentioned coming to live here."

Arthur and I had been emailing each other since our trip in Europe, and I couldn't remember him telling me about coming to live in California. He ended many of his emails with "*A bien tot,* Sis" ("See you soon"). But he never specified any time.

Dad said, "I learned he's applied to a university there."

"He's never told me."

"I don't believe you. How could he keep something like this from you? I'm sure you encouraged him."

"Honestly, Dad ..."

He cut me off. "I'll never forgive you for this." Then, he banged his telephone on the receiver.

I've never heard from him since.

I understood why Dad was angry. Angrier than when I called the family legacy tradition sexist. Arthur was expected to inherit much of the family fortune and with it, the management of its holdings. The life and future of the Martinez family rested on Arthur's hesitant shoulders. I understood then that Arthur was brought up by my grandparents to prepare him for his presumed role as the future *pater familia*rs.

My father could see Arthur was not like him. Tradition did not mean as much to Arthur as it did to him. And Dad thought it was me, during the months Arthur and I meandered across Europe, who convinced Arthur that the choice on where and how to live was his alone to make.

Knowing Dad, I was sure he wouldn't give up easily. Arthur was young, and Dad believed he held the trump card. Having had control over the first four decades of his life, he would grant Arthur that same freedom. Meanwhile, Dad would do all he could to make Arthur see and accept his family responsibilities.

I might have complicated his task, but ever confident of himself, he was sure he could undo the effects of my interference. Dad believed in the power of his wealth. The power that could entice Arthur to do as Dad wished.

Chapter Thirteen

Late November 2000

Who Stole the Manuscripts?

A couple of days later, Nathan and I meet at the Emeryville Peet's. It's late afternoon, and only four or five customers are in the coffee shop. I order decaffeinated mocha with whipped cream before I join Nathan at a table near the entrance, a place that seems to be taken every time we've met before.

Nathan says, "Your London trip was worth it, wasn't it? Thank you for the work you've done. It's definitely a step forward."

"Yes, but now we have to find out who stole it."

"That will be harder. The art dealer could have given us a good lead if he had disclosed who the sellers were of those manuscripts."

"That's a dead end, don't you think?"

"Maybe not. If we tell him we have strong evidence they're stolen, he might get rattled enough to reveal the names of his clients."

"You think he doesn't know they're stolen."

"I think he knows. Or at least suspects the sellers gained possession of the manuscripts through means that aren't exactly legal. Unscrupulous dealers are out there. They'll sell fakes and original art pieces of questionable provenance with no compunction. And too many collectors covet artworks enough to turn a blind eye. They feign ignorance of buying or owning stolen art. And all of them—dealers and collectors—get away with impunity."

Shocking to me, this wheeling and dealing in the art world. How could they? But I say, "Wouldn't an art dealer be more wary if he's shown evidence he's selling stolen goods?"

"We hope so. That's why the information you gathered from the art loss registry is quite valuable."

"I don't think the Swiss dealer will reveal who the sellers are."

"You're right, but he might take the manuscripts off the market. That tells us something. And it buys us a little more time to zero in on the thief. Do you have a date the church reported the manuscripts missing?"

"Yes. I made copies." I open the folder I brought with me, leaf through the church files and point to the date on a report.

"June 1945." Nathan mutters to himself.

"The church inventoried the contents of the boxes they hid in the cave in early April, 1945. When they returned to retrieve the boxes after the German surrender, they noticed that items in two boxes were missing."

"The ones which held the manuscripts."

"And a few other items still missing." I point to the small items under the illuminated manuscripts on one of the registry's lists.

"We need to find out who controlled the area where the cave is located at the time the church reported the missing items. It should be fairly easy. I've done it before. It will only take me a phone call to the National Archives on World War II." He looks at his watch. "Six o'clock. Too late."

I close the folder and push it towards Nathan. But he says, "Keep it for now. We'll look through them again later."

I reach across the table to retrieve the folder. "We're closer to uncovering the truth, aren't we?"

"I think so. But my phone call won't give us the identity of the thief."

"No, but we're inching closer."

He smiles. "I like your optimism. Yes, we're inching closer. By the way, have you narrowed down the subject of your thesis?"

"I'd like to focus on the fifteenth-century manuscript, partly because I'm familiar with *The Utrecht Psalter.* So, though I've only seen the cover and several pages of that stolen manuscript, I presume to know something about it. Besides, to me there's a connection between this Psalter and the picture books of my childhood. In both, images enhance, if not completely take over, the functions of narrative language. But no matter which manuscript I focus on, I'll address their having been stolen and kept by the thief for such a long time. In doing so, I expect to gain insight into the value of art for individuals. The content of the manuscripts must have some deep meaning to the thief that would explain why he hang on to them."

"Fascinating. Analyzing the thief's relationship to the manuscripts can tell us what it is about art we value. Sometimes so deeply our obsession with it, or our greed leads to crime."

"Yes, I still think this particular theft might not have been done for profit or self-aggrandizement, at least not initially.

Like you said, it's not the usual art pieces thieves steal. Did the thief develop a genuine love for these manuscripts? And did that love make it impossible for him to part with it?"

"Careful," Nathan says, still smiling, though he's shaking his head. "I know it's hard to be objective about art, but watch out. Don't romanticize your thief. Remember you yourself said he might have kept these manuscripts because he was afraid of being caught."

I laugh. Self-consciously. "Thanks for reminding me. I know you'll be an objective critic of what I write."

"We'll keep each other on track."

The thudding of chairs on table tops tells us it's time to go. "Can I drop you off at your apartment? It's getting dark."

"I prefer to walk. My place is only ten minutes away." It actually takes me a half hour to walk, but why quibble about it?

"You sure? It'll only take a few minutes."

"Thanks, I need the exercise."

At the sidewalk outside the coffeehouse, I expected us to part ways, but Nathan stops for a moment. He's assumed his characteristic thoughtful look.

"You accomplished a lot at the registry. Going through reams of records is never fun. I wanted to go with you, do my share of the tedious stuff. But I couldn't." He hesitates. Uncertain what to say next? Deciding not to say any more?

"I might as well tell you."

I wait. Is he opening up? A little, at least?

"I haven't completely left medicine. I trained in internal medicine rather than specializing in one of those areas my parents wanted me to. A friend from medical school works at a free clinic. He needed to take a vacation and asked me to fill in for him last week."

"Oh. Nathan, that's ..." Why does my brain draw a blank the second I need it?

When I remain mute, he waves goodbye, and strides briskly towards the parking lot.

"... wonderful ... admirable." Clichéd compliments, but I mean them. Compliments he's too far away by now to hear.

I amble on towards my apartment, reflecting on the encounter. He hesitated to tell me about his volunteer work. But why? It's something he should be proud of.

The following morning, Nathan calls me at the Art Office. He has talked to a lady at the World War II archives. American military forces controlled the zone in and around the Harz area, and guards were posted at various caves to safeguard everything stored in them. We finally have the information to support Nathan's suspicion that an American soldier stole the manuscripts.

Chapter Fourteen

December 1945

Home At Last

He couldn't believe he was spending Christmas at home. But as one of those deployed at the beginning of the war, he had earned more than enough points in Operation Magic Carpet, the military's demobilization process, to be among the first to be sent home.

Now, here he was, impatient to reunite with the unusual souvenirs he had mailed home. Spoils of war, he corrected himself.

After the tearful but joyful reunion with his family, he retreated to his room. He was impatient, but he would have to wait a few more hours until everyone had gone to bed.

He laid down to rest before the special dinner his mother and sister were preparing. They were determined to celebrate his homecoming for a whole day. He planned to show his spoils of war to his family, but he was not yet ready. He wanted to spend some time gazing at them, admiring them, alone in his room.

He was going to wait for another night when the fuss over his return had died down. After dinner, preferably, away from leftover food and dirty dishes, and after everyone had washed and dried their hands.

He fell into a shallow slumber, dominated by a recurrent dream that started on the battlefield when he could snatch an hour or two of sleep: A field of flowers, yellow and blue, up to his knees. Swaying in the wind. He stands in the midst of it, holding his rifle. Alone. Where was everyone?

He hears a soft voice calling, looks around, but sees no one. Someone lays a warm hand on his. His name again, in that soft voice. He jerks his arm to dislodge the hand.

He awoke, staring at his mother's face, alarmed but braving a smile. The field of flowers, he was sure now, helped keep him alive.

A few nights later, after dinner, he announced he had war souvenirs to show them, but they had to wash their hands first and join him in the living room.

As each object passed from one hand to another, his family briefly examined these oddities, but didn't know what to make of them. Despite the unusual covers, they were less awed by the old books than by the casket and the small crystal-encrusted reliquaries.

"They're so cute, these crystals. And so fragile," his sister said, "You can see there's stuff in them."

He said, "Peek into them but please don't open them."

"I won't. I might break them."

"Thanks, Ginnie. You did everything as I instructed."

"Those books are obviously old, but they're impossible to read. I opened them when I received them, but I couldn't make out the words. They're not in English. The one with the simpler cover was nicer. You couldn't read the words, but the drawings of little figures doing things were so cute. If they had been enclosed in frames, they would look like comic strips."

"Why did you get these old books anyway? For the stones on the covers? Are they precious?" his brother asked.

"The books are beautiful. It doesn't matter that you can't read them. Besides, they're quite old and they're part of German history. Maybe the stones are precious, but I don't intend to sell those books. Who would want anything German, anyway?"

As soon as he said this, he realized he was contradicting himself. He had taken these items—most likely precious—from boxes hidden in a cave by a German church. The cave had not been among the mine shafts where Hitler and his commanders had hidden their loot.

When he first opened the book with the tarnished gold cover, he was awe-struck by the words all written in gold ink and the first letters of each page embellished with gold leaf. He couldn't read the words any more than his sister could, but he knew they weren't printed but handwritten on parchment made from animal skin more durable and long-lasting than paper. Technically, they were manuscripts and should date farther back than the middle of the fifteenth century when the printing press was invented in Germany.

His sister said, "But are those stones real? Worth a lot of money?"

"Like I said, I don't know. I didn't bring them home to sell. They're for me a reminder of what I went through and suffered in that war. I'll always have them to show me that I survived and gone back home. That the side I was on won."

What he didn't tell his sister was he was convinced that if he were to sell the golden book, it would fetch thousands of dollars. The cover alone was worth that much.

The second book was less richly decorated, but he agreed with his sister. The illustrations of figures running across each page were like a comic strip.

After the holidays, he went to the city to reunite with old friends who survived the war. Before their meeting he went to his bank to store the casket and his other little treasures in a large safe deposit box. A time might come when he would have to sell them to cover his personal expenses in the city.

He also visited the university library where he had earned his fine arts degree. He vaguely remembered reading about ancient manuscripts in one of his art history textbooks. But at that time, his main interest was portraiture, not medieval illustrated books. Now that he owned a couple, he must find out more about them.

His old books were called illuminated manuscript or manuscript illumination, because words, decorations and painted illustrations in them were gilded. Usually with gold leaf, or sometimes silver.

Gold made the manuscripts shine. He suspected all that gold was a metaphor for seeing the light, which was appropriate for books of a religious nature. The first manuscript had illustrations of evangelists and Jesus every so many pages. The second featured a gilded full-page painting, followed by pages of sketches of religious rituals in ink and watercolor that he was sure illustrated the texts on the same page. Gilded colorful vines and flowers adorned the bottom of every page.

The items he took from that cave were treasures. He had bagged some of the best trophies of the war. Only fair, he thought. He had gone a young man and returned an old man. His hair had receded, his cheeks were shrunken, and the skin on his head was so parched he imagined he could see through it to his skull. He looked ghastly. Ghostly. Jumpy. Plagued by nightmares. He cringed every time someone touched him. He had lost his youth, its hope and promise stolen by Germans in a war he couldn't grasp the meaning of, started by an arrogant race bent on destroying races and cultures they thought inferior to their own. He fought as he was told, but he resented having to fight a senseless war.

Maybe his resentment helped him survive, but he had aged beyond his years. For all he had suffered, he deserved all he had taken, including the silver ornaments from the Jewish home. For those, though, he felt an occasional pang of guilt.

Every piece he had brought home held the most important years of his life. Those four years were a lifetime lost in a theater of international war more brutal than the last. His trophies of war compensated for his injuries, both physical and spiritual. He would display them, and people he had yet to meet would know he had been in the war. He had helped vanquish evil and had survived with all his body parts intact. And yet nothing, not even his trophies, could ever bring back his lost youth.

He bowed his head and cried.

Chapter Fifteen

Back To Work

On Monday morning, I'm back in the Art Office, sitting across Professor Fischl as he hands me the pop-quiz answer sheets from the previous week. He says, "You'll be doing double duty on those answer sheets this week. I plan to give another pop quiz on Thursday."

"That's okay by me, Professor. I owe you. You've been generous giving me time off to do research."

"How's the research going?"

"I think we're getting somewhere. Have you talked to Nathan?"

"No. Busy, you know."

"He's the Nathan Adler I met in Europe."

His eyes gleaming with curiosity, Professor Fischl says, "You don't say. You mean he trained as a doctor? Like his parents. I would never have suspected. I always thought art and journalism were his passion. It was he who convinced his parents to buy two of my paintings. Two scenes of workers picking grapes in the Napa Valley. I wonder why he left medicine."

"I don't think he's totally left it. From the little I know, he works part-time at a clinic."

"Well, well! Interesting. Maybe it's time he and I have that dinner. I'm a nosy old geezer, Ms. Clarissa, in case you don't know that yet. I'd invite you to that dinner as well, but Nathan can be guarded."

"I understand, Professor. I know that about Nathan. His guardedness, I mean."

He watches me, an eyebrow raised. "How well did you know him?"

"He was really more my brother's friend," I say, amused. The professor is a nosy geezer.

"I see. So, tell me what you've learned so far. And is it getting you closer to a decision on your master's thesis?"

"I think so. I'm doing an illuminated manuscript, for sure. In the medieval style. I'll concentrate on the fifteenth-century manuscript for the content."

"Not the older one which is likely to be sold for at least three times as much moolah?"

"The golden gospel. That might be of greater interest to Nathan because of its age and how much it would sell for. It would attract more readers to his book. But my interest isn't based on monetary value, or age, but on what the manuscript as a work of art means to me."

"Is that what it's called? *The Golden Gospel?*"

"No, it's the name I give it because it's written in gold ink. Makes it easy for me to distinguish it from the fifteenth-century manuscript when I talk about it."

"You've seen them."

"Not the originals. Pictures."

"Better for the manuscripts, I think. They're so old and shouldn't be handled too much. What are you calling the fifteenth-century manuscript?"

"For my purposes only—the *Utrecht Repro.* Sooner or later, we'll learn which ones these two are. More than likely, they were produced in German scriptoria rather than transported to Germany from France. The church that reported their loss claimed having owned them for centuries."

"You're saying they're not part of the Nazi loot and it's not the church that's selling them now."

"That's right. The church reported they were lost and want them back. We don't know how the sellers acquired them but it's probable they were stolen at some point."

"Very good, Ms. Clarissa. I think your thesis might be one of the most fascinating I'd have the privilege of evaluating."

"I hope so, Professor," I say brightly as I rise from my chair. He seems to have become more open to my thesis proposal.

"Call me Adam, Ms. Clarissa. Most of my students do."

"Thank you, Adam. I'll try to remember that." I wanted to ask him to stop calling me "Ms. Clarissa". It actually bugs me. To those who know his habit, it may mean nothing. But to strangers, it has a ring of pretentiousness that I'm afraid they'll attribute to me.

I'm more Issy, the nickname Arthur gave me when we were kids and which he calls me now when he's not using "Sis." Mom calls me Issy, too. But, I have to be on a more intimate footing with someone for me to disclose my nickname to her or allow her or anyone else to call me Issy.

*****

In the afternoon, I attend Adam's art history intro class. I've missed two weeks of it.

I don't hear from Nathan for the rest of the week. But Arthur has come every evening bringing take-out dinner. Once, on Thursday, Jeffrey comes along.

I watch them bantering, horsing around. Arthur is nineteen and Jeffrey might be thereabouts, but to me, they still seem like children. Childlike, though, rather than childish. They're in tune to each other's thoughts and feelings, their mutual trust unquestioning. For the first time, I envy my brother.

On Friday evening, I tell Arthur we should go on a short trip after Christmas."

"Just the two of us? Or with Nathan, too?"

I crinkle my nose. "Not sure about Nathan. Why not Jeffrey?"

"I'm sure he'd be thrilled. He was looking for an excuse to shorten his Christmas visit to Arizona. Maybe he can use this trip as his excuse. You sure about Nathan?"

"I'm afraid we may end up talking too much about work. Our meetings have all been about illuminated manuscripts. I need a break from it, a little fun. We can visit the Getty Museum in Los Angeles if you really want to see illuminated manuscripts. They have a few on exhibit. Besides, I've never been to LA. We can hit a few other famous tourist spots."

"Haven't been there, either, as you very well know. And neither has Jeffrey. I'll see him tomorrow. Tell him then and he can give his parents a heads-up. Too bad, though, about Nathan. I do want to see him again. He can be a lot of fun."

"Why don't you go see him yourself?"

"I might do that." Arthur puts his arm around my shoulder and plants a kiss on my cheek. "Can I stay here tonight? I do miss you, you know."

"The couch has your name on it, kiddo."

That night, sitting on my bed, I think about my parents again. I haven't heard from them since I arrived in California. But to be fair, I haven't called them, either, though I've sent them a few emails neither of them has answered.

I pick up one of the framed pictures on my night table, possibly the last they had together. Mom and Dad are standing in front of a volcano, smiling for the picture-taker, a foot of space between them. On the back, Mom had scribbled: *In front of the Mayon Volcano, a near-perfect cone.*

Dad. Tall, straight, and handsome. Not above bragging about his thick black hair with hardly a streak of grey even in his mid-fifties. He blamed me for Arthur's choice to join me and make California his home. Even if it were true, could he not forgive me for that?

Mom. Grasping the strap of her shoulder bag. Her abundant reddish-brown hair pulled back and beginning to grey. She turned heads for a long time with her tantalizing green eyes and her long flowing tresses. I miss hearing her voice. How she'd change it to match the characters in the stories she read to me. In my teens, she began to retreat into a shell.

I'm concerned about her. Dad is highly respected in his country and assured of a fortune as the first son of a retired general who owns several plantations. But Mom, estranged from her immediate family and forging a new life for herself, faces challenges worse than mine. My eyes are moist gazing at her standing next to Dad.

"What's happened to you, Mom?"

I wish I'd asked her before she left why she told us not to contact her. That we should wait for her to call us.

I had sensed a desire in her—maybe a need—to cut ties completely with us, and build herself a new life. At the time we parted, I was too anxious and preoccupied with what was ahead of me that I didn't probe into what might have been going on with her.

I'm sure she still loves us—me, Arthur and even Dad, despite the problems they had in the last few years of their marriage. Maybe she has dreams she wants to pursue. Dreams she can only go after, freed from responsibilities to her family.

She majored in art, too, though she didn't graduate. She married my father instead. She dreamt of writing children's books that she, herself, would illustrate. My father, at the time a recent West Point Military Academy graduate, whisked her off to California where he did doctoral work in international studies. And where both Arthur and I were born.

I kiss the picture twice. Once on Mom's face and the second on Dad's. I utter a silent prayer for us to connect again in some way, across the thousands of miles that separate us.

Chapter Sixteen

December 2000

Back on the Trail

At the Art Office, I'm once again at my desk, surfing the internet. Back to the tranquil noon hour when everyone else is out to lunch and I'm alone relishing a sandwich. A peaceful hour in a familiar place indulging a daily habit.

I spent two weeks of the last month in Europe, in cities familiar to me from having visited or lived there in the past. And yet, in these recent visits, a sense of being unmoored bothered me. Was it because I missed that sense of security my parents gave me when they were there with me? Thankfully, I had work to do. Work that shaved the edge off that near panic.

The phone on my desk rings but I hesitate to pick it up. It's my break time. And I refuse to spend it on anything other than what gives me pleasure. Besides, my phone has never rung during the lunch hour and I've never had the dilemma of whether to pick it up or not. The ringing stops and I sigh with relief. But the silence is a short two-minute reprieve. The ringing starts again and goes on longer. Defeated, I pick it up.

Before I could say hello, a voice answers. "Hello Clarissa. I need your help."

Nathan. Sounding pressured, and not in his usually cool manner.

"Nathan. Is anything wrong?"

"Nothing, if you can help. I know you have school and a job that need you as well, so I thought I'd work on our search by myself for a while." He hesitates.

"But?"

"I need your presence. I've been following up on your research at the art loss registry. I came across a guy. German. A kind of maverick with a mission to recover looted art and return them to their rightful owners. He's willing to meet with us. Share what he knows."

"Sounds like you've already talked to him."

"Over the phone, yes. I informed him of what we're doing. And I learned one of his clients is a German cultural organization anxious for the return of items stolen from what he called a Stiftskirche—a church, I believe. He has narrowed down his search to a list of suspects for the theft of the lost manuscripts. He can use our help to identify who in the list is the likeliest culprit and he'll share with us all he's gathered about World War II looting. We need to meet with him."

"Does this require another trip to Europe? To Germany?"

"No, fortunately. He lives on the East Coast and is willing to meet us halfway. But I offered to pay for plane tickets and hotel accommodations for him to come here. He agreed. He also agreed to a weekend meeting. Said it was better for him. And if we can help, he hopes he can strike that particular case off his list."

"When?"

"This weekend. Short notice, but he sounds like a busy guy. Travels between here and Europe quite a bit."

"Where?"

"We need a quiet place so I suggested my house. Is it okay with you?"

"Of course."

"We also have to prepare a little so we should meet before the appointed time to talk."

"Okay. When and where do we meet?"

"I don't want this to interfere with your work schedule, so you choose time and place. I think we'll only need an hour."

"Thank you for accommodating my schedule. The coffeehouse closes shortly after six. Are you okay coming to my apartment on campus?"

"Shouldn't be a problem. I've been there once."

"Thursday, around six?"

*****

I come home half an hour earlier on Thursday to tidy up a little before Nathan arrives. The night before, I went to a nearby grocery for bottles of water, coke and beer, and a bag of pretzels. I know little of the social conventions for when an acquaintance or business partner comes to your home for work. Arthur and Jeffrey are the only visitors I've had. Other than making sure they have beverages and snacks to munch on, they ask for nothing and entertain themselves. So, shouldn't those suffice for Nathan as well?

Nathan arrives on time. Casual in blue denim jeans, a black sweater, a black windbreaker, and his ever-present messenger bag. He dispenses with the usual pleasantries and says, "Where should we work?"

"How about the counter?" The folder containing the files from my search at the London registry of lost art is lying on the counter.

"That should do pretty well." Nathan puts his messenger bag on the counter and sits on a bar stool.

"Can I offer you something to drink? Coke? Water? Beer?"

147

"Water is fine."

I push the folder away from the messenger bag and put two bottles of water next to the bag. I sit on a stool with a third water bottle. I face Nathan who's guzzling water until it's down to a quarter of the bottle.

He says, "I guess this meeting with Mr. Wilhelm is like a job interview. He worked hard to put his list together and he wants to ascertain you and I can do the task before us."

"And we want to know the source of his information and how he put his list together."

"Yes. Reliable, verifiable information."

"Should I have copies made of the data from the registry of lost art?"

He glances at the folder on the counter. "We should have those on hand in case he wants to see them." He takes a folder out of his bag and reaches over to put it on top of my folder. "I made you copies of files I received from the National Archives of World War II."

"Thanks, I'll look them over."

"Mr. Wilhelm is way ahead of us and has sources directly accessible to him but not to us. He's been in this business for the last twenty years. We're neophytes compared to him. He's a lawyer, too."

"He's beginning to sound intimidating. How did you find out about him?

"Someone at the National Archives told me about him. He had already done what I had intended to do. He was there for days rummaging through their records. The staff got to know him well. He sounds like a genial guy with what one of them called a 'weird sense of humor.'"

"Maybe it's the German sense of humor. Your finding him is a lucky break for us, though, isn't it?"

"A promising start. But I anticipate a lot of legwork tracing the footsteps of his suspects and zeroing in on one of them."

"What if most of the people on the list have died?"

"That's more likely than not. Then we'll have more work to do."

Nathan takes the second bottle of water and drinks it, more slowly this time. I watch him—this guy who almost always has something to say that's worth listening to—quaff his water in silence. He must have come from the clinic to be this thirsty. He gazes back at me, his eyes crinkling with a touch of amusement. I smile, arching an eyebrow.

"I was parched," he says, putting the empty bottle down on the counter. He looks at his watch and gets off the stool. "I have to go, but one last thing before I do: I don't know how long our meeting with Mr. Wilhelm will last, but I ordered dinner to be delivered to my house. I'm working at the clinic in the morning. So, if something comes up and I'm delayed, can you be on hand to receive him and the delivery?"

"When does the meeting start?"

"He flies in the morning and we scheduled the meeting for three o'clock."

He takes a key out of his keychain and lays it on my palm. Holding my gaze, he says, "*A la prochaine,*" and walks towards the door.

I follow him, more than a little amazed. How much French does he know?

Chapter Seventeen

Mr. Wilhelm

After a bus ride, I walk several blocks in a neighborhood of California bungalows to reach Nathan's house. Ten minutes early for our scheduled meeting, I'm not in a hurry. A deer or two in Santa hats wink at me from one house. Colorful lights and fat Santas add a festive air at other houses. It's a misty December afternoon, the promise of rain hanging in the air so still you can see moisture suspended in the atmosphere.

Like most houses on the street, a short walkway leads to a few steps up a small covered entry porch to Nathan's house. On both sides of the porch, rhododendron and ceanothus bushes past their flowering season have shed some leaves. I sit on one of the short concrete walls bordering the steps to wait for Mr. Wilhelm and the dinner Nathan ordered from a restaurant.

Nathan called me half an hour ago. He has been detained at the clinic and will be a bit late. He hoped no more than fifteen minutes.

The walk warmed me up, but it doesn't take long before I begin to shiver in the cool, damp air. I regret not having put on a thicker jacket. I could go into the house to warm up. Nathan did lend me a key. But I feel uncomfortable intruding into his space while he's not here. "It's all about boundaries,"

I could hear my mother say all those years ago. Everyone has a sacred space another should not enter until she's invited.

I will have to open the door to let Mr. Wilhelm in, so what's the difference if I enter the house now? Because, I tell myself, his coming changes the dynamics. Letting us both in becomes all about work, part of the responsibilities implicit in a work partnership.

I rise, exasperated at my scruples. But, I guess, like everyone else, I'm a captive of my past. I pace up and down the short walkway until a cab screeches to a stop behind me.

A blond, fair-skinned, tall man climbs out of the cab and with quick firm steps approaches me. This must be Mr. Wilhelm. He's right on time. He extends his free hand to me, and I grasp it. He's carrying a portfolio with his other hand.

"Hello there, I'm Kurt Wilhelm," he says, shaking my hand, smiling widely, wrinkling his eyes, and animating his whole face. He must be about Professor Fischl's age.

"Clarissa Martinez. Welcome, Mr. Wilhelm."

"Call me Kurt, please. Something tells me we'll have to put up with each other for quite some time." He barely has an accent I can detect. And yet, like me, he doesn't sound American. Or maybe I should say Californian, the only American I really know.

I smile back, searching for what may be the usual response to his remark; to his casual, friendly—and to me—disconcerting demeanor. But my mind is blank. All I can do is lead Kurt up the few steps and open the front door. I let him in first. As I'm about to enter, the delivery guy from the restaurant arrives with two bags of food.

"Mr. Adler's order," he says.

"Do you need me to sign anything?" I say, taking the two bags.

"Nope." He pivots on his heels and rushes back to a red car in front of the driveway, its engine still droning.

"Here, let me," Kurt says, relieving me of the bags. He raises the bags to his face and sniffs. "Hmm, something smells good in here."

"Nathan ordered dinner," I say, as I unlock the front door.

"Ahh. I can't wait."

We step into a large open space, a couch, armchairs, and tables on one side of the foyer and a dining table, a matching buffet, and chairs on the other side. Kurt unburdens himself of the bags of food on the dining table.

He joins me in the seating area where I've remained standing. I sit down on one armchair. He goes for the couch.

"Nathan will be a bit late. He couldn't leave work right away."

"No problem. You and I could get better acquainted. May I call you Clarissa? Maybe you have a nickname? I love nicknames, you see. Because I don't have one. Kurt is a hopeless case. Could not be any shorter."

He laughs and I can't help laughing with him. Why is it so easy for certain people to put other people at ease? Arthur has the same gift. Jeffrey, too.

"Clarissa is fine. How was your flight?"

"Uneventful. Which is how I like it. I travel a lot but I'm not fond of being buoyed several thousand feet above the ground."

"I've traveled a lot, too. Europe mostly. Lived in Berlin a couple of years when I was a child."

"I'm from Munich myself. Your father must have been a diplomat."

"He was, yes. But he took early retirement and I'm sure he's having a blast back in the Philippines."

"You're Filipino?" He seems incredulous.

"Half. My mother is white. From deep in the mid-west. I was born in California." I've never revealed those facts about myself on first meeting someone. And not in one long breath.

"It must explain your big, beautiful gray eyes. An enchanting mélange of East and West."

I'm not used to compliments, and a flush creeps up my cheeks.

Kurt seems to sense my discomfort. "I do shoot my mouth off sometimes. Anyway, I'm excited to finally see a bit of California. Don't tell Nathan, but I changed my flight to give me two days to spend in San Francisco. Maybe I'll go to Sausalito and the redwoods, too."

I laugh again and he smiles. I say, "Me, too. I need to grow up and learn how to handle it when someone pays me a compliment and those around me all turn to ogle me."

"But weren't you the center of your parents' attention?"

He's assuming I'm an only child, but I don't correct him. "I guess that's my problem. I wanted them to leave me alone sometimes."

"Well, I have the opposite problem. I have three kids who all want to be the center of attention all of the time and at the same time."

We both laugh again, and at this lighthearted moment the front door opens and Nathan steps into the living area. He stares at us, a bit bewildered: two people in his living room—

The Golden Manuscripts

strangers to each other—laughing as if they've known each other a long time.

Kurt gets up, approaches Nathan with an outstretched hand. "Kurt Wilhelm. Pleased to meet you, Nathan."

Kurt shakes Nathan's hand vigorously and Nathan returns the hand shake with equal energy.

"Truly honored to know you, Kurt. I've googled you and your work after we talked on the phone, and I am quite impressed."

Kurt shrugs, a blush spreading across his cheeks and down his neck. He turns to me. "You see, Clarissa, I also don't handle compliments well."

I purse my lips, trying to suppress a smile of amusement.

Nathan's inscrutable gaze darts from Kurt to me. "Something to drink before we begin? Kurt? Clarissa?"

Before either of us can answer, Nathan turns towards the dining area, picks up the bags of food on the dining table, and goes through a door into what must be his kitchen. He returns a couple of minutes later, carrying a large tray of an assortment of refreshments in bottles: water, coke, ginger ale, and beer.

Chapter Eighteen

So Now What?

Nathan sets the tray on the coffee table. Kurt reaches for a
bottle of beer and Nathan asks me what I'll have. He hands me
a bottle of ginger ale and takes beer for himself. He sits on the
armchair across the table from me.

For a minute or two, we imbibe our beverages in silence.

Kurt, sitting at the end of the couch closer to me, turns to
Nathan. "I like your place. Open and airy. Glass sliding door
to your backyard, a high ceiling and not many walls to bump
into. Is this a California bungalow?

"I've heard it called that."

"Have you lived here a long time?"

"In this house? Four years."

"I saw kids playing in the front yards of some houses. Do
you have any?"

"I'm unattached."

"Well, you're still young. I married in my mid-twenties and
I'd say wait until you're thirty."

Nathan answers with a polite smile. Kurt turns his
attention back to his beer.

Moments later, Nathan says, "How long have you lived on
the East Coast, Kurt?"

"Thirty years at least. I went to Georgetown, got a law
degree, did graduate work in International Relations, met my

wife, and decided to stay. She was born in New York, but her family originally came from Jamaica."

"Do you have kids?"

"Three boys who keep me on my toes." Kurt goes on to talk about his sons and the youngest's latest mischief. He's clearly proud of his children.

I'm content to take swigs of ginger ale and listen to the men talk—Nathan with his short direct replies and Kurt with his stories.

At a pause in Kurt's storytelling, Nathan says, "Kurt, you were going to show us the information you have collected. And we will show you ours. Shall we move to the dining table? We'll have plenty of room to spread out."

Kurt gulps what's left of his beer and swipes his portfolio off the couch. Nathan and I finished our drinks minutes ago.

Eight chairs flank the rectangular dining table of dark stained wood. Nathan, who brought the beverage tray, deposits it at one end of the table. He gestures for Kurt to sit at the other end. We take the chairs on either side of him.

Kurt and I lay out the folders we've brought. Nathan takes his from the top of the buffet against the kitchen wall.

Kurt begins, going down a list with the information he has gathered. I can tell from the exchange that ensues between him and Nathan that they have already discussed much of the information on Kurt's list.

Kurt, who has morphed into a formal take-charge persona, came with two copies of his list of suspects which he passes on to Nathan and me.

He says, "The owners of those medieval manuscripts we're after—a Stiftskirche, a very old collegiate church from the twelfth century—was in a town controlled by the American military when the church reported them missing. But other armies did pass through the area at the time: Russians, British, Canadians, for instance. It's impossible to know who went into the cave between March—when the church hid things they wanted to protect—and June of 1945 when they discovered a couple of manuscripts and several other treasures were missing from two crates. The only thing we're sure of is which American battalion first arrived in April to secure the cave. Later, there was some confusion and military personnel went into the cave without permission. Some Russian officers, I learned, insisted on going not only into Nazi loot but museum repositories as well. So, they could have gone into the cave."

"They had their own mission towards the end of the war," Nathan says. "They collected masterpieces they have refused to return, arguing they recovered them from Nazi loot. They believe those artworks now belong to Russia, maybe as compensation for the devastation the Nazis inflicted on their country. They also took art that escaped Hitler's scorched-earth policy on Slavic countries to annihilate both their populations and their cultures. So today, if you want to see those masterpieces, you have to visit the Hermitage and Pushkin museums."

I was outraged at hearing this. We're going after one or at most a few people for stealing two precious manuscripts. And yet, here's a whole country who did in-your-face massive looting and no one seems to have raised a fuss about returning their plunder to their owners. We as a society must also be culpable: What if we didn't value things the way we did? What if we had some kind of standardized scale which determines the price of a piece of art. Would a Matisse still sell for more money than a work of equivalent creativity and beauty by a lesser-known artist? Would art thieves still be tempted to steal the more famous artwork?

My outrage hits me so hard I couldn't help blurting out, "I love art and I keep digitized copies of my favorite artworks in my laptop. Maybe, I could even appreciate other presumably precious things like diamonds. But the value of these treasures, translated into the prices we attach to them, isn't inherent in them. Is it?"

Nathan and Kurt stare at me, dumbfounded.

I stare back, from one to the other. "Well, is it? Maybe if collectors didn't pay so much money for certain artworks, there wouldn't be massive art looting." I probably sound naïve, but I don't care.

His gaze steady and his voice controlled, Nathan says, "Actually, there are recent studies to show artworks have inherent value. We appreciate them and see beauty in them because of certain characteristics they possess. Characteristics like pattern, symmetry, and color that have universal appeal. We may have an inborn response to beauty. Some neuroscientists are researching what parts of the brain are stimulated when people look at artworks.

"We collectively agree human life is precious, and so are food, water, and shelter to keep us alive. We're also feeling, thinking creatures. We need social connections, things to nourish our minds—ideas, accomplishments, creative activities, maybe a quest for beauty and an entity we believe are of a higher order than we are. Art feeds into that part of us."

"Very well said, Nathan," Kurt says. "Before I took on cases of stolen artworks, I knew very little about art. I rarely visited museums. Didn't stop to wonder what art means to me. But as a lawyer, it bugged me that there are people who steal them with impunity. Having met clients distraught over a painting or a sculpture that meant a lot to them, that their family has owned and treasured for generations, I began to see. Now, I understand what Keats says about a thing of beauty. We all need beauty in our lives. Beyond giving us pleasure, we have art to help ease pain and hardships, or to remember and honor people we love."

He wraps the back of my hand with his. "I think it's good you brought up this issue, Clarissa. We do go through a lot when we undertake any kind of mission, and it helps to be reminded why we do it."

Nathan says, "I agree with Kurt. We need to be reminded of why we're doing all this. I believe those medieval manuscripts are cultural property, part of that country's patrimony. They belong to a specific German church and there are laws of ownership people must obey, statutes of limitations notwithstanding. Owning cultural property assumes the church has the privilege of owning them, and in return for the privilege, they must them safe and preserved for posterity. The church is trying to do so and we're doing what we can to help them."

I believe, like the two of them, art fulfills a human need and can serve as a palliative, but I wanted them to know those old manuscripts meant so much to me regardless of how society values them. Meaning so personal that it might be hard for others to understand. Art is precious not only for what an artist tries to express in it, but also how a viewer reacts to what she sees. Good art is a bridge between the creator and the engaged viewer.

But it's futile to prolong the argument.

I must apologize. Not because I've been chastised by one or both of them. They have been reasonable. More than that, they understood how I felt, Nathan especially. It has become clear to me these artworks have personal meanings for them beyond the tangible outcomes of publishing a book or returning artworks to their rightful owners.

Contrite and admitting the uneasy reality I am naïve compared to these two men, I say, "I'm sorry for my outburst. I suppose I'm overwhelmed by how much work lies ahead of us. And we're not certain we'll succeed in finding out who stole these manuscripts so they can be returned to their owners."

Neither of them responds. I look up, my eyes shifting between Nathan and Kurt. They gaze back at me, neither of them anxious to break the silence around us. I read empathy in their eyes and the smidgen of a smile on their lips—all I need to reassure me I can be open with them.

It's Kurt who proves unable to endure silence for too long. He clears his throat twice and taps the list with his ballpen. "Shall we proceed?"

Nathan and I nod in agreement. His gaze holds mine some seconds longer, a fleeting expression in his eyes suspending the breath in my chest. He looks away and turns his attention back to the document.

Kurt points to the list in our hands with his pen. "The list I gave you—I really didn't have much to go on. It includes names of soldiers and officers I gathered from military archives who have been suspected, accused or brought to trial—in some cases after the war—for stealing art, jewelry, and other objects that could be sold for thousands of dollars. It goes without saying the list isn't complete. Things were most likely taken that could have qualified as thefts but were considered spoils of war."

I say, "What do you suggest we do if the people on this list are dead?"

Kurt says, "Many probably are. But we must assume these manuscripts were either passed on to heirs or sold. The manuscripts are on the market as we speak. I thank God for that. At least we have proof they haven't perished. Too many manuscripts did. But these can be retrieved. Too many other artworks were destroyed when, as Nathan pointed out, the Nazi army left utter devastation in cities like Warsaw and Leningrad—St. Petersburg as we know it now—because Hitler believed Slavs were inferior to the Aryan race. The siege of Leningrad is particularly horrendous, resulting in civilian casualties some historians believe constitute genocide. One historian says it's 'the deadliest blockade of a city in human history.' Later, more artworks and other cultural artifacts were lost to us when the Nazi armies bombed places they retreated from. They wanted to deprive the Allies of those treasures."

Nathan says, "Allied bombing also destroyed cities and treasures."

It took me a moment or two to fully grasp what Kurt and Nathan said about Warsaw and Leningrad. Murdering a whole race, then stealing from them and wreaking devastation on their culture, including their artworks. Why?

Tears begin to sting my eyes at the unfathomable hatred and cruelty that drove a group of people to annihilate others. I reach for a few tissues from my purse to dab my eyes before anyone notices my moist reddening eyes. My sadness overwhelms me. My whole body is in turmoil. Out of anger.

And hatred. For murderers of innocent people, who most likely suffered no remorse for what they had done.

A little more in control of my emotions, I dab my eyes dry once more. As I tuck the tear-stained tissues into an outside pocket of my purse, I catch a glimpse of Nathan watching me.

Nathan looks away, shifts his attention back to the list. "Before we go after the names on this list, I think we should go back to the art dealer. Inform him he's selling stolen property."

Kurt shakes his head. "I tried. Didn't budge them one bit. I think the dealer and the seller are hoping to make an under-the-table deal."

"I was afraid of that. Did they know you're representing the church that owns those manuscripts?"

"They did. They dropped hints they'd be open to negotiations with the church. They would return them in exchange for a fee."

I say, "Would the church go along?"

"I wouldn't advise them to consider such deals. They own the manuscripts."

Nathan says, "Why couldn't the church sue for their return?"

"The statute of limitations has expired. Too much time has passed since the crime was committed. The dealer was aware of that fact and they're using it to their advantage. It boils my blood sometimes how people could be so greedy they ignore the right thing, the moral thing to do."

Nathan and I say nothing as we let Kurt simmer down from his anger. It doesn't take him long.

"I'm leaving a folder with you. It contains files I could compile about people on the list. Summaries of trial proceedings, testimonies, transcriptions of oral reports from possible witnesses, things of that sort. It's quite thick, as you can see. I tried to organize them a little, so you'll find documents clipped together." Kurt puts the folder in the middle of the table.

Nathan says, "Do you have the names of the American soldiers from the first battalion who arrived to guard the cave?

"Glad you asked. Those people would normally not be on the list by my criteria. But since they were the first Allied soldiers who came, I put the name of the battalion commander and the squad leader assigned to guard the cave at the bottom of the list. And as you see, I've placed asterisks on their names."

Nathan says, "Great. I'm inclined to begin with those names."

"So you believe American soldiers would steal essentially unprotected artworks?"

"Kurt, you're not asking a serious question."

"No. Art that's there for the taking can be too much of a temptation for anyone to resist, especially if you have some idea of its value."

I say, "Yeah, and those manuscripts could easily be hidden inside an army uniform."

Kurt says, "Frankly, I myself would have started with those names. They were there for sure and the first to enter the cave. If we rule them out after examining the data we have on them, you'll still have other leads to follow."

None of us expected we'd resolve anything this evening. But we can't stop talking, rehashing what we've already said until Nathan announces it's seven o'clock and he's starved.

He has stored our dinner in the refrigerator, and except for the salad, the other dishes only need reheating in the microwave. I volunteer to do the heating and Nathan sets the table.

Kurt walks around the living area, its walls white and bare, except for one painting about four feet wide and nearly as tall. A seascape Kurt stands in front of for a minute or two.

He comes back to the dining area as Nathan and I place dishes on the table. "Nathan, is that a Turner on your wall?"

"Not really. A reproduction."

"Good enough to pass off as the original?"

"Yeah, the artist is exceptional at making copies. But it won't pass tests of authenticity. It's not signed, for one. As far as I know, Turner signed all his works."

Kurt says with a wicked smile, "Well, there should be a forger or two who could sign it and some unsuspecting collectors who'll bite. Aren't you tempted?"

"Do you think I'll admit that to a lawyer like you?"

Kurt laughs and we laugh with him.

He surveys the dishes on the table. "California cuisine? I can't wait to taste it."

Nathan says, "You're in luck. This has been prepared by Chez Panisse, the best in the area."

Our dinner stretches into two delightful hours of savoring delicious dishes and a rambling conversation Professor Fischl would call small talk.

This is the first time I've seen Nathan talk and laugh so freely. Kurt, his stories, and maybe the wine and tasty dinner have loosened Nathan's tongue. For every trivia or funny anecdote Kurt relates, Nathan has one of his own to share. He is indeed shedding his scales.

After dinner, Nathan offers to drive Kurt to his hotel and me to my apartment on campus. Though Kurt's hotel is farther away than my place, Nathan drops him off first.

Kurt gets out, but before he closes the car door, he shares another joke we all laugh at.

As he drives away from the hotel, Nathan glances my way. "What do you say to doing a little work tomorrow? That is, if you have nothing else lined up. It's Sunday, but this way you won't be taking time off your work and classes."

I wish I could tell him I have a date. It would make me sound more like my peers—normal. But the fact is I also can't wait to wade deep into Kurt's files. "Sure. But I'm a late riser on weekends so can we start ten-ish?"

"No problem. I can pick you up at ten o'clock and we'll work at my house if it's okay with you."

"We left the files on your dining table so it's like we just took a break from our work."

Chapter Nineteen

The List

Nathan arrives promptly at ten, stops in front of the entrance to my apartment building where I have been waiting.

"Thank you for agreeing to do some work today," he says as I climb into the front passenger seat. From his manner and the expression on his face, he seems to have receded back into his shell. Or maybe like Kurt, he has a formal face and manner for work and an easy and open one for leisure and play.

At his house, he offers me coffee before we start, which I accept. All I've had this morning is a breakfast bar I munched on as I ran down the stairs from my apartment.

He leaves a thermos of coffee, carafes of cream and sugar, and a plate of cookies on a tray at one end of the table. A nice gesture. One that, by afternoon's end, proved to be an antidote to the mind-numbing effect of poring and sifting through hundreds of words. After a while, they begin to sound the same.

We sit down to work at the other end of the table. Nathan hands me the files on the commander of the battalion, a general, assigned to the regional area where the German church is located.

The general's history is straightforward. He came from a family of soldiers, went to West Point and had been in military service for nearly thirty years. His record was impeccable. He arrived in the Saxony-Anhalt region in July, 1945, days before its control was assumed by the Soviet Army.

"The general isn't a suspect," I say, setting his records aside. "We can strike his name off the list."

Nathan looks up from the records he has been absorbed in. He's been examining the squad leader's records. He waits for me to explain.

"He didn't arrive at the Harz until July, a month after the church noticed the manuscripts were missing."

Nathan nods. "Okay. Let's strike his name off the list."

I can't help adding, "The general went to West Point."

"Like your dad."

"How did you know that?"

"Arthur. When we were getting acquainted in Europe. He said your father went to West Point to please your grandfather."

"I didn't know. Grandpa was a graduate of the Military Academy in the Philippines. He's a general. Maybe Dad fulfilled his father's dream."

Nathan grins. "So, you're the army brat of military elite."

"Hardly. Dad was never in any war. Not even in Vietnam. They groomed him as a diplomat but he says his superiors were convinced a military title and uniform might help when he's involved in certain negotiations. I guess endorsement from the military leadership of his county helped him go to West Point and fulfill his father's wish."

Talking about my father has made me aware my parents are always there in my subconscious more than I've admitted to myself. For a second or two, a familiar and comforting sight flashes before my eyes: Dad, erect and distinguished as he finishes buttoning up his uniform and Mom hands him his officer's hat.

My grandparents weren't the only ones who glowed with pride over my father's admission to West Point. Mom did, too. She often said foreign students were rarely admitted to it and we, his children, should be proud of him.

A wave of nostalgia wells up from my chest and before I can check myself, I say, "I miss him, my dad."

"Where is he now?"

"He's back in Manila."

"With your mom?"

"No. She went back to Illinois. I miss her even more."

"Why not go for a visit? Christmas is a mere few days away."

"I can't." Two short words heavy with regret.

Nathan gazes at me for a wordless moment or two. "I know what it's like being estranged from your parents."

I stare at Nathan who's averted his gaze and is sifting through the files again. It's back to work for us, clear enough.

He takes a few records from the pile he's been going through and hands them to me. "Since we've crossed off the commander from our list, help me with these files on the squad leader. There are things in them you'll find quite interesting."

I take the files, wondering what Nathan's remark about parents implied. But it's not the time to indulge in speculations. I pick up the document on top.

They're transcripts from the university the squad leader attended: Art History 1, Art History 2, Beginning Drawing, Design 1, Color, Composition, Figure Drawing ... The list of art classes goes on from one page to the next. He was a Fine

Arts major, focusing on painting. By the end of the war, he was promoted to lieutenant.

"This is unbelievable. A little too easy. This guy fits right into what I guessed the profile of the manuscript thief would be."

Nathan says, "Because he does doesn't mean it's him. I bet you'll find one or two others on Kurt's list with similar academic backgrounds. In fact, this guy might have been chosen to guard the cave precisely because of it."

"You're right," I say, but my excitement isn't dampened.

"But we don't write him off. Right now, he's high on our list of suspects."

"A list with only one name on it, so far."

"It will grow."

I find a few more facts about the man I dub "the lieutenant." He was among the first to be deployed to Europe in late 1942 when his battalion was sent to Italy, then to Normandy and other parts of Europe. His platoon arrived in Germany in mid-April 1945. Less than a month later, Hitler drank cyanide and blew his head out, and a week after that, the German military surrendered. The lieutenant was in Germany to witness the end of the most destructive war in human history.

He didn't go home soon after, but stayed a few more months teaching art practice classes while waiting for orders to demobilize. Surely, these facts on when he arrived and when he might have left Germany strengthen the evidence that this lieutenant is the manuscript thief.

Nathan interrupts my musing. "Look at this. This guy was accused of stealing silver cutlery and other ornaments from a Jewish family. The matter was investigated and he was fined and ordered to return the items except for a few ornaments he denied taking."

"That might be damning evidence. He doesn't seem to have had qualms taking things that didn't belong to him."

"It's not in his favor, that's for sure. But in war time, can a lawyer justifiably argue such objects as spoils of war?"

We finish examining Kurt's files by the end of the afternoon. The lieutenant maintains his rank on our list which includes three more names, a woman and two men. All three were American officers caught for stealing valuable items from a rich German family who owned a considerable estate in a neighboring town. The family fled the country before Allied troops arrived, but returned shortly after Germany surrendered. Their story sounds vaguely familiar, one Nathan might have talked about, or I may have encountered in an earlier internet search.

The three confessed, were tried, and found guilty. But all the stolen items were sold to some unscrupulous dealer and were never recovered. A regrettable and unfair outcome for the theft victims.

Nathan and I agreed these three were quite likely not the thieves of the manuscripts. We found no records to indicate they were ever around the Harz cave. Besides, wouldn't they have confessed to stealing the medieval manuscripts as well?

Nathan says, "Anything in the records you have of where our main suspect is from?"

"Yes, a small town in Texas."

"We'll dig deeper into his past after the Christmas break. It was easy singling him out from the list. I wonder why Kurt didn't see that right away."

Nathan rises from his chair and turns on a couple of floor lamps in the living area. He gathers the documents on the table and puts them back in the folder.

So engrossed was I in the events Kurt's files revealed that I hardly noticed it has gotten darker. I rise from my chair.

Nathan says, "I owe you dinner. We already missed lunch. My fault. I'm sorry."

"The cookies helped. But I'm open to some quick Chinese."

We drive to a nearby Chinese restaurant Nathan says serves traditional dishes made with fresh ingredients. As we did while feasting on the fancy Chez Panisse takeout at his house, we enliven our Chinese meal rehashing the work and outcomes of our recent research.

*****

A couple of days later, Nathan tells me he called Kurt about the lieutenant. Kurt did study the information on his suspects and reached the same conclusion we did.

As to his reason for not disclosing all he knew when we met, Nathan quotes Kurt, "I thought you should discover this information for yourselves. I could have missed something that could change conclusions we draw from the research. I also think such revelations will be received better from an American team rather than a German. So, it's up to you to make it known."

Nathan protested that it was premature to share what we know. We need more specific facts to show the lieutenant was at the cave where the church treasures were hidden.

Nathan continues, "He agreed and also suggested we go back to Switzerland, confront the art dealer and tell him we have the name of a suspect who could have stolen the manuscripts."

"Can we do that before we have more concrete proof of the theft?"

"Sometimes you need to take a risk to discover the truth. If he has enough of a conscience, the dealer will withdraw the sale. He faces a jail sentence if it's proven he's selling stolen items, especially ones valued in millions of dollars. Taking the manuscripts off the market will keep the manuscripts stored in one place. Prevent or at least delay them from changing hands so we don't lose track of them. The dealer might also become more cooperative. Drop a hint or two about who the sellers are."

"But can't your lawyer call him? His word might have as much or more weight. And it will save travel money and time. Your money, I might add. I surely can't afford it on my assistantship."

With an impish grin, Nathan says, "He can. But I was hoping we could go on another trip together. Inject a bit of fun into our work."

Warmth creeps up my neck to my face, and I turn away. "I'd hate to ask Adam for another favor."

"Please don't take what I said too seriously. I was trying to lighten us up. We've been too absorbed in this search for a thief. But I don't have Kurt's easy manner and sense of humor."

"Okay, I understand. Adam says I don't do small talk so we're not too different on that score. But yeah, I'd like us to lighten up a little in our work."

Chapter Twenty

A Christmas Break

As planned, Arthur, his friend Jeffrey, and I drive to Los Angeles in Jeffrey's old Volvo for a short vacation the day after Christmas. On our limited budget, we share a room with two large beds—one for the boys and the other for me—in a cheap hotel about ten miles from the Getty Museum. In deference to my being the oldest and the only female among the three of us, I also get to use the bathroom first upon waking up in the morning.

The city has a lot of touristy spots, but we agree to do museums first and the Getty is our first stop. We're there not only to see its main attractions, but also its exhibit of medieval manuscripts on the ground floor. It's reputed to have quite a collection of illuminated manuscripts, maybe the best in the US. The museum website presents a sampling of their manuscript acquisitions and a plan to run a special exhibition of illuminated manuscripts sometime next year.

The Getty Center is nothing like the museums I've been to in Europe. It opened its doors only three years ago in a complex of newly built modern buildings sprawled on top of a hill overlooking Los Angeles. Complete with a fountain and a garden. Older European museums usually took over venerable old buildings located in historical city centers.

Two of my favorites, the Louvre in Paris and the Accademia in Florence, were established as museums in the 18th century, and were housed in buildings several hundred years old. My other favorite, the Musée d'Orsay was transformed into a museum in the 1970's, only a couple or so decades before the Getty on the hill. But unlike the newly built home of the Getty collection, the d'Orsay is a renovated train station, built a century ago.

Arriving at the Getty Museum is a unique experience. We park on a lot at the foot of the hill and ascend via a tram to the complex, as if we're being lifted to a place of refuge. Up there, above the smog and away from the racket of modern life, we can leave everyday cares behind for a few hours and immerse ourselves in the beauty and grandeur of some of the best master works man's creative mind and soul can conjure up.

Before we see any other artwork, we visit what might be the museum's most famous piece, Van Gogh's *Irises* in the gallery of 19th century paintings at one of the Museum Pavilions. A crowd has already gathered in front of it.

We stand behind everyone else ogling the Irises. But we outlast most of them and advance to the front row as viewers move on to other works.

It's an arresting picture. Bright, vibrant colors fill the canvas. Thick, dark serpentine lines define shapes. Somehow, even in a painting of nothing but a flowering plant, Van Gogh manages to evoke intensity, movement, and tension.

Arthur says, "I love it. The irises look so alive. Their leaves are like green snakes rearing their hands. And those colors, wow!"

Assuming his self-appointed role as Arthur's art teacher—
or art illuminator as they now call it—Jeffrey says,
"Complementary colors. Blue and orange. But harmonious
ones as well. Green and blue. But look at that single white iris.
Why do you think it's there?"

"An accent maybe? Or maybe that's how Van Gogh saw it."

"I'd like to make a copy of this painting. A bigger one.
Would you like to do a copy, too?"

"No. I can't even draw." Arthur says.

"Try it. I'll help you. What do you think, Clarissa?'

"Sure, Jeffrey, why not. I've copied paintings and they
don't have to be in the same medium. They don't even have to
look much like the original. I did a Georgia O'Keefe red poppy
in gouache once for a watercolor class assignment. The
original is in oil and that change in medium was disappointing.
The picture lost its life, its brilliance."

Jeffrey perks up. "See that, Arthur. You're free to paint
any way you please and I'll be there to guide you along."

"We'll see. Anyway, I'd like to see your painting of the red
poppy, Issy," Arthur says.

"Sorry, I don't have it anymore. I gave it to Mom. She asked
me for it before she left."

Someone in the crowd shushes us, prompting us to amble
on to the other paintings on either side of Van Gogh's Irises:
one of the many Degas paintings of bathers, a Monet haystack,
another Monet study of the church in Reims, and one of
Cezanne's apples. Subjects these artists have painted before.
From the gallery, we go to a special exhibit of Raphael
drawings, and finally, to the illuminated manuscripts on the
ground floor, the main reason we came to this museum.

The exhibit in a small room includes only a couple of manuscripts and a few leaves from each, all enclosed in glass. Unlike the crowd at the *Irises*, only a handful of people are viewing this exhibit. I think it a shame—the lack of interest in books as artworks. But I must look at this absence of interest with an objective eye. This genre of art doesn't attract much publicity, unless something sensational happens like the theft of an art piece valued at millions of dollars. Or it resurfaces for sale years after it's been reported lost. Publicity draws attention to an artwork and people become curious enough to want to see it.

Jeffrey nudges me with his elbow as we reach the last leaf of a manuscript on exhibit. "What do you think?"

"Frankly, I'm disappointed. Getty is known to have a good collection of manuscript illuminations and I expected more."

"I'm okay with it. All I need is an intro and this does it for me. But Arthur seems to be engrossed in it." He points with his thumb to my brother who has lagged behind us.

Arthur is gazing intently at the cover of one of the manuscripts. I approach him—Jeffrey trailing behind me— and I touch his arm. He cranes his neck towards me. "Is this what you want to do with your thesis?" he asks.

"You mean produce an illuminated manuscript?"

"Something like that, yes." He points to the exhibit in the glass case.

"I've sort of committed to doing it, but I'm not sure I'm up to it. I'll have to learn to do certain things depending on the style and practices of the medieval period I choose to do it in. I'll be creating an artwork and essentially writing a short book as part of that artwork. It'll be more than the usual thesis. An art project with written content."

"Wouldn't it be more fun and more challenging?"

"It'll be all that. Plus, a lot more work. And more intimidating, for sure. I don't know if I'm up to it."

"I'm pretty sure you're up to it, Sis."

Chapter Twenty-One

Looking Inward

Arthur's confidence in me is unshakeable, my inner voice asserts several times during the rest of our four-day visit to Los Angeles. In our last conversation at the Getty Museum, he has, in effect, challenged my commitment to the thesis I've blithely promised Professor Fischl. An art project that might prove to be the making or undoing of me.

Riding back to the Bay Area on Interstate 5, a route of unchanging landscapes that can lull you to sleep in the steady speed of a car, my thoughts alternate between fantasies of successfully pursuing an unusual art project for my master's thesis and the reality of the prodigious amount of learning and work it would exact out of me to accomplish it. It would be unique, but am I up to it?

My inner voice kicks in. Why not paint another large picture? Not a landscape, nor a still life, but some depiction of everyday life—like the French realists and impressionists did, but in my own style and alluding to current issues.

That's what the professor wanted me to do. But I've been there, and my first-year project is a canvas painting. I need a fresh challenge. One that requires skills I must learn. Like illuminated manuscripts. They hold me in a grip that won't let go.

Inner voice says I win. But I should be prepared. Unforeseen events are bound to happen when I plunge into something new.

When we arrive at my apartment in the evening, Arthur takes both his luggage and mine out of Jeffrey's car. He tells Jeffrey he's staying with me for a while. I suspect Arthur wants to follow up on our conversation at the Getty.

Scowling, Jeffrey opens his mouth. Closes it, pressing his lips into a thin line. He's disappointed.

Arthur sighs. "It's late, Jeffrey. Gotta go."

"When can I expect you back at the dorm? Gotta prepare for term finals, you know."

"Relax, Jeffrey. We have four more days. I'll see you in a day or two. I brought my laptop so I can start. You do the same."

In my apartment, I deposit my bulging backpack at the foot of my bed. Arthur drops his on the floor by the couch. I come out of my bedroom with a towel on my shoulder and another in my hand that I pass on to Arthur.

"I'm taking a shower," I say.

"I'll make us some tea," he says as I close the door to the bathroom.

An hour later after we've showered and scrubbed off the grime from our trip, we sit on the couch in the living area, slowly sipping warm cups of earl grey tea. Arthur bought a box of these tea leaves a while back and stored it in my kitchen shelf. We've savored it with milk a few times.

Arthur finishes his tea and puts his cup down on the coffee table in front of the couch. He says, "I want you to promise me you'll do that art project."

"Why?"

"Because it's something unusual. Something more challenging than writing a boring thesis in the old boring way. It's who you are, Sis. Why not flaunt it?"

"I'm not writing a boring thesis. I'm doing graduate work in art practice, so I have to produce art."

"Isn't an illuminated manuscript a piece of art?"

"It is, but illuminated manuscripts are passé. Making them is more like marching to the beat of ancient drums."

"Yeah, but I'm confident you'll give your project a new twist."

"At this point, I have no idea what that would take. Doing it the old way would be quite a feat in itself. I can't see myself stretching, drying and cutting animal skins into 8x10 pieces and writing thousands of words using some old script—that's font to you modern men."

"Is that what it takes?"

"Well, the form did evolve once printing machines were invented."

"There you go. Who says you have to write in cursive? Use your brand-new laptop. I bet you can find a medieval style font. Stop making excuses, Issy, and dive into it."

"I wish it were that easy—diving in. But I promise I'll give it serious thought. You must promise in return not to bug me about it."

"Promise. Am I allowed to ask you anything about it at all?"

"Yeah. About once a month. But don't expect details."

Chapter Twenty-Two

January 2001

New Responsibilities

A new year, a new term at the university. But it's not back to the old grind. On my first day back at the Art Office, I wave a greeting at Professor Fischl, who's already in his office. He beckons me to come in. Still saddled with backpack and lunch bag, I go directly in.

I catch a whiff of peppermint as I sit across from him. He's chewing gum. Something I've never seen him do before. An open packet of gum sticks lies on his desk. He picks it up and thrusts it in my direction, "Want one?"

"No, Professor, thank you."

He opens the front drawer of his desk and throws the packet into it. "I need to make changes to your schedule, Clarissa."

He's dropped the "Ms." Another change. I can't help wondering what's going on, but all I say is "Okay."

"You've attended one term of my intro class." He pauses a little to chew some more. "I want you to take over one class every two weeks. Would you be up to it?"

He has wasted no words stating the third change. A bombshell that takes me some seconds to process. "I guess I have to be."

Should I have said, "Yes, I am?" An answer he would have found more reassuring. But the fact is I have no experience teaching. And unlike Arthur's challenge, this responsibility leaves me no choice but to do what I can. And teaching assistants do occasionally teach.

Chewing his gum, Professor Fischl stares at me, weighing my answer. A moment later, he stops chewing and says, "Right. Let's talk about what you need for this class. You have a copy of my syllabus. We pretty much follow the textbook, as I'm sure you've noted, but I'll give you some journal articles, lectures I've written and discussion topics to engage the class. They'll help you prepare before the days you'll be teaching. And if you want, I can sit in for about half an hour on the first two or three sessions you teach. Then I can give you some feedback on how you're doing. But I'm sure you'll do okay."

"I think your feedback will help a great deal. Thank you."

"Good. Of course, you'll still be doing answer sheets and recording."

"I understand. Can I ask a favor, though? Can we schedule your pop quizzes on the day I take over, at least for the first three sessions? To ease me in. It'll give me at least thirty minutes to get used to standing before the class before I lecture. This is the first time I'd be teaching a class."

"Okay, good idea. I have lists of test questions for every chapter in the textbook and you can pick 20 questions for every test you give. I'll include those with the teaching materials I give you."

"Thank you, Adam."

"Well, that's about it. I know you didn't expect this and I'm sorry to spring it on you, but I wouldn't have made this change if I didn't think you can handle it."

"Thank you for your confidence, Professor." I raise my right hand. "I swear I'll do my best. It's a challenge and a good learning experience for me."

He chuckles and shoos me out of his office.

Later, Randall confirms my suspicion. The professor is under pressure to finish his mural by March. The deadline set when the project began—end of December—has come and gone. He told his clients he needed at least five more months, but the bank only granted him three.

Like Randall and the two other assistants, I'm inheriting the pressure the professor is now under. Having worked with the professor for the last two years, Randall seems unfazed. He says Adam has never finished a project by deadline.

I know the material of the intro class quite well, so I think I can handle it. I'll have to focus and schedule my time to accommodate the new tasks. Write my lecture a few days before I deliver it. And rehearse it with Arthur.

Chapter Twenty-Three

On to Texas

I call Nathan before I leave the office to inform him about my new responsibilities.

He says, "I was waiting for something like this to happen. When it comes to making art, Adam has no concept of scheduling. We'll have to adjust as we go along."

"Thanks for being accommodating. I'd like to keep working with you. You've taught me a lot."

"You've taught me a few things, too. And I've had more fun following the trail of the manuscripts with you."

"I'm glad," I say, though looking back, I remember he only started having more fun since Kurt's appearance. Before that, he was formal and always on task. He might have learned how to become more open watching Kurt, who's more willing to engage in "small talk."

I bring up the topic of the lieutenant, the lead we said we'd follow up on before we parted on Christmas Eve. "What are we doing about tracking down the lieutenant?"

"We need to go to Texas. I scoured the Texas phone book for people with the lieutenant's surname during the holiday break. I found four in a town around El Paso, including a business establishment, Maddox Hardware Store."

"I'd like to go to Texas."

"I'll have to talk to Kurt first. We may need a lawyer. You never know what could happen. When we go will depend on his being available."

*****

A few days later, I find out what adjusting to my new duties at the Art Office exacts out of me when Nathan calls me again.

"We're going to Texas, Kurt and I. To track down the lieutenant."

"Can I go, too?"

"You could if we're going on a weekend, but it seems Kurt can only come weekdays. We fly on Thursday."

I am disappointed but I have no choice. I've been harboring some hope—or maybe it's a fantasy since he might already be dead—that I could meet and talk to the lieutenant, find out why he stole the manuscripts and why he has kept them all these years.

I say, "How long will you be there?"

"A day, maybe two or three. Hard to say. Depends on how hot the trail is. We don't know if the lieutenant is still alive. He should be in his eighties by now."

"What if he's already dead?"

"I don't trust what that art dealer said. He was protecting his clients, so he could have been lying."

Nathan, the skeptic. But that skepticism has served him well. It has made him persistent and hopeful that his search for truth will be rewarded.

"Can you keep me posted? Text me or call me on Arthur's cellphone. I think he'll lend it to me if I ask him."

"I will and I'll see you when I return. Kurt is flying from North Carolina and going directly home the following day."

On the day they arrive in Texas, I receive this text message from Nathan on Arthur's cellphone:

Kurt and I are standing in front of Maddox Hardware. About to go in.

In the evening, he emails me:

This is a small rural town. A few thousand people. I think we were tagged 'strangers' from the moment we got out of our rental car. We both wore casual attire. Faded jeans, sneakers, and windbreakers on top of our shirts. Like everyone else. But we didn't fool anyone. The few people we met on the street stared at us as if we were aliens. It didn't faze Kurt, as you might have guessed. This guy can teach me a social skill or two.

At the hardware store, we picked up some items to buy. At the cash register, a man in his sixties waited on customers. But aside from us, there was no one else. I asked him—as casually as I could—if he knew someone by the name of Joseph Maddox. The cashier said, "Of course. He opened this store eighty years ago, but he's dead now."

I said, "I'm sorry to hear that. My grandfather fought with him in the last world war." Grandpa was in that war, but it was unlikely they met.

"Oh, you must be talking about the son, Joe Junior. He was the one who fought in that war. A real town hero, he was."

"Where's he now?"

He didn't answer while he took his time bagging our purchases. By the time he spoke, his manner had changed from somewhat friendly to cold. "You'll have to ask the family."

He gave us our merchandise and walked away, leaving us standing by the cash register.

We're in the right town, that's for sure. And Joe Junior is most likely the thief of those manuscripts.

We'll try to snoop around some more. Kurt has to return home tomorrow and I may be here for a little while longer, but I'll be back on Sunday.

That's the last information Nathan sends me from Texas, but on Sunday evening, he sends me another email. He's back, and would I be okay meeting tomorrow after work when my classes and teaching assistant duties at the university are done for the day? He has information to share.

"Okay," I email right back.

We agree to meet at his house.

Chapter Twenty-Four

Closing In

Half-past five. Nathan arrives on time. As I settle into the front passenger seat, he says, "What's it like, standing in front of a class and lecturing?"

"I haven't started. Ask me week after next. That will be my first time."

"You nervous?"

"No. I might be, as I get closer to Wednesday. But I start out giving the first pop quiz of the semester, so I won't have to talk for a half hour, or maybe an hour. Anyway, I've arranged to try out my lecture on Arthur and Jeffrey, so I won't be too anxious."

"Who's Jeffrey?"

"Arthur's friend from the university."

Nathan says no more as he turns his attention to the slow and hectic traffic we must negotiate to reach the quiet road to his house.

Minutes later, at his house, he takes out a paper bag from the trunk of his car. I catch a whiff of roasted meat and spices sifting through the bag.

Nathan says, "I have something for us to munch on first. I can't think on an empty stomach. I think we have enough food here to call it dinner."

"That's thoughtful of you. I haven't eaten anything since lunch."

In the living area, we sit at one end of the dining table, and he takes out two sandwiches, two small foam containers, two big cups of smoothies, napkins, and plastic utensils out of the bag. "Two grilled chicken sandwiches. I think you also ordered a chicken sandwich on our trip to Switzerland. Two cups of coleslaw. Two smoothies—one is mango and the other is very berry. You get first pick."

"This is definitely dinner," I say, choosing the mango.

Nathan says, "I knew you'd take that."

"Why? Because I'm half-Asian?"

"I guess. Is that racist?"

"Maybe not. But you're stereotyping me."

"I'm sorry. I didn't mean to do that."

"Actually, I chose the mango because I thought you'd prefer the very berry. Maybe, I was stereotyping you, too. I think it's inevitable. Human nature, maybe? When you don't know someone well enough, you resort to stereotypes."

"I think we're getting to know each other better working together researching the provenance of these manuscript illuminations," Nathan says, handing me a sandwich.

I smile. *Yes, we are.* But I leave that thought unsaid.

Half an hour later, we clear the dining table of paper wrappers, containers, and napkins. Nathan collects them, dumps them in the paper bag. and throws them in the trash.

Seated back at the table, he takes out a notepad from his messenger bag and reads from his notes. "I sent you a text after Kurt and I left the hardware store."

"Yes. I've saved it in my computer."

"Let me start from there. Anyway ... Kurt and I didn't snoop around the town like we planned to. Instead, we brainstormed. His goal is different from ours. It's to repatriate the manuscripts and the other treasures taken from the cave to the church which owns them. Mine is to show it's not only Nazis who looted. Allied troops—Americans, in particular—did, too. My end goal is to present an unbiased version of the looting of treasures in the second world war, with special focus on illuminated manuscripts and other rare books. I want to awaken American consciousness, and their conscience. If people know of other valuable objects that have been stolen—not spoils of war, but artworks or other objects of meaning and value to a country, a town, or a city, or even to individuals, they'll do what they can to help return such objects to the rightful owners."

"Those are noble causes, yours and Kurt's."

"It isn't just war loot at stake. Collectors and museums don't always bother to find out the provenance of items they buy. They could be buying stolen property and not know it. The good news is there's growing awareness among museums to pay more attention to where the artworks they buy come from."

"You mean like the Provenance Research Project the Metropolitan Museum of Art in New York started last year to ascertain if they acquired artworks that might have been Nazi loot?"

"Yes. Many other American museums are doing provenance research—The Getty, the National Gallery of Art, and the Art Institute of Chicago, for example. So do many European museums, such as those in France, Germany, and the UK. A few don't seem to pay it much attention. Russia, as you know, refuses to repatriate their World War II art loot. Spain has also been slow to do so."

"Maybe given more time, they'll do the right thing."

Nathan says, "We hope so. Anyway, before I go on, can you tell me how you're progressing on your thesis? I know you want to do something different with what we learn from our research."

"Yes. I'd like to focus on the manuscripts, especially the 15th century one. I do want to include something about art looting and from there, go deeper into the content, especially the illustrations and paintings in them. Did those illuminations influence the thief to keep them? Or did he take them just because those manuscripts were there and they were unique and valuable spoils of war?"

Nathan nods. "I understand. Genuine interest as opposed to opportunity."

He doesn't have that frowning Nathan-the-skeptic look on him, so I assume he must like my ideas at least a little.

"Okay, moving on. Before I go into my small-town Texas adventure, let me tell you what else Kurt and I agreed to do. We decided to see what more we can dig up at the National Archives. Kurt volunteered to go. It's in Washington D.C, a car drive from his home. About the same distance from San Francisco to Los Angeles. He'll see if there are any more records he can find on the lieutenant. But his interests go beyond the manuscripts. He's also on the trail of the other treasures stolen from the cave in Harz. He knows the church reported the theft to the monuments men. There's a chance they at least began investigating it."

"Began? Are you saying they didn't follow up on it?"

"Those were chaotic times, and after the war Germany was divided into east and west. Control of the Harz Mountain area was taken over by the Soviets and it became part of East Germany. The monuments men were officers of the Allied forces and could only work within West Germany. So, they stopped investigating."

"A lucky thing for the lieutenant if he is, in fact, the thief."

"He might also have deduced the owners of those manuscripts couldn't go after him."

"I can't wait to hear what Kurt finds out."

"I hope we'll get another breakthrough. It's real progress narrowing our search to one of our soldiers. And we might even have his first name: Joe Junior."

Chapter Twenty-Five

Nathan: Testing His Comfort Zone

Nathan says, "You know I'm not exactly a gregarious person. I don't have Kurt's gift for casually approaching people and putting them at ease before he wrings information out of them."

I can't help chuckling. "I know. But you have your own tactics. A bold-faced lie such as the one you came up with to see the manuscripts in Switzerland. It worked, too. Well enough anyway for you to see pictures of covers and pages of the manuscripts and conclude they're real."

"But a lie can be risky. And it can cost you. I'm working hard to find the truth about these manuscripts, so they can be returned to the church without me having to buy them."

"You also lied about your grandfather knowing Joe Junior."

"That one isn't too bad. I'd call it a white lie. A lot of journalists use that 'tactic,' as you call it, because it's effective often enough at ferreting out information."

"So how did your snooping go?"

"Well, the first thing I had to do was search the local phone book for addresses of people with the Maddox surname. I found only four. It's a small town, and the streets where they live didn't take a whole lot of time to track down. Once again, the problem was how people regarded me in those neighborhoods. In the first place, I'm clearly a stranger. And unfortunately, I don't think I look approachable."

"But you're a journalist with a few tactics up your sleeves."

"Being a journalist is a problem in a small town with two or three large churches in it. We can be a pesky presence to many people, especially when they believe we're intruding into their space. Rural folks hate intrusion. The tactics I used in the past, in other settings and situations, won't work there."

I stare at Nathan, clean-cut and unruffled in his indigo pants and white shirt. "You know what, though? You look more like a doctor than a journalist."

"I just came from the clinic, so I should look like a doctor. Anyway, even if you're right, it doesn't mean people who don't know me will trust me. In a city, maybe, or a college town, a doctor can inspire a certain kind of trust."

"All these things you've been saying—do they lead to you telling me your snooping came up with nothing?"

"Frustrating, isn't it? After all the trouble one goes through, only to end up with nothing. But guess what? I did get somewhere."

"How?"

"You might call it luck. On one of the streets I checked out, I saw this bunch of kids—teenagers in shorts—one of them twirling a basketball on his finger. They were talking in loud voices. They looked like they had just come from playing ball. I thought: these kids may still be excited from their game and they're in a group. So, they might be less wary, less suspicious of a stranger coming up to them. Also, they're young, and I hope, more trusting. I sauntered to where they stood, smiled brightly, and said, 'Hi guys!' Most of them ignored me, but a couple did turn towards me. I said I was looking for Joe Maddox Junior. That I have some information for him regarding his past military service."

"Another white lie."

"Well, it worked. By then, they all seemed curious. They turned toward me and told me the street his house is on. Described it as 'the blue house with peeling paint'."

"Did you go there?"

"I did. There were three blue houses on a street of well-kept homes, but only one had badly peeling paint. Once there, I hesitated, thinking I don't want to screw this up. I can't barge in unannounced and expect them to be truthful with me. Well, they probably won't be truthful, anyway, if they so much as suspect I'm looking into one of their own stealing the treasures that the family is now selling. I left, mortified that I failed, but vowing to return another time with some strategy to help loosen their tongues. I'm still at a loss, though, as to how to do it."

"Do you think they might trust a woman more?"

"Like you, you mean?"

"Yes, why not? Of the three of us, I'm the only one who wears a skirt."

"They might not trust you more, but because you're a woman, they might find you less intimidating."

"Ah, yes, the weaker sex. When do I go?"

"You're excited about this, aren't you?"

"Won't deny it. I've imagined talking to Old Joe Junior."

"I have to admit, going to the town made me more curious about what kind of person he is. His motivation, first of all.

This is the place that shaped him. What was it like growing up in a closed community like that? There must be clues about the town that would help us understand why he stole. I already suspect one—the three Baptist churches. Residents probably tend to be religious."

"But wouldn't that be more of a deterrent to stealing?"

"Yes, but these are religious manuscripts. Did they hold a specific fascination for him? The town also looked to me like a largely white enclave next to towns with more diverse populations. I would bet the residents are generally conservative."

"Why should that be a factor?"

"I don't know, for sure. A strong hatred for the enemy that justifies taking things away from them?"

I withhold judgement. Instead, I imagine talking to Joe Junior, hearing the reasons directly from his mouth. "So, when do I go?"

"Let's wait to hear what Kurt finds out. It could tell us what to look for. I expect his call by the end of the week."

Chapter Twenty-Six

Our Man

On Thursday evening, Nathan calls me to say Kurt called him straight from the National Archives in Washington DC.

Nathan says, "Kurt being Kurt, the first thing he says is 'I caught a bug in Texas. I felt awful on the plane back to North Carolina.'" Then he laughs and adds, "I think it's punishment for disrupting the pace of life in that sleepy town."

"He had some good news—good for the book I'm writing, anyway—more evidence of Allied looting. Kurt learned there was an Art Looting Investigation Unit—the ALIU—composed of art experts from museums and universities who researched precious objects reported lost by institutions, as well as by individuals. They kept good records and among them is a case file on the missing treasures from the Harz cave. Guess who was listed as a suspect."

"Lieutenant Joseph Maddox."

"Yes, it's incredible how things are coming together. The file included transcripts of short interviews of soldiers in the lieutenant's regiment. Two or three soldiers guarding the cave said he came out of the cave once with a sack containing something in the shape of a box."

"Was he charged?"

"No, unfortunately. The ALIU lost its jurisdiction on the case when the region was incorporated into East Germany. Joe

Junior was saved by the division of Germany into East and West."

"What about now? Germany is one country again. Can't they reopen the case?"

"Not against Joe Junior. The statute of limitations saves him this time. His relatives could be charged for selling stolen property though. We'll have to ask the legal expert."

"Kurt, you mean."

"Yes. But he tells me the German cultural foundation he works for isn't interested in bringing criminal charges. Their priority is the return of the treasures. Not only the manuscripts, but other objects as well—reliquaries and a box nearly as old as the ninth-century manuscript."

"I bet he's not happy with that. I remember him saying he would advise the church against negotiating with the current possessors of the manuscripts."

"He did say that, but this case is complicated. Several countries are likely to be involved. Countries that might have different laws. There might not be international laws dictating what should be done. In any case, if this is brought to court now, it may take a long time to prosecute, and all the church wants is to get those treasures back."

"Have those other objects been found?"

"Kurt thinks they're being kept in the same place where the manuscripts are."

"Some bank, according to the Swiss art dealer."

"He thinks there's enough evidence to petition the court for his firm to inspect the manuscripts and the other treasures."

This, to me, is good news. It revives my hope of one day seeing these manuscripts. In their original form, if that's possible. But I'll settle for a facsimile.

Chapter Twenty-Seven

Back to Texas

My father's diplomatic assignments took us to big cities and we seldom ventured into the smaller towns and cities of the country we were living in. Even in California, I've so far traveled only to San Francisco and Los Angeles. So, I found the small Texas town where I end up ... quaint. I don't know how else to describe it. It's nothing like I've seen before in the major cities of Europe or Asia.

Every big city has its own flavor. That much I know from my limited experience. And it seems, so does every state, and every city and town in this country. But maybe, it's not so much the buildings and landmarks of a place as it is the people who inhabit it that give it character. The business district here doesn't stand apart from those I've seen in small cities we drove by on our after-Christmas trip to Los Angeles. And it seems this place also has near-derelict neighborhoods and more affluent areas with large homes and manicured lawns.

Anyway, ten minutes after stepping out to the streets of this town, I understand what Nathan said about feeling out of place.

In a big city, your anonymity protects you. Everyone around you is a stranger hurrying to go about their business. If they bump into you, they move on. Few bother to even mutter a quick excuse.

Here, people I'm about to cross paths with step aside a little, increasing the space between us as we pass each other. They look at me, and I know they're wondering what I'm doing here. That I have no business being here. What was I thinking insisting on coming to this town by myself?

But I'm here and these last few months working with Nathan and Kurt have toughened me up a little. And I'm not totally without ideas. I've come attired so people would peg me as an artist going around, looking for places to sketch. Sneakers, faded jeans, and a loose brown shirt spattered in a few places with paint. Long hair twisted into a bun, clipped to the back of my head. Backpack stuffed with a big bottle of water, boxes of Conté crayons and pastels, and a foldable stool, its legs sticking out of the pack. A tablet of sketchpads and a portable half-size French easel in its own carrying bag, light enough to tote around in one hand.

In many European cities, it's not uncommon to find some artist doing exactly what I intend to do: sketch or paint where people go by. Passersby get curious. They approach and take a peek at what you're doing.

Some artists offer to do cartoons or realistic portraits of anyone willing to sit for it and pay a fee. My gig is sketching town or cityscapes that I'm not offering for sale. I'm hoping that in this town, some people will ignore the fact that I'm a stranger and be interested enough to come and look at my work, giving me a chance to talk to them. To ask questions.

I'm now on the long and straight main street where Nathan told me I can find the Maddox Hardware Store. On this street, commercial buildings stand no taller than two stories.

I'm looking for the hardware store, my gaze shifting between the stores to my right and those across the street to my left. After traversing a few cross streets, I find Maddox Hardware Store on the opposite side of the main street from where I'm standing. A concrete building of dirty red, it declares its store name in large letters painted a contrasting color of dull yellow orange. On the sidewalk, a foldable sign advertises items on sale at the store.

I look around for a place where I can sketch. Somewhere I wouldn't be in anybody's way as they walk by, and still have a view of the hardware store. In the Western European cities I've been in, I always found an outdoor café where I could take some refreshment and sketch. I've also sat on public benches around parks, churches, and monuments while I drew scenes that I occasionally turned into paintings.

But from what I've seen of it, this town has no public benches and no outdoor cafés. And across the street from the hardware, no space stands out as being better than any other. I decide to set up my portable easel and foldable stool against the front wall of a drug store directly across from the hardware. But before I do, I go into the store to ask the lady at the counter for permission to park myself at her storefront and draw. She throws a cold glance at me, but nods her head.

After about an hour of sketching with pastels, a woman and a girl, maybe about eight years old, walk by. The child lags behind while the woman, blonde and pretty, who I assume is her mother, goes into the drug store. So far, I've seen less than a dozen people pass by, and only a few of them enter the store. The child comes close enough to look at my work. She watches me for a few minutes and says, "What are you drawing?"

I smile at her. "The stores across the street. Would you like to see?"

She nods and I bring the sketch closer to her. She says, "It's nice. Are you using crayons?"

I hold up a box for her to see. It's divided into rectangular compartments of pastels of different colors. "They're more like chalks. Would you like to try one?" I say, handing her a red chalk.

She seems hesitant to take it from me. She looks up.

Her mother is coming out of the store. She calls the child's name, "Bella, don't bother the lady."

The child looks up but doesn't move. The lady approaches us. She says, "Sorry, ma'am. I hope my daughter isn't bothering you."

"No, not at all. She's curious so I showed her my sketch." Though the lady doesn't ask, I add, "I'm going around different towns for landscapes I can paint."

"Well, good luck." She takes her daughter's hand, and they walk away. The child looks back and waves at me. By late afternoon, no one else has come to watch me draw and I've finished a few sketches and one pastel painting of the hardware store.

I drive out of the town to stay the night at a hotel in El Paso Nathan recommended. I feel somewhat discouraged. Maybe, my strategy won't work. Still, I have two more days of my extended weekend to try again.

The following day, Sunday, I return to the same spot. At ten in the morning the hardware is closed but the drug store is open, country music floating softly out of it. The street would look and feel desolate were it not for that music. I go into the drug store to tell the lady at the counter that I'll be sketching again.

She nods and I saunter out. But before I'm out the door, she says, "Hey, miss, can I see some of your drawings from yesterday?"

I turn around and say, "Sure."

I take the sketches but not the pastel painting, out of my portfolio. She looks at each of them, points to a couple and says, "I like these. Can I have them?"

I'm taken aback. I've never been asked so directly for my artwork. People in the cities I've sketched in seem to understand that artworks are not something the artist gives away freely. Then, it dawns on me that, maybe, she considers them payment for letting me sit outside her store to sketch.

She stares at me, challenge in her eyes. I know I have to give in, but I'll do it my way. "What if I do a couple of sketches of your drug store? Wouldn't you like those better?"

She perks up. "Would you? I'll frame them and display them on this wall behind me."

The wall is full of ads, but she can probably take out a few and put up my sketches. Not exactly what I would have done.

Before I leave the store to go across the street for a better view of her store, she says, "Can you sign them, too?"

I nod, hesitantly. I've never signed any of my previous drawings. On canvas paintings I've submitted for art classes, I've written my name in full on the excess fabric folded at the back and stapled to the supporting wooden frame. The ones in Mom's possession aren't signed. The drawings I will give the drug store lady are the first works I'd sign on the lower right-hand corner, the customary place for artists' signatures.

I draw the drug store in colored Conté crayons and finish the sketches before noon. But I wait to give them to the drug store owner.

In late afternoon, she shouts at me across the street. "Hey, miss, where are my drawings? I'm closing in ten minutes."

I fold up my easel, stuff all my art paraphernalia back where they belong, and rush across the deserted street.

"Here they are," I say, holding up my first sketch of her store and then the second.

She takes one and then the other, examining them. She smiles and seems genuinely pleased. "Thank you. I like that you did them in colored pencils."

I'm tempted to correct her and tell her I didn't use pencils, but I don't.

She glances up at me briefly. "Now, I can boast that I also own drawings signed by the artist. And they're of my store."

"I'm glad you like it."

She reads my signature at the bottom: "C. Martinez Are you Mexican?"

Once again, I'm taken aback. I think her question too intrusive. No one has ever asked me what I am. What does it matter to her? I hesitate for a moment or two and answer her in as neutral a tone as I can muster. "No, I'm not Mexican." And I leave it at that.

She says, "Oh." I think she expected me to tell her my ethnicity, but maybe she picked up something in my tone that held her back.

I regret my reaction and try to make up for it. I smile at her as sweetly as I can. "See you tomorrow."

I have met and talked briefly to three local residents. While I cannot brag about that number, I have two more days to test my strategy in another part of this town.

Chapter Twenty-Eight

The Dim Light at the End of the Tunnel

Back at the drug store the next morning, I thank the owner for letting me sit outside her drugstore and draw. I also tell her I'm going to find a residential area to sketch, hoping it opens her up and she'll tell me more about her town.

She says, "You can check out my neighborhood. If someone gets suspicious and asks you why you're there, tell them I sent you. There are a few other streets I'd recommend but try ours first. You'll find good people there."

Pointing to the hardware store across the street, she says, "We're neighbors—us and the owner of the hardware store."

I turn my head in the direction she's pointing at. "Maddox—is that the name of the owner?"

"Yes. But it's the older brother of the man now running the hardware store who was our neighbor. It's their father who built their business years ago. Joseph Senior was highly respected in this community. The current owner, Joe Junior is in his eighties. He's nice, but not very outgoing. He's not living in his house anymore, though. One of his nephews and nieces

215

comes to check the mail, or water his plants about once a week."

"Where's Joe Junior now?"

"Nobody knows where he is. He could be in some old folks' home. He'd been sick and I heard he's lost his memory."

"I'm sorry to hear that. How long did you know him?"

"Since I was a little girl. My father said he fought in World War II. Came back a hero. The family displayed some of his medals in their store. There was also other stuff he brought back from the war—souvenirs, Dad said. Beautiful things, maybe French, that he sometimes showed people. I saw them once myself, but I can't remember them except for a couple of very old books. They were quite unusual. They had fancy covers I'd bet you couldn't find anywhere else but a museum."

"Who's running the store now?"

"His younger brother. You must have seen him come in and out of the hardware. Balding. Kinda surly. Always scowling."

"Yes, I think I did see someone balding smoking outside the door to the hardware. Big burly guy."

"That's him. Mr. Maddox," she says with a sneer she doesn't bother to hide. "He's not as nice as Joe Junior. Their business isn't going well with him running it. Been going downhill since Joe Junior got sick."

"Did you know Joe Junior well?"

"Not really. He's my dad's generation. But I liked him. Most of the town liked him. He didn't mix much with people around here. But he was gracious when he did. And he was generous."

"Does he have a family of his own who could take care of him?" I realize as I asked this question that I felt sad for Joe Junior, though I can't say why.

"You mean a wife and children? Well, no. Nobody talks about it, but everybody knows he's queer. There were always guys from out of town who came to visit him, stay in his house a while."

The conversation is becoming gossipy. And not relevant to tracing the fate of the illuminated manuscripts. Not exactly where I want it to go.

Looking at my watch, I say, "I have to go. I'll be leaving for another town tomorrow. You've been so kind and helpful. Thanks again."

She smiles. "You're welcome and thank you for your drawings. If you come again, you'll see them on my wall."

The houses on Joe Junior's street are larger and their front gardens well-tended. The families in the neighborhood might be among the most affluent in the town. The drug store lady might have steered me here to show me a better image of the town than passing visitors ordinarily see.

The blue house with peeling paint is easy enough to spot. The street is narrower than the main street and buildings on each side are closer. There are no sidewalks. At the moment, the street is quiet and deserted. There's no doubt I would look conspicuous here, no matter what I do.

I drive down the street, uncertain if I could casually set up my stool and start sketching. And maybe someone might be curious enough to come out and ask me what I'm doing. Someone like the drug store lady, but older, who might have known Joe Junior well enough to tell me more about him.

I came here intending to knock on his door, saying I'm an art student doing studies of small-town USA. I hoped he would be willing—maybe eager—to talk to me based on our common engagement in art. But since he no longer lives here, I've lost that option.

I pass the blue houses and at the next cross street, I turn right and cruise back to Joe Junior's street. This time, I see a plump, white-haired woman in a flowered house dress hosing her lawn. I stop the car.

In a few unhurried steps, I stand outside the gate to her house. She looks up. I like her grandmotherly look. She says, "May I help you?" Her tone isn't hostile, but it isn't friendly, either.

"Good afternoon, ma'am. I was wondering: Do you think it would be okay if I do a few drawings of your neighborhood?"

"Young lady, this is a free country. You can do whatever you want."

That's not quite true. There are laws that won't allow you to do certain things. Kill or rob, for instance. But no use saying anything but "Thank you" with a smile of gratitude.

She shoos me away with a wave of her hand. I take out my sketchpad and box of pastels. I don't bother with the stool. I've painted standing for hours. I do a quick sketch of the old lady in front of her house. Then, I do a few more of the blue houses, including Joe Junior's. In the hour or so I've been sketching, I've seen no one else come out.

I amble back towards the old lady's house. She's finished watering her lawn, but she hasn't gone back in. She's sitting on a white wicker chair on her porch. I think she's been watching me.

I wave at her and say, "Thanks again."

She gets up, raises a hand in answer to my wave, turns toward her house, opens her screen door, and disappears into her house. She has made it clear she wants nothing more to do with me.

As I walk back to my rental car, I wonder whether I'm wasting my time waiting for someone to come out. I'm seized with the urge to leave this area. As if it has become suddenly oppressive. Anyway, there's no reason for me to stay if I can't talk to Joe Junior, whose whereabouts are unknown, according to the drug store lady. Knocking on someone else's door to ask questions also seems futile.

Back at the hotel, I repack my few belongings and call American Airlines to ask if there's a flight to San Francisco tonight that can accommodate me. Luckily there is and I have enough time to drive to the airport in El Paso.

I call Arthur to ask if he and Jeffrey can pick me up at the airport. But I can't reach him, and I have barely enough time to drive to the airport and check in to board my flight. I have no choice but to call Nathan. It will be past eleven when the plane touches down in San Francisco and I expect him to say he can't come. But I'm wrong. He will be there. I think he's eager to learn the outcome of my trip.

One tiny step forward—that's all I've accomplished on this trip. I've confirmed Joe Junior was in the last world war and he brought home some "beautiful things" from the war. But we already knew all that. What I had hoped for was to meet him, engage him in something like a heart-to-heart about what the manuscripts meant to him and why he never tried to profit off of them. Didn't he know they were worth millions?

We can keep looking for him, and with some luck, we'll find him. But if he has lost his memory, would we learn any more about why he's kept the manuscripts all these years?

Chapter Twenty-Nine

Could Have Ended Better

"So, how did it go?" Nathan asks. "You're back a day early."

He takes my easel bag and my luggage, and we stride out of the airport to where he parked his car.

I don't answer his question, maybe because I can't think of something simple or trite with which to dismiss it. Instead, I say, "Thank you for picking me up. I'm sorry it's rather late. I didn't expect you to agree to pick me up."

"Why did you call me then if you thought I wouldn't come?"

"I couldn't get a hold of Arthur, but I felt like I needed to see a familiar face when I arrive. I couldn't stand the prospect of getting into a cab with a stranger."

"I'm flattered I'm your second choice."

Do I detect a hint of sarcasm in Nathan's voice? Is he somewhat hurt or offended?

"There's no one else I could call. And I'm so thankful you came." I say, appalled that my eyes are getting moist.

I must sound pathetic admitting I had no one else I could rely on to pick me up at the airport in an ungodly hour. I had to turn to someone with whom I have nothing but a formal working relationship. Someone I regard as my boss.

We reach the parking lot in silence. I follow Nathan towards the back of his car, where he unhooks my backpack off my shoulders, and stores it with my easel and luggage in the trunk. He throws me a quick glance, and I smile at him as a way of thanking him once again. He says nothing, and it's too dark for me to see the expression on his face.

He opens the passenger door and I climb in. He drives to my apartment in silence. I wonder if I should say something, start some small talk to ease the discomfort I sense in the silence between us. But I'm too spent in both body and mind to want to break it.

In the visitor's parking lot at my apartment building, he unloads my belongings, locks his car, and carries my backpack and luggage up to my apartment. Neither of us has spoken.

I unlock my door and go in. He follows me, closing the door behind him. Inside, he puts everything on the floor next to my couch.

He straightens up, gazes at me a moment. He says, "Believe it or not, I was glad you called me, Clarissa. I was worried about you. You didn't call or email while you were in Texas."

I return his gaze, blinking to hold back tears welling in my eyes. I've only been gone three days and I never expected Nathan to admit he worried about me. An admission that stirs up a mix of emotions I can't fathom.

He puts an arm around me and leads me to the couch. We sit down, side by side. "I'm your friend, Clarissa. You can trust me, open up to me. I'll always be straight with you. What happened in Texas? You seemed so fired up when you left and now, you look like you had a massive letdown."

I am depressed, though I'm not sure why. I'm also disconcerted facing this compassionate side of Nathan. And yet, I shouldn't be surprised. He's a doctor, after all.

"I think I failed in what I set out to do. Maybe I expected too much." My voice is a little shaky.

I relate what transpired in Texas in more detail, including what I learned about Joe Junior.

"You didn't fail. You got someone to talk to you, who gave you information that corroborate what we already know. That's good. It means we can be more confident of the data we've gathered. It makes our case stronger. You also learned something new about Joe Junior that we can follow up on. You've brought back important information. Kurt and I didn't get as far as you did.

"I think you're disappointed you didn't talk to Joe Junior. You wanted so much to know what the illuminated manuscripts meant to him. But he wasn't there, and even if he was, he might not have wanted to talk to you, anyway. You could continue looking for him. Or you can change your end goal, go for what you can realistically accomplish."

I say, "Searching him out to talk to him is futile. The drug store lady says he has lost his memory. I should let it go. Move on."

"Why is it so important to you to find out what the manuscripts meant to Joe Junior?"

Why, indeed? I've never articulated the reasons to myself. Maybe it's intuition, which to me has always been a real, but vague, thing. Nathan watches me with concern as he waits for my answer.

"I've never actually thought about why. But I think it's not often that you could meet someone who truly understands and appreciates medieval manuscript illuminations. So, maybe, I fantasized Joe Junior does, and felt a kind of kinship with him. And yet, at the same time, I think I was angry with him. He's kept for himself treasures that should have been available to all of us. How could he justify that?"

"You can agonize over these questions, but we might never know the answers. For this evening, though, are you okay letting go of this ..."—Nathan seems to be searching for a word—"...this quest? Let it simmer for a while?"

I look at my watch: 2:20 am. "Oh my God, it's morning already. I'm sorry to keep you here this late. You've been so kind and understanding."

"I'm glad I could help clarify things for you. And I don't mind staying up this late. But I do have clinic duty tomorrow."

"Oh. I'm doubly sorry."

"Don't worry about it. I don't start until three in the afternoon. But I do need to get some sleep."

We rise from the couch at the same time. Nathan goes towards the door, and I follow him.

He stops at the door, his left hand on the door knob. He turns to me. "Will you have dinner with me sometime this week? I mean a relatively fancy one, not take-out sandwiches over documents we're poring over."

I don't answer right away, unsure how to respond. I wouldn't go out alone to dinner with Professor Fischl who, I'm sure, would never think to ask me. To me, Nathan is as much my superior as the professor is, though he's nowhere near as old. When he joined Arthur and me on our tour of Europe, I thought of him as an equal. But since we agreed to work together researching the fate of the illuminated manuscripts, I've accorded him the respect I give my professors.

Nathan notices my hesitation, "I'd like you to accept me as a friend and not just someone you work with. Or, worse, someone you work for."

Embarrassed that he might suspect I have interpreted his dinner invitation as asking me out on a date, I say, "Yes, dinner would be a nice break from work. I'd like us to be friends, too."

Chapter Thirty

April 1970

War Loot Twenty-Five Years Later

Twenty-five years. That's how long he'd had possession of the treasures he took out of a cave in a mountain in Germany. He was amazed that the colors of the illustrations hadn't faded. They were still bright and intense. Not long after he acquired them, he had become obsessed with them, starting each day gazing at them, marveling at the colors, the gilding that exuded light.

He almost lost them. The church, which owned the treasures, had reported some items missing from the crates in the cave, notably, two very valuable manuscripts. The monuments men had looked into the report, obtained detailed descriptions of the missing treasures, consulted with art experts, and declared the items as cultural property valued at millions of dollars. After interviewing soldiers who guarded the cave, they had opened an investigation.

Soldiers in his squad had whispered among themselves about who the most likely thief was of the missing treasures. Though no one had dared to say his name aloud, he had known they suspected him—the leader of the squad assigned to guard the cave.

Who else could their suspect have been? For a week or so, he had issued a command to let no one, including his men, enter the cave. He alone had access to its interior and the crates stored in it while he did an inventory of its contents.

He had been aware he faced the threat of another court martial. And this time, the consequence would be more serious than when he was first tried for stealing silverware.

Despite the odds against him, he had hung on to some hope. The military court would have trouble proving he stole the lost church treasures. They were no longer in his possession. He had sent them to a secure place across the Atlantic. Unless the military court's search for evidence extended to his hometown, they were unlikely to ever find the treasures.

Still, he had spent some agonizing nights debating with himself. Should he come clean and return the treasures? They had been spoils of war to which he was entitled. Compensation for the ravages on his mind and body, wrought by a war initiated by murderous Nazis who sought to annihilate not only Jews, but also homosexuals, gypsies, the sick and disabled, the Slavs—anyone and everyone they believed inferior or degenerate.

No one in his platoon knew he was among the people the Nazis hated so much and would have had no compunction wiping off the face of the earth. Had he been European and a Jew, he would have been gassed right away. Or, if not a Jew, he could have been pursued and mauled to death by rabid dogs, a fate rumored to have befallen a French man in a concentration camp, who had been fingered by another inmate as depraved.

In either of those possible scenarios, he would have escaped the fate of those unfortunates, but the Nazis would still have thrown him into a concentration camp, where, according to rumors, he would have been abused by both soldiers and inmates, tortured, sodomized with blunt objects, raped, and treated as the lowest form of human being. He shuddered. And told himself he would have survived. He was born with the grit of his Southwestern ancestors, and an American soldier, trained and experienced in combat.

Then, the unexpected happened. In August, 1945, a shuffling of the post-war control of Germany by Allied Forces had resulted in the Soviet Army taking control of the eastern section of Germany. The cave in which the church had hidden their treasures was located in that zone. American Forces had had to leave, and the monuments men had ceased their investigation of the treasures missing from the Harz cave.

The Soviets who had assumed jurisdiction over all matters pertaining to the area never took up the case of the missing manuscripts. How could they have when they had done their own looting?

He was free. Free from the threat of a court-martial. Free to keep his treasures all his life. Free to enjoy them and do whatever he wanted with them.

He sighed in deep relief every time he recalled those events. He didn't attribute them to luck. To him, they constituted Destiny. And Justice. Events had fallen into place at their proper time and in proper ways to ensure he discovered the treasures, and obstacles were eliminated to his owning them. The treasures had fallen into his lap to possess, savor, and use for as long as he lived. Was there a sweeter victory than that?

A few weeks after he returned home, he had fashioned a wooden box of oak and a thick plexiglass cover in which to shelter the manuscripts side by side. Except for those times he had shown them to friends or customers at the hardware store, they had found a permanent home in this box on top of his night table. He could gaze at both manuscript covers every morning and every night without lifting the plexiglass.

He had tried a few times to read the old manuscripts. Maybe he could glean some wisdom out of them to guide his life. But the letters required great effort to decipher. He had recognized a few letters well enough despite their fancy decorations, particularly those at the beginning of chapters. He had recognized a few words as Latin, a language only specialists bothered to learn. He wrote them down, anyway, intending to translate them with the help of a dictionary in the library. He gave up after a while. The meaning of the text would forever elude him. He was okay with that.

He focused his pleasure on gazing at the images. He surmised the books were either bibles or prayer books, since the gilded and colorful illustrations were of saints and religious rituals. That he was the one who found these books of faith constituted proof for him that he was somehow singled out, though he couldn't say what for. His faith in God was deep and uncompromising, but he was not much of a church goer. He only went to attend religious rituals like baptisms and celebrate certain religious holidays.

The pictures had astonished everyone to whom he later showed the manuscripts. Family members, the rare neighbor he felt comfortable with. Long-time friends, as well as transient friends who stayed in his house a few days and vanished later.

He occasionally displayed the manuscripts inside their glassed-in box at the hardware store. But customers only saw the manuscript covers. Many glanced at them, uncertain what they were, and resumed the business of choosing and purchasing items they came for. Those curious enough asked about the unusual covers, and seemed puzzled when he told them they were covers of rare old books. They eyed the stones and relief sculptures a little longer before moving on.

During the first few months after his return, hardly anyone had asked how he came by these souvenirs. When someone did, he had jokingly said he found them in a gutter in Strasbourg—he liked dropping names of places alluding to his World War II service—on the French-German border after Allied forces had bombed specific targets. No one had ever wondered how the manuscripts could have survived bombing and not turned into detritus in gutters. They accepted his little lie.

But then, this man came into the hardware store one day to buy a couple of cans of paint. An out-of-towner, he was visiting a friend whom he was helping renovate the interior of his house. He saw the manuscripts in the glass shelf.

He started asking questions. He knew some art history and had seen illuminated manuscripts in museums. It turned out he was also an artist, a sculptor. They talked about art until some other customers came into the store. Before they parted, he asked the man if he wanted to have some coffee in his house later that evening or the day after. To continue talking about art. He came to his house that evening. And stayed the night. They agreed to meet again.

For three months, they saw each other every weekend at the same time at a hotel in El Paso. It was bliss until one weekend in the third month.

He had brought the manuscripts with him. His lover had only seen the covers before that weekend. When he saw the illustrations, he was impressed by the details in each picture and their bright, pure colors. He asked how he came by such rare manuscripts. He told him the story.

His lover said, "You took them? Just like that?"

He said, "Spoils of war. Nothing like Nazi loot."

He didn't know his lover would go to the library to research art theft in World War II.

The next time they met, his lover said he must return the manuscripts to the rightful owners, whoever they might be.

"They're Germans," he said. "They must pay for what they've done."

"It doesn't matter. Art this old and precious is a cultural legacy."

That was the last time they saw each other.

Chapter Thirty-One

May 2001

Arthur and Me and Cooking

The day I'm back in the office, my brother calls me during my lunch hour.

"Issy, I got your voicemail. I'm sorry we didn't connect. We really should buy you your own cell phone. It would make it easier for us to talk to each other."

"I haven't saved enough money yet."

"How much more do you need?"

"A hundred, I think."

"Okay, I can do that. I'll save a month of wages from my cafeteria job."

"But what about wine and take-out dinners?"

"We'll have to go without. What's a month, anyway? Maybe we have to learn to cook."

"I'm good at hamburgers and omelets."

"See, that's my problem. I'm sick of hamburgers and eggs. Lola's a great cook. I miss her adobo and kare-kare."

"I know adobo. What's kare-kare?"

"Everyone knows adobo. Kare-kare is pork or beef and vegetables, usually cabbage, eggplant, and green beans stewed in peanut butter and water that's reddish orange from achiote seeds that have been soaked in it. I like it best with ham hocks

233

cooked until the meat is falling off the bones. You never had it?"

"No. Mom's a good cook, too. She always tried recipes from each of the countries we lived in. The ones we liked, she kept. She did make adobo, from a recipe Dad gave her. Her beef stew is a Provençale dish to which she adds olives. It's yummy with noodles or baguette to sop up the sauce."

"You're making me hungry. Can you hear my stomach growling? Anyway, we should get together soon, for that night we promised ourselves. Sharing our experiences growing up apart. "

"Okay. How about this weekend? Saturday night?"

"You're on."

*****

I don't hear from Nathan for the rest of the week. Either he's busy at the clinic, or he's giving me time to recoup from the disappointing outcome of my trip to Texas. Maybe time to reflect, as well, on how I intend to incorporate the information we have so far gathered on the illuminated manuscripts into my thesis.

He does call on Saturday evening, while Arthur and I are muddling through a recipe for adobo we downloaded on the internet. After we talked on Monday night, I decided Arthur and I should start our Saturday rendezvous trying our hands at cooking something we both enjoy.

Nathan says, "Hello Clarissa! Feeling better today?"

"Actually, yes. I think it's good to take a break. Arthur is here and we're trying to cook our very first adobo. We've never done this before, and we'll probably mess it up. But how hard is it really to make this? It's a stew. You dump everything in the pot and let it simmer."

"All you need to do is mix all the ingredients together and let it simmer until it's tender and the sauce has thickened. Don't bother browning the meat and don't forget the bay leaf."

"Have you made this before?"

"I've tried it once. I can cook, so long as the process isn't complicated. And I have time. Stews are relatively easy."

"Nathan, you haven't ceased to surprise me yet."

"Good, I'll keep the surprises coming as long as I can. Anyway, I'm freer next week. Shall we go out to dinner some evening next week."

"Saturday night is good. It will feel less like something we're doing for work."

"Great. I know a place you'd like where I can get a reservation. Pick you up at 5:30?"

I'm a bit bewildered that he's picking me up that early, but maybe he has to go to work on Sunday. All I say is, "Sounds good."

When I hung up, Arthur says, "Did you just agree to a date with Nathan?"

"It's not a date."

"Work, then, on a Saturday night?" Arthur lifts his left brow, mischief in his eyes and his grin.

"No, we're going out to dinner."

"A non-date date, then."

"Call it whatever you want. He's my boss. I don't date my superiors."

"Such scruples. Nathan was a friend before he was your boss."

"May I remind you: Nathan was your friend, not mine."

It's nine in the evening when the adobo finishes cooking. A late hour for dinner, but a homemade meal is worth the wait. We're happy enough with the results. Arthur declares it's good, but not as good as Grandma's adobo. We have used two pounds of pork to make the dish, half of which we consume, much of it by Arthur.

Arthur packages the rest in a covered glass bowl to store in the refrigerator. He says, "Can I bring some of this leftover with me tomorrow?"

"Of course. But leave me a little bit. I'll take it to work on Monday."

At eleven, when we've cleaned up, we settle on the couch together. With a bottle of icy coke in his hand, Arthur is fortifying himself for an all-nighter. He has a few more bottles in the refrigerator, one of which he offers me, but I refuse it.

I say, "Truth time, eh? That's why you're here instead of studying with Jeffrey at the dorm?"

"I'm doing more than okay in school, but I've had this prickly feeling—whatever it is—and it's been bothering me. Now it's like an itch I must scratch."

"And you want me to help you scratch it?"

"You could say that. I'm sure you have an itch or two to scratch, too. So, tell me what it was like growing up with Mom and Dad. I'd like to know what I missed."

"Maybe nothing. I was happy enough, though I admit the frequent moves were unsettling. Mom did her best to make it easier for me, but when I was older, it occurred to me we've never lived in a place where I could say we settled. There was always somewhere else we would be decamping to. How about you? What was it like growing up with grandparents?"

"Uneventful and boring, but they loved me and took very good care of me."

"Sounds like neither of us has much to complain about. Not perfect childhoods, but no child abuse. Mostly loving. So, where's the itch?"

"How did we end up thousands of miles from our parents, who're thousands of miles from each other? What's more, our mother doesn't want anything to do with us. We're a broken family."

How, indeed, did we end up estranged from our parents? And why does it matter? I don't have answers to Arthur's questions, so I say the obvious, "Each of us had to make a choice. And we did. And Mom hasn't cut ties with us. She asked for some time to find herself."

"That's a cop-out answer. Why did you choose California?"

"Born here, though not raised. I'm an American citizen."

"So am I. But you could have chosen to live in some other country in Europe or Asia. People immigrate all the time. It's no longer that hard to apply for citizenship in other countries."

"It's easier in some countries. Maybe I'm bothered by philosophical questions I can't articulate, much less answer. Or maybe home to me should be a place not too far from Mom. She's left me something of herself I'll always have. She nurtured in me a love of art, particularly picture books."

"But we don't even know exactly where Mom is. All we have of her now is an email address. Anyway, to me, she's a stranger."

"I know, and it's sad. She's back in her hometown, or thereabouts, looking for herself."

"She asked us to leave her alone until she contacts us. How screwed up is that? Frankly, I don't care a damn fig."

"Do you resent them taking me, and not you?"

"Isn't it obvious? Why didn't they take both of us?"

Arthur turns away from me, eyes narrowed. From the muscles on his jaw, I can tell he's gritting his teeth. This is the first time I've seen him this angry.

"Do you hate them?"

"They're my parents. I can't hate them. They're good people and I know they love me. But why didn't they take me? I would have loved to live in all those different countries."

"Do you resent me because they took me?"

"I did, for a long time, until we went on our tour of Europe together. I was naïve—or should I say ignorant? But you took care of me. You made me feel you'd never do anything to hurt me. Our parents made the decision to leave me behind with Lolo and Lola. But you were there at a crucial time."

"I think it was mostly Dad's decision to leave you, although Mom said Lolo advised it. If he's anything like Dad, he'd also be a military take-charge person who had to have his way most of the time."

Arthur nods, "That's Lolo."

"I think that's why Mom left Dad. She felt she'd been swallowed by him, lost in his grand persona."

"Rejected."

"Negated, which might be worse. It implies you're nothing."

"I'm not sure I know what you mean. Lolo never made me feel that way. I've never thought of myself as a nothing."

"You're a guy. It makes a difference."

"Are you saying Dad and Lolo are sexists?"

"Maybe racists as well. It can go both ways, you know: Whites discriminating against Asians and vice-versa."

"Those are heavy accusations."

"You decide for yourself. As much as I love Dad, I'm actually glad Mom left him. And I hope she finds what she's looking for."

"Do you hate Dad for being racist and sexist?"

"No, not at all. He and I don't agree on some things, but I know he loves me. I do love him. He devoted some time to me. He was my bedtime-story reader on weekends." Anxious to draw the focus away from me, I add, "How about you, growing up away from us?"

"I love Mom and Dad in my own way. They profess to love us, and I believe them. They've done what they could to be good parents. We haven't been abused. Jeffrey told me his dad was a strict disciplinarian. Used a belt when he got angry. I guess I should feel lucky. But I don't. Jeffrey's family is intact. He has a place he calls home. He belongs. We don't."

"You would have a home if you chose to live with Dad. You'll even have grandparents nearby. And an extended family of aunts and cousins. You grew up surrounded by a big family."

"Then, maybe it's me. I never felt like I fit in in that country. Remember, like you, I was born here. And after Europe, you're the one I feel closest to. You're kinda quirky, too. Like me. I've never met anyone obsessed with musty ancient manuscripts."

"Oh, they're out there."

"They may be quirky, too. Outliers like us."

"I don't see how you're an outlier. I think you've adjusted better than I have."

"You don't know everything about me, Sis."

"True. But you're so young. How can you already have secrets?"

"Someday I'll tell you."

"So, we're not doing truth all the way tonight?"

Arthur averts his eyes and becomes pensive. "I don't think I'm ready."

"Why? Are you afraid of how I'll react? You know I'll always love you no matter what."

"Maybe I have to learn to accept myself first."

"It seems to me the itch you're talking about has more to do with yourself than why we're thousands of miles from our parents, and have no place we'd call home."

Chapter Thirty-Two

Arthur Opens Up

Arthur eyes me for a few moments, thinking, maybe vacillating. He gets up for another bottle of coke, rejoins me on the couch, and drinks his coke to the last drop, deep in thought. He puts the empty bottle on the table and cranes his head towards me. "What do you think of Jeffrey?"

"I like Jeffrey. Nice kid."

"Is that how you think of us? Kids?"

"He's your friend and you're my kid brother. It may sound silly, but I guess it's why I think of you as kids."

"Are you a virgin, Sis?"

His question startles me. Blunt. To the point. And too personal, even from a brother I trust. I can't answer right away. Then, I remind myself: We have agreed to be truthful. So, returning his unflinching gaze, I say, "Yes, I am."

"Well, I'm not. So, you see, I'm not a kid anymore."

"No, you're not." I say, racking my brain for any references he has made to a girl. Nothing. It's Jeffrey he's always talked about. Somewhere in my subconscious, I retrieve a suspicion I might have refused to articulate earlier. A suspicion that the two of them were more than friends. "Is it ... Jeffrey?"

"Yes. We've had a thing going since we returned from our visit to LA." He watches me, the serious, thoughtful expression on his face replaced by anxiety. Searching for distaste or disapproval I might feel for his unexpected disclosure.

I pull him close and put my arms around him. "Oh, Arthur. All I want is for you to be happy. Any choices you make are okay by me. Well, so long as you don't rob or kill anyone."

He hugs me back tight and doesn't seem to want to let go. I feel his chest rise and fall fast against me and I realize he's crying. I hold him, stroking his back slowly. After a few minutes, the heaving of his chest slows to a regular rhythm.

He disengages from me, wiping his tears with the back of his hand. "You don't know how much this means to me. I'm sure Dad would never accept a son ... like me. And I've reconciled myself to the idea that he would disown me. It's the other reason I chose to come here instead of living with him and all those noisy, nosy relatives. As to Mom, I don't know her enough to tell how she'd react."

"I'm sure Mom will accept you as you are. Dad won't take it well, but with time, he'll learn to accept it."

He lays his head on my shoulder and says, "I hope you're right."

We sit in silence. Arthur's revelation is so new, and for me, unexpected, that we seem to implicitly agree words are superfluous as I soak in this new truth about him, while he's relieved he has confessed, and nothing has changed between us.

I don't know how long we wallow in silence. After a while, the weight of Arthur's head begins to numb my shoulder. I pat him on the thigh. "Would you like another bottle of coke?"

He nods and I fetch a couple from the refrigerator. I hand him one. I take the other.

After a few sips, Arthur says, "I need to tell you one more thing. It concerns Nathan."

I sit up, apprehension inching up my chest.

"You know why Nathan and I haven't kept up with each other?"

I shake my head.

"I was a seventeen-year-old kid when we first met. He was very nice to me, even solicitous. I didn't know at first why he got me all excited when I'd see him. I used to put my arms around him all the time and he never stopped me. I would even playfully kiss his cheeks and he'd smile. I fell in love with him. He was my first love, and I interpreted his kindness and caring to mean he felt the same way I did. Then, one day, I kissed him on the lips. He didn't pull away. He let me. But then he said, 'I'm sorry Arthur. I prefer women.'"

Arthur pauses, as if to let Nathan's declaration sink deeper. I suspect he has said it to himself many times: "I'm sorry Arthur. I prefer women." At seventeen, discovering who he was, and trusting Nathan, he took it to negate who he is. Hurting him terribly. Stoking anger. Fueling an impulse to strike back.

"I took what he said as a rejection. Not only of my sexuality, but all of me. I owed him my insight into myself. It was how I felt when we were together that made me aware of what I am. He came to mean so much to me that when I laid myself bare to him, I took what he said as a betrayal. I became angry, resentful. Said some things I have regretted ever since. I accused him of having led me on, and he should be jailed for corrupting a minor. All he did was stare back as I vented my anger, his eyes inscrutable. Then, he said, 'Arthur, you're a wonderful and loving person and I like you very much, but as a friend.' It wasn't what I wanted to hear, and he seemed so calm. I shouted back, 'I hate you and I never ever want to see you again.'

"On looking back, I realize I was so hurt and angry, I said all those awful things to him. I blush every time I recall telling him he was corrupting a minor and should be jailed. He never touched me anywhere but my arm or my shoulder. I know now he treated me like a kid he was fond of. There was never anything physical between us like I now have with Jeffrey."

"Have you ever told him you regret what you've said?"

"No. I hoped ... Actually, I never thought we'd connect again. Anyway, after that kind of outburst, texting or emailing him to apologize for the things I said didn't seem good enough. I felt I should do it in person to show him how sorry I was."

"Where did this kissing incident happen?"

"On the last leg of our tour. In Florence. When I kissed him on the mouth, I guess I wanted to let him know how I felt before we parted."

"But you went on the same flight to California."

"Actually, I changed my flight before all that happened. I had meant to stay with you for at least another week. But I wanted to be with Nathan for as long as possible and was hoping we could talk on the plane about meeting again. Instead, my return home started as a ten-hour nightmare. I had reserved the seat next to his. This man I had convinced myself by then was vile and hateful.

"I was a wreck by the time we landed at SFO. He, however, sat next to me cool and collected. He even smiled at me as he rose to disembark. I hated him even more after that."

"Maybe his smile was his way of telling you he didn't resent you for how you reacted to what he said."

"I know that now. He might have understood and maybe he has never resented me. But I have to apologize to him in person before I can totally forgive myself."

We take swigs of coke until Arthur finishes his. Mine is still half-full. He puts his empty bottle on the coffee table, and lays his head on my shoulder again. "I'm sorry, Sis. Dumping all of this on you."

"We did agree to tell all tonight."

He stretches his legs and massages his belly. "I think I drank too much coke." He glances up at me, grinning. "I don't believe you've told all. Why are you still a virgin, Issy? Twenty-two and untouched in this day and age. I hope you don't turn into a cantankerous old maid."

I shrug and don't answer.

"What are you looking for Sis? Have you never been in love? Never wanted to have sex with someone you're attracted to?"

"I've been sublimating sex into my art," I say.

He raises his head to face me. "You're joking."

"Only half-joking. I've met guys. A couple of whom couldn't wait to get into my pants. But I've been too busy hopping across different countries, squeezing in school and artmaking. Serious relationships didn't fit into my schedule."

"Maybe you never met anyone who swept you off your feet."

"Well, I did have one experience that might take me a long time to forget. And it all happened in one afternoon."

"Oh yeah? This, I gotta hear."

"It wasn't a case of being swept off my feet. To an observer, it could have looked like a dull conversation between two people. All we did was talk. For five straight hours. That was what was extraordinary about it. Somehow, we never ran out of topics or issues to argue over. And yet, we were strangers to each other and we parted without even knowing each other's name. But there was this palpable connection between us, maybe from finding many things that interested us both."

"Where and when did this extraordinary experience happen?"

"Aboard the overnight steamer we took from Corinth to Brindisi, Italy. You and Nathan were somewhere. I deposited my luggage in my room and wandered around a bit. I was hungry, so I went to the snack bar, stood in line behind this bearded American, and somehow we started talking."

"What was he like?"

"He was an electronics engineer who built microcomputers for electronic toys. He seemed shy, at first, but I'm usually not gregarious either, and maybe we sensed we had that in common. He turned out quite articulate and fascinating."

"I think I remember seeing you two. Nathan and I were strolling around the steamer, stretching our legs, and saw you wrapped up in conversation with this guy. We didn't want to disturb you. Nice-looking guy, blonde hair. My God, Issy. Was it the romance that might have been?"

"Who knows? But we both sensed we'd never meet again."

"No physical attraction?"

"I don't think my heart has beaten faster, nor have I ever tingled meeting an attractive guy for the first time. The long conversation with this blonde, bearded guy was ... intellectual. A meeting of minds between two introverts."

"Oh, Sis. I don't want to see you shrivel into old age a sorry virgin. I want to see you happy."

"I'm reasonably happy. And being a sorry old virgin might not be so bad if I make a name for myself as an artist."

No, I don't really mean that, do I? I do want to experience what it's like to love, even if it ends up in heartache. Mom and Dad loved each other, and though they're now apart, I know they had happily loved each other most of the time they lived together. I sensed it. The love between Mom and Dad.

I leave my thoughts unsaid.

Chapter Thirty-Three

Patching Up A Broken Friendship

I stay awake that night, my mind replaying Arthur's revelations. It never occurred to me all those months we traveled in Europe that he fell in love with Nathan. And that his unreciprocated feelings had caused a permanent rupture between them by the time our trip ended, and we each went our own way.

When Arthur met Jeffrey—or maybe because he met Jeffrey—Arthur had matured and reassessed what had happened between him and Nathan. He no longer saw Nathan's response as a rejection. And yet, he's protesting too much, too anxious to make me believe that, in accepting the truth, he can again admit he missed Nathan, and not for any romantic reason.

I envy my little brother, who has tasted life in ways I haven't. He's chewed on heartache from which he emerged wiser. Wiser than me, I'm sure. Still, there are certain things I can do to help him clarify his feelings. Bringing Nathan and him together, for instance. There had been a genuine camaraderie between them that's worth reviving.

Arthur says he's ready to reconcile with Nathan, but he's unsure how to go about it. Leave it to me, little brother. I can orchestrate a reconciliation. It won't take much, and it will give Arthur another chance to face reality, not only of his feelings for Nathan, but also of the nature of Nathan's regard for him.

The next morning, over coffee, cream cheese and reheated bagels, I ask Arthur what he thinks about inviting Nathan over for adobo he and I would cook a day or so before.

"Yes," he says, enthused. "I did consider sending him a long email once about how sorry I am. But I prefer face-to-face. When do we do this?"

"This coming Saturday. The day Nathan and I agreed to have dinner together."

"Oh, no, no, no. That's a date."

"It's not a date. At least not the kind you imagine. No more than a chance for us to get to know each other so we would be more comfortable working together. A dinner here can do that, too. And it would be more informal with you around. Put us more at ease. Like how we were in Europe."

"But what if he actually expected to be alone with you?"

"I'll tell him what I'm thinking of and if he's not okay with it, we can plan for another time when the three of us can do something together."

At the Art Office the next day, I call Nathan.

"This is unexpected," he says.

"I'm calling about our Saturday dinner."

"Has anything come up to change your mind? Or the day you can come?"

"No, neither of those. But I was going to propose a bit of a change. See if you're okay with it. If not, we can go ahead with our Saturday dinner."

"What's on your mind?"

I detect a change in Nathan's tone. A little more guarded. Reestablishing some distance between us.

I hesitate, but tell myself it was he who wanted us to be more like friends who can be direct with each other. "How about you come to my apartment for dinner with Arthur and me? We'll make adobo, Arthur and I."

It takes Nathan a long moment to answer. "Well, that may actually be a good idea. Arthur and I have texted each other, but it's not like we used to be. Maybe this is a way to reconnect."

"He wants to apologize."

Again, a short silence. "Did he tell you what happened in Florence?"

"He did. But I'll let him talk for himself."

"Will you have dinner with me, anyway? Just you and me? After this Saturday?"

"I'd love to."

*****

Arthur comes on Friday with three pounds of boneless pork butt. "My contribution. More than we can eat. We'll have leftovers for a few more meals. Anyway, they taste better a day or two later. I also emailed Lola. She said to simmer it until it's tender, and on the day we serve it, cook it down to a thick sauce. Then, panfry the meat for some crispiness. I think that's what I liked about her adobo. The meat gets coated in sauce and the edges are crispy."

"Sounds yummy. Let's go, do it."

The following evening, we hear a knock on the door at half past seven as we're clearing up the coffee table. Arthur and I planned an informal dinner, with plates, utensils, and the dishes we're serving all laid out on the table.

"I'll get it," Arthur says.

"You sure?"

"Better now than later when we're eating."

I stand by the coffee table, as anxious as I believe Arthur must be. I watch him advance towards the door. When he reaches it, he stops and looks back at me, a tremulous smile on his lips. He turns towards the door, and—unhurried and almost meditative—he unlocks the deadbolt, twists the doorknob, and pulls the door inward.

Through the open door, I see Nathan in casual khaki pants, a navy blue shirt, and the navy blue linen blazer I've seen him wear a few times before. His eyes are smiling, looking at Arthur. For a moment, they both stand still. Then, Arthur surprises me, and maybe Nathan as well. He steps towards Nathan and puts his arms around him.

Nathan's surprise only lasts a few seconds. He returns Arthur's embrace, as his gaze meets mine. His smile deepens and—another surprise—he winks at me. It's a playful gesture, like surprising me with the unicorn.

They pull apart and Nathan says, "It's been a while, hasn't it? I'm truly happy to see you, Arthur."

"Me, too. And yeah, too long," Arthur says, placing a hand on Nathan's arm and leading him into the room.

Nathan says, "Your adobo smells so good. Did you both make it?"

Arthur says, "With a little long-distance coaching from Lola. That's what we call our grandmothers in the Philippines."

"Must be pretty special, then."

"Wait till you taste it, and if you like it, we'll tell you Lola's secret."

I say, "A little something to drink, Nathan? An aperitif of white wine with crème de cassis? The only one I know how to make."

"A kir cocktail, you mean."

"Yes, a drink Mom often made for Dad. She used champagne, I can only afford Riesling."

"I like kir," Nathan says.

"Three glasses of kir coming up," Arthur says, taking a few steps to the kitchen counter where a bowl of kir is waiting to be scooped into wine glasses.

I say to Nathan, "You like kir. When did you first have it?"

"Do you want the short or long version?"

I glance in Arthur's direction. He's placing half-filled glasses of the cocktail on a tray and will be joining us in a moment. "Short is okay."

Nathan says, "A summer trip to Paris before I went to med school. My first trip to Europe."

"Okay, guys. Here it is. Shall we all sit down?" Arthur stops next to Nathan and hands him a glass of kir. He gives me a glass, and lays the tray on the coffee table.

Nathan takes the armchair. I sit on the couch at the end farther away from Nathan. Arthur has no choice but to sit closer to him.

"Tell us the long version of your first taste of kir. I heard you say it was on your first trip to Europe," Arthur says, picking up the third glass.

"Credit my education to a French couple I met at a café in Paris. I was alone sitting at a table next to theirs. They were so close, I could reach out and touch them. The man had a thick document he was reading and writing notes on. The young woman who must have been at least ten years younger than him, was sipping espresso, looking mellow and unperturbed. She had been casting glances at me for a little while. Maybe she was bored or annoyed being ignored by her companion. Anyway, she started talking to me."

Arthur leans forward, rapt up in Nathan's story. His eyes shine and he lets out a gasp or two as Nathan tells his story. I've seen Arthur react that way before. At the café in Paris two years ago. I didn't think anything of it then, but now it worries me.

Nathan continues his story. "We talked for quite some time. I was eating a sandwich, the first meal I've had that day. It was getting dark by the time her companion was done making notes on his document. He got up to leave. She did, too, but on impulse, she said to me, 'Why don't you come with us? We're going to a bar on Place des Vosges that serves some delicious cocktails.' The guy didn't look too happy, but he agreed. At the bar, the guy ordered us all kir royale, which uses champagne instead of white wine. Then, he introduced me to absinthe."

Eager to show his knowledge of French culture, Arthur says "Cafés are so essential to French social life, aren't they? They invented a café culture that lives on to this day. That's how you and I met."

"Yes, and I'm glad we did," Nathan says, his gaze drifting to meet mine.

Arthur says, "How did you like absinthe?"

I don't wait for Nathan's answer. I get up to refill their empty glasses of kir. He may have related a long version, but I suspect there's more to the story than he's telling us. But it's of no consequence to me. What concerns me is Arthur's reaction. He seems to me a little too excited and eager to please. I can't help wondering if he might still be in love with Nathan.

As I hand them their half-full glasses I tell them I'll finish preparing dinner. Arthur offers to help, but I say, "No need. I got it. And I can hear you from the kitchen."

Arthur continues to talk about French café culture. I heat the adobo per Lola's instructions, dress a package of greens with a Vinaigrette, bring out plates, napkins, and utensils.

At some point while I was finishing the dishes we're serving, I see Nathan lean forward. Arthur is talking in hushed tones. Nathan listens intently. Arthur must be telling Nathan how much he regrets all those things he accused Nathan of.

After dinner, when Nathan is about to leave, they talk again by the door. Arthur may be repeating his apologies. Before Nathan leaves, he pulls Arthur close and hugs him. Arthur hugs him back. Nathan waves his goodbye to me before he opens the door and closes it as he walks out. Arthur stands by the door a few seconds before he turns around.

He approaches me. "I think it went well. Thank you, Sis. I can't believe how understanding he is. He said he bore me no grudge, that I was a kid, exploring and finding out who I am. If he hurt me, he didn't mean to. We just happen to be different. He also said that he thought, and still thinks, I'm a wonderful, caring person and he's touched, but envious, at how well you and I get along."

He's smiling, but I catch a fleeting shadow in his eyes.

"Arthur, are you sure it went well? Can you truly say you don't care for Nathan the way you used to?"

"Absolutely. Nathan is a friend. I don't get that same excitement being with him the way I do with Jeffrey. In fact, I think I'll go back to the dorm. Okay with you if I don't sleep here tonight, Sis? Suddenly, I miss Jeffrey so much."

A couple of hours later, I stay awake in bed, fidgeting and unable to let go of my apprehension. Something continues to bother Arthur.

Chapter Thirty-Four

The Fate of the Illuminated Manuscripts

On Tuesday, Nathan calls me to meet him at the Emeryville Peets' after work. He has news from Kurt about the fate of the illuminated manuscripts.

He's already at the coffeeshop when I arrive, sitting at one end of the banquette as usual, sipping an espresso, perusing a newspaper, one of several that some customers bring in to read with their coffee and leave for others. As I take the chair across the table from him, he looks up, folds the paper, and lays it on the banquette.

"Sorry, I'm late," I say.

"Five minutes or so, that's all. Everything okay at the university?"

"Not as crazy as usual. Spring semester is over. Summer sessions have begun, and there aren't as many students on campus. And in case you haven't heard, the big news is Professor Fischl's mural is finished."

"Good for him. And good for his graduate assistants."

"Yes, although two assistants who worked on his mural are worried their assistantships may not be renewed in the fall."

"Yours is secure, I suppose."

"He teaches the same classes every semester, so I think he'll keep me."

"I'm glad for you. Would you like a café au lait?"

"No thank you. It'll keep me awake tonight."

"How about decaf or some iced tea? It might help digest Kurt's news when you hear it."

"That bad?"

"No. Most of it is good actually, but ... wait until you hear it."

"I'll have some water, then."

Nathan goes to the bar for a bottle of water, leaving me to imagine what Kurt's news could be. I've been itching to find out the "fate of the manuscripts" since Nathan called me earlier today. As far as my own interests are concerned, the worst that could happen is if some anonymous collector has bought the manuscripts, intending to keep them for his private collection, making them out of reach to the rest of us. To me, the best place for rare old books and manuscripts with historical value is at museums, or university and national libraries like the British Library in London or the Bibliothèque Nationale in Paris where people can request access to them.

Nathan comes back with a bottle of water and a glass with some ice cubes in it. He twists the cap off the bottle and pushes it towards me along with the glass. He waits for me to pour some water, take a few sips, and put the glass down. He's not in a hurry to share Kurt's news, and he's putting me in unbearable suspense.

Impatient, I say, "What's the big news?"

He knits his brow and holds my gaze for what seems like an eternal minute. He's put on the stern professorial look I remember from our first meeting at Peet's. Is he annoyed at my impatience? He's being needlessly dramatic, and I'm diverted. I suppress an urge to laugh in amusement.

Finally, he speaks. "The manuscripts are going back to the rightful owners, along with other treasures Joe Junior stole—a casket studded with precious stones, and a few smaller religious reliquaries."

A grim undertone to his voice reins in my amusement and puzzles me. "That's good news, isn't it?"

"It is, and it isn't. The good thing is these treasures are back to where they belong. The not-so-good part is the church paid a few million dollars for their return. And as you can imagine, Kurt protested. He had advised against paying to retrieve the treasures. But the church obviously had the final decision."

I'm incredulous. And dismayed. "How could the church pay to get them back? The manuscripts were clearly stolen, and we have some good evidence that points to one culprit."

"I suppose that's the art world for you. You can't judge it by the same rules and principles you do for most things."

"Sounds like the church paid ransom for them."

"It does sound like ransom payment. Not only for the manuscripts, but for the other treasures as well."

"How much ransom money did the sellers get?"

"I think it's somewhere to the tune of nine million, in total."

"That's a lot of money. Joe Junior is nine million dollars richer for stealing treasures. I understand he stole during the chaotic aftermath of a world war, but he could have returned them."

"As a couple of French soldiers did who came upon illuminated manuscripts more famous and more valuable than those Joe Junior stole. The French Army raided a German train carrying Nazi loot at a station in Berchtesgaden in the Bavarian Alps. One of the officers stepped on what, at first, looked to him like a brick. On picking it up and examining it, he realized it was an illuminated manuscript. So, of course, he took it, stashed it in his bag. Upon his return to France, he showed it to a friend who worked at the local library. The manuscript, as it turned out, was *Très Belles Heures*."

"The Duc De Berry's *Très Belles Heures*! The one I have a printed copy of. One of the most famous and most valuable."

"Yes, that one."

"What happened to it?"

"It was returned to the owner, the then Baron de Rothschild, who reported it missing. He later donated it to the Bibliothèque Nationale."

"Why couldn't our American soldier have repatriated the ones he found?"

"Why indeed? I think he knew what he had and was aware of their value. So was his family, who intended to profit from them. The family lied about how they acquired the manuscripts and the other treasures. They took the treasures to Switzerland where laws were more lenient because they were afraid of prosecution. Throw in unscrupulous art dealers and lawyers and the rightful owners who wanted their treasures back and the outcome is inevitable."

"The owners agree to pay ransom."

"Those profiting aren't calling it ransom money, but a 'finder's fee.' I suppose there's a convoluted way in which you can argue the payment is a finder's fee. Joe Junior is our thief, but he's not listed as a seller. The art dealer is. He can be said to be the finder, which isn't unusual. It's common practice for art dealers to find and buy artwork they sell later. This art dealer will pocket a percentage. And so will the sleazy lawyer hired by Joe Junior's family."

"Has a figure been quoted on how much these treasures would sell for?"

"If they were sold at auction, the most recent estimate for all of Joe Junior's stolen treasures—manuscripts, casket, ivory comb, and reliquaries—amounts to two hundred million dollars. The manuscripts account for much of that sum."

"Two hundred million! That's mind boggling. But I guess the manuscripts alone are priceless. Still, it makes me wonder all over again what determines the value of an artwork."

"Have you been to an auction?"

"No."

"I've only been to one. It's a unique experience for us, the uninitiated. Obviously, a competition where the highest bidder wins. On the surface, the atmosphere is casual, even friendly. Many in the audience know each other, might even have bid against each other in the past. To me, the tension is palpable, though it's held under wraps. In the end, what the artwork sells for depends on what the highest bidder is willing to pay. And quite often, it's way above the initial appraised value."

"Does the intrinsic value of an artwork figure in its monetary value?"

"Most serious collectors hire experts to advise them, so you could say intrinsic value does count. But experts don't always agree and there's a lot of ego involved in the bidding. Collectors are a highly competitive bunch. Some collectors become obsessed with acquiring and owning certain pieces. Some like to show off the pieces in their collections. Most of them consider the art good investments. Extraneous stuff like that drive prices up. Sometimes way above intrinsic value."

Not a picture to be proud of, hacking away at my idealistic view of the art world. A disenchantment to reflect on alone in bed and deep into the night.

I say, "In a kidnapping case involving a ransom, the perpetrators—when caught—are brought to trial. Shouldn't the sellers, including Joe Junior, be charged?"

"They should be, from a moral point of view. Legally, I don't know. There are statutes of limitations and other legal issues you and I are ignorant of. Ask Kurt. He can answer such questions."

"I guess I should look on the bright side. Those legal issues aren't relevant to my interest in the manuscripts. The church has regained possession of the manuscripts, and I can request access to them for my thesis work. I do find that particular outcome favorable to my interests. But when you consider everything, it's not only disappointing. It's depressing. A major crime goes unpunished. Worse than that, it's rewarded."

"Legal issues are also outside the purview of what I initially wanted the book to show and prove. I wanted Americans, and—yeah—the world, to wake up to the fact that Allied soldiers did some looting during the last world war. That no one is immune to temptation. I wanted to look into the differences between those who do what's right and return found art and those who keep them. But we may have to address legal issues in some form to understand the cogs that drive the art world."

Nathan is—as Arthur would say—being "collected" about the resolution of the church treasures, but he's not exactly calm about it. Now, I can see what brought on the stern expression and grim tone to his voice. The recovery and repatriation of the treasures is a major victory that deserves to be celebrated, but the fact that people can profit—in a big way, in this case—from committing major crimes goes against our sense of what is right.

I'm flabbergasted that every piece of evidence we've unearthed to prove that the church treasures were stolen by Joe Junior has counted for nothing. I'm disillusioned that everything I've learned to be legally and morally right has been ignored in deciding the fate of the illuminated manuscripts and the other church treasures.

As I struggle with this reality, I search for some way to stop or at least minimize this barrage of conflicting thoughts and emotions. Maybe it's human nature. We search for a palatable way to explain dissonances. I'm aware that's what I'm doing when I say, "Well, the finder's fee is a small fraction of the total value of the treasures."

Nathan says, "Nearly five percent."

"The return on what the church pays is so huge, I can see why they agreed to pay a finder's fee to get their treasures back."

"I know. And aside from the monetary value, there's the weight of history that adds to the church's decision to settle. The manuscripts were a gift from a king that the church has

owned since the twelfth century—a priceless reason for paying
for their repatriation."

I might have hoped Nathan would contradict my
rationalizing the finder's fee. Instead, he's cited other reasons
to justify it. Reasons I can't deny. Consider the bigger picture,
I tell myself. Aloud, I say, "Should we also take into account
motivation and context in judging this theft?"

"What do you mean?"

"Well, unlike Nazi looting and the Isabella Stewart
Gardner Museum art heist ten years ago, the theft of the
church treasures is a crime of opportunity as the war was
ending. Nazi looting and the Gardner Museum heist were
planned, and the perpetrators knew what they were after."

"I suppose if the theft of the church treasures were to go to
court, the jury would take motivation and context into account
and Joe Junior and family might not be judged as harshly
compared to an art theft that has been planned. But who
knows what would happen? The fact is Joe Junior committed
a major crime."

"The artworks stolen from the Gardner Museum in Boston,
if I remember correctly, were also valued at $200 million ten
years ago, weren't they?"

Nathan says, "Yes. And at that time, they set up a $1
million dollar reward leading to its recovery."

"None of those artworks has been recovered."

"They're too hot to sell. Unless, of course, they've been
privately sold."

"So, the German church has been luckier than the Gardner
Museum."

Nathan gazes at me, frowning for a moment. "You're
making a point I haven't totally grasped."

"I'm not making a point. I'm extremely disappointed at the outcome of the theft of these illuminated manuscripts. They're worth about as much. And yet, they haven't attracted as much attention as the Gardner heist artworks."

"The Gardner Museum heist took place while much of the world was at peace, and the thieves took pieces by famous, highly regarded artists: Rembrandt, Vermeer, Degas, and Manet. One Rembrandt piece is being singled out by the art world because it's the only naval piece he painted. I'm betting the value of these artworks will surpass that of the treasures Joe Junior took."

"I see. I understand the theft of these manuscripts can't be compared to other cases of art thievery. But doing so helps me cope with my disappointment."

"I'm rather disappointed myself. But we can't change the outcome. We must learn to accept it."

"Was the outcome ever in our hands? Did our investigation help in any way?"

Nathan stares at me, his eyes soft with concern and something else that, I hope, isn't pity. But I'll take compassion. It implies understanding and sharing.

He says, "Of course, it did. If Kurt, you, and I didn't bring the truth out in the open, these treasures might have been sold for a lot more money than the sellers finders' fee. They would have profited so much more from their crime."

"They could also have sold them to some private collector who would store them in his repository until he can resell them for a profit. Meanwhile, they're lost to the rest of the world."

"These aren't paintings in frames you can hang on walls to show off. We would hope that anyone who collects such manuscripts realize they need great care. Right temperature, protection from dust, air, and light. Also, oils and other organic matter from handling them."

The coffeeshop has dimmed its lights and Nathan looks at his watch. "This place is closing in fifteen minutes. Let's go. I'll take you somewhere nice to eat. A Japanese restaurant where we don't need a reservation. You do eat sushi?"

"I love sushi."

"Good. You look a little depressed. I heard raw fish helps get you out of a depressed mood."

"I never knew that."

"Because it's probably not true. I wanted to distract you a little." Grinning, Nathan throws me a quick glance.

"See, now you're smiling. Anyway, focus on the brighter side. The church treasures have been repatriated. The manuscripts are safe and have become accessible to the public. You can request to see them or have the church make copies so you can study them. If they had been sold to a private collector who stores them in a vault, they'd be lost to all of us."

"And there goes the illuminated manuscript I wanted to create on the fifteenth-century manuscript I wanted to study and analyze."

"Time to get serious, then. Call Kurt. He'll have information on how you can contact the church."

Chapter Thirty-Five

June 2000

Joe Junior

He sat on a wheelchair in the garden at the back of the old folks' home. Bruno, the aide who had wheeled him out, spread his ample bottom on a bench to his right, humming a tune and tapping his fingers on his thighs.

His gaze roamed the landscape. Everything was a blurry green with patches of red, white, and yellow here and there. Bruno had forgotten to put on his glasses. He could have asked for them before they left his room, but it seemed too much of an effort to open his mouth.

Why didn't his family let him die from the stroke he suffered two years ago? He would have preferred it to living in this place. The aides and nurses cared for your physical shell, made sure you were clean and fed. On nice days, which was much of the year, they pushed you around the garden path and parked you near a bench for about half an hour. Occasionally, residents were treated to some entertainment. But he paid no attention to those. He had television in his room that the aide turned on after breakfast and turned off at bedtime. But he barely watched it. Instead, he stared at the ceiling, a blank white space that calmed his mind. When his eyes smarted from dryness, he closed them, and before long, he fell asleep. The few times his mind wasn't vacant, he indulged in a world in his head of experiences and places he could still remember.

The staff left him alone and he saw no one again until the next mealtime, or the sunny afternoons when Bruno wheeled him out to the garden, and an aide put him to bed. This was not living.

Maybe they could do nothing more for him. His stroke blunted his reactions. He had become a rag doll with straw for brains. And all he wanted now was for them to let him recede into permanent oblivion. The quicker the better. But he couldn't even tell them that. Most days, his brain couldn't summon the words to say what he wanted to say.

On rare days like this day, he awakened with his mind lucid, his memory harking back to a distant past. A past when the first thing he had done to greet each day in his own home was to sit up, swing his legs to the floor, and open the special box on his nightstand containing the old illuminated manuscripts. He had feasted his eyes on the manuscripts lying side by side in the box. He lifted one and opened it to each of four pages of illustrations: Mark, Matthew, Luke and John, the gospel writers.

The first manuscript back in its usual place, he picked up the second. Unlike the first, the illustrations in the second manuscript ran along the top of every page. They were not of the gospel writers. Instead they depicted figures engaged in actions described in the psalms.

Debilitated by his stroke, he could no longer swing his legs. But with his arms and hands, he could still heave his body towards the edge of the bed to gaze at his old manuscripts. He rarely opened them these days. He didn't touch their covers, either. Such simple movements had become too taxing for his shaky arms and hands and his fading body. And without glasses, everything around him was blurred. All he could do now was to reassure himself his old manuscripts were exactly where he expected them to be.

Minutes later, he pushed the button to summon an aide to help him dress and bring him his breakfast, half a glass of warm milk and a donut hole. The staff knew that when he summoned Bruno instead of waiting for him to come, he was as close to a normal old person as he could possibly be. In fact, he had more lucid days than he let on. But it was also on such days that he sometimes wished he had died the day he had a stroke. Being more aware of what went on around him was, for him, a curse. While he could watch and understand what was going on around him on such days, he still could not do anything on his own. Not take a walk. Not read. There was only the television. Almost always, though, those days were followed by many more days of apathy and obliviousness.

On a lucid morning a month later, he pushed his body to a sitting position, and turned his head toward the nightstand on which lay his box of old manuscripts. The box was not there. It had vanished.

He froze for a few seconds before his body collapsed on its side. Low raspy wailing issued from his mouth. Wailing that grew louder and raspier until a couple of nursing staff barged into his room. He tried to tell them what happened but the words he uttered sounded like babble to the alarmed staff. Unable to be understood, all he could do was to keep pointing to the empty tabletop.

One of the nurses left the room. Less than two minutes later, she was back, a syringe held chest-level in her right hand, ready to administer a tranquilizing injection. A third aide followed her.

Bruno, who usually pushed his wheelchair out to the garden, understood what he was trying to say, reminding him that his brother and sister had visited him a few days before.

But he didn't recall that visit. It must have been on one of his foggy days. Only they could have taken his box, Bruno said. He would call them and ask about the box.

*****

His brother and sister visited him a few days later, when his mind was fogged up, and he sat still on his chair, his face betraying neither thought nor emotion. His sister spoke, kept on speaking, the same words sputtering out of her mouth. She pointed to the empty side table.

For a moment, the fog in his head cleared. He focused on his sister who seemed to be holding back tears, trying to explain what happened to the box, to the treasures that, after the war, had given meaning to his life. Through them, he had met new friends, and attracted new lovers fascinated by the manuscripts and curious about what kind of a man would own them. In the last two years, those manuscripts gave him a reason to endure living when he was most depressed.

As he understood more of what his sister was saying, his body began to tremble. He could not accept what his sister was telling him, but he was helpless. All he could do was surrender his grasp on reality to the comfort of oblivion. His eyes clouded again, and he closed them. His mind blocked out the sounds around him, and he retreated into his shell, back into a vacuum.

Days later, he woke up with a clear mind, and found himself in a strange room. He had not slept in his own bed, in his own room at his own home. Where was he? Scanning the room a few times, the last incident with his sister began to creep back into his consciousness. His sister in tears, telling him they had no choice but to sell his precious manuscripts. They were their only hope to keep the hardware store going. They owed it to their father, to him, and to their children to preserve their father's legacy.

He muttered to himself repeatedly that they had no right. No right. What kind of a legacy is a hardware store? How could they even think of comparing it to historical works of art of incalculable value?

What had he done? He could have returned the treasures. The military command would have considered the terrible conditions of wartime as extenuating and meted a relatively light punishment. If only he had done the right thing.

But was he capable of doing the right thing at that time? Those treasures were his reward, his salvation. The price he exacted out of the Nazis for the irreparable harm they did to him and his fellow soldiers.

Helpless and despairing of his loss and his uncertainties at what he should have done, he could still hope that his treasures were now in the hands of someone who could value them and care for them as much as he had done. But could hope spare him the unbearable agony of his descent into purgatory? He was sure that was where he was going. He had killed, but it was to help rout evil. He had stolen treasures, but it was wartime and victors looted with impunity. He had committed acts forbidden by the church, but he had not hurt anyone in doing so.

The following morning, the aide found him cold and still as a statue, his face frozen into a grimace of pain. Or maybe, he was smiling. Hard to tell on this old man, Bruno thought.

Chapter Thirty-Six

Summer 2001

Moving On

Summer break. No school for me and no graduate assistant duties. At least until fall semester starts. Professor Fischl has renewed my assistantship and I'm grateful. I wouldn't need a student loan for my last year of graduate school.

In the days following the return of the golden manuscripts to the church, I couldn't help dwelling on the abrupt and disillusioning conclusion to our search for truth and a just outcome to the theft of two valuable illuminated manuscripts. It distracted me from focusing on crafting a proposal for the written part of my two-pronged master's thesis. But I have persisted.

The content part of my thesis proposal is finished. I have chosen my topic, tentatively titled it *From The Utrecht Psalter Towards the Art of Modern Picture Book Creation.* There's more work to do when I write my thesis. But for now, the literature review for the paper I did for Professor Fischl and the research and ideas I've gleaned working with Nathan and Kurt, have been enough for me to flesh out this aspect of my proposal. Before I submit it to Professor Fischl, I email a copy to Nathan with the short message: "What do you think?"

On Thursday noontime, he calls me at the office. "Your proposal looks good. Could do with a few more details. I wrote a couple of comments, but I'm sure Adam will approve the concept. The most challenging part is still ahead of you, though. Do you have a good idea of how to present your content as an illuminated manuscript—materials, illustrations, that sort of thing?"

"I initially wanted to create my illuminated manuscript in the medieval style, although I admit I'm intimidated by what it would require. Besides, I haven't even started, and I've already come up with a big problem. Parchment is available, but prohibitively expensive. A precut 8 by 10 piece can cost 20 to 50 dollars a sheet, depending on what kind of animal skin is used. Imagine what it would cost if I ordered a special size like 10 by 15."

"That is a lot of money, no matter how you cut it."

I catch a pun in what Nathan said whether he intended it or not. I say, "I'm not cutting each piece. I'm folding it in the middle, so each sheet makes two pages inscribed on one side. With the 10 by15, the dimension of the manuscript will be 5 by 7½."

Nathan laughs. "You got me there. But seriously, it's conceivable you'd end up with a fifty-page thesis at least. That's beaucoup bucks for material to write on."

"Certainly is, for a graduate student making just enough for day-to-day existence. Besides, I'll need material for the manuscript cover. Plus quills, ink, tempera, and gold leaf for writing and illustrations. On top of all that, I'll need to search for a medieval-style font or make up my own and practice writing it with a quill. I'll have to learn to bind a book. I don't know if I'm up to doing all that."

"I don't think medieval scribes bound the books they produced. At least, by the fifteenth century, various tasks of bookmaking were done by different artisans. In fact, one illustrated manuscript might have used several artists when many illuminations are required. Or one scribe could write the text and someone else might do the initial letters and titles to different sections of the manuscript."

"That's good to know, but again, I'll need money to pay someone to bind my manuscript. Anyway, I do want to learn how to bind a manuscript. It can't be that hard."

"You're in control, Clarissa. It's your artwork. Talk to Adam. He'll be the one evaluating that aspect of your thesis."

"I may have to reassess this whole project. I haven't given up on doing a medieval manuscript. Maybe there's some kind of paper out there I can substitute for parchment. Something like papyrus or Asian rice papers. Those have also been around for centuries. I think they might have predated parchment."

"Look at it this way: Strictly speaking, you can't be producing a medieval manuscript, because you live in the modern era. Instead, you're creating a modern illuminated manuscript in the medieval style."

"You're splitting hairs."

"Yes, but it might free you up. There is, as they say, more than one way to skin a cat. You'll come up with a unique piece when you change a few things. Medieval scribes and artists did. Remember what you said about *The Utrecht Psalter* creator taking something that already exists and making it his own? A manuscript with a touch of Asian or Egyptian roots, for instance, would be more a propos of our times. Art, like a lot of things, adapts itself to what's current. Anyway, I've emailed you back your study proposal with my comments. We can talk about it some more over dinner. You haven't forgotten, I hope."

"No... But, I thought, since those German manuscripts have been returned to their rightful owners, the work on our project is done."

"We still have a book to write. Our plan was for you to write a couple of chapters. I know your thesis is your priority, and I've always expected you'd focus on that. But I'm confident you'd finish it months before our book goes to the publisher for editing and book cover design. And remember I'm still your de facto thesis adviser. Or have you fired me from that position?"

"No, of course not. I value your opinion and your advice."

"Saturday then. Pick you up at 5:30?"

"Why so early?"

"We're going to a popular tapas bar. They don't take reservations, so it's better to be early."

"Okay, 5:30, Saturday."

As soon as he hangs up, I open my email app and eagerly read Nathan's comments. The first: "You need to have a clear idea of how to produce the illuminated manuscript and include it in this proposal before submitting this to Adam."

His comment echoes my misgivings on my ability to produce an illuminated manuscript in the medieval style. I do have a bit of a problem with being impatient or acting on impulse. I agree it's wise to do more research on the process before submitting my proposal to Professor Fischl.

The second: "Find out from Kurt how to get a facsimile of the recovered German manuscript. You might not have to include this part in your proposal, but that facsimile is essential."

I guess I didn't make it clear enough that I must do that.

People say, "a couple of ... things, comments, days." They don't mean it. It's a shortcut for more than one. In addition to his two early comments, Nathan wrote shorter notes throughout the proposal, pertaining to specific phrases and ideas.

The third, at the end of the proposal: "You write very well. Ever considered writing for a living?"

This last comment is a balm to my somewhat bruised ego. Nathan's feedback on the content of my proposal has been honest, thoughtful, and prompt. I'm grateful to him. He has agreed to help me without compensation for his time and the knowledge he has shared with me. But, like everyone else, I'm sensitive to what I perceive are criticisms of my ideas, my projects. My first impulse to nurse my bruised ego has always been to take a break, usually by sketching or painting.

I close my email app. Out of a drawer in my desk, I take out a sketchpad and a box of well-used Sennelier pastels I bought at a store in Paris. The dirty plate, glass, and fork I used for lunch are still on top of my desk. I place my uneaten peach on the plate and immerse myself sketching a still life of this montage of my customary weekday noon hour.

*****

In better humor in the evening, I email my father about the master's thesis I'm planning to produce. If he answers, maybe I can ask him for a little financial help.

I have been sending him emails whenever new or important things happen to me and Arthur, a continued attempt on my part to repair the rift wrought at our parting in Rome. He has not responded to previous emails I've sent him since that time, and he might remain silent on this one as well.

But I continue to hope. He is my father and we're bound by blood. We have a history of shared experiences sown in my growing-up years.

I'll always remember the day he told me that in his culture, familial loyalty is in the blood. And that loyalty assumes blood ties remain strong, regardless of past animosities. To drum that lesson into my head, he recounted stories of family feuds in his country—feuds that arose when a conflict between individuals from two different families escalated to include other family members. They often ended up in violence including murder that claimed victims on both sides.

So far, though, our blood ties haven't helped my efforts to heal the rift between us.

Chapter Thirty-Seven

Getting More Comfortable

On Saturday evening, I welcome a respite from reliving past regrets. I dress up a little for dinner with Nathan, but I'm doing it for myself as well. I need a mood booster. I don an outfit I last wore at a soirée with friends from my graduating class last year—black sequined tank top, a black pleated skirt that ends above the knee and a short taupe leather jacket that drops just below the waist. I hook on gold hoop earrings and slip several gold bangles on my wrist, jewelry I've rarely worn since Dad gave them to me two years ago.

Nathan and I stop at the entrance into Cesar's at a quarter to six, already packed with diners when we arrive. A two-year old tapas bar in Berkeley, it's a casual, lively restaurant, fronted by two large doors open to the sidewalk.

A waiter greets us, and weaving between occupied tables, Nathan and I follow him to an empty one deep inside the room. As soon as we sit down, the waiter hands each of us two separate menus. One for drinks and one for dishes.

Like the tapas bars in Spain, Cesar's serves small plates, snack-sized dishes meant to go with alcoholic drinks. In France, these dishes may be served as entrées, the first course.

Appetizers, if you'd rather call them that. I've always been curious how the word "entrée" derived from the French word "entrer," to enter, got translated into "main course" in the American menu. In France, the main course is listed as the "plat principal," literally main plate or main dish, served after an entrée.

Nathan asks me if it's alright for us to share each plate we order. That way, we can sample more dishes. We can always order more of tapas we like. Good idea, I say.

I had my first taste of tapas in Sevilla, a southern historical city in the Andalucian region of Spain, where Dad took Mom and me on our first stop to celebrate Mom's fortieth birthday. From there, we went to a restaurant for roast suckling pig. It was a memorable night I treasure, a night of feasting and laughter that lasted until midnight.

A high-ceilinged ground-floor room in a centuries-old building, the Sevilla tapas bar was smaller and much older, but grander, than Cesar's. Chandeliers hung from the ceiling, and what might be centuries-old mahogany cabinets lined wood-paneled walls. A long marble service bar was laden with plates of various tapas. Despite its quiet majesty, the atmosphere among its clientele was informal. You could order drinks and tapas from the waiter or go to the service bar and carefully pull out plates of tapas laid out or stacked up on it. You could eat and drink your tapas standing at the end of the bar free of dishes. Dad opted for a table and we ordered from a chalked-on menu on a board behind the service bar.

While the names of dishes at Cesar's are in Spanish, their descriptions are in English. The first tapa I search for in the menu is boquerones fritos, fried fresh anchovies, a dish found in many cultures. The Greeks and Italians make them, and it was the first tapa Dad ordered to remind him of his home country. Done well, it's crisp on the outside and tender on the inside, and I could eat the whole thing, bones and all, in a couple of bites. Along with jamon iberico de bellota, it's what I remember best from my Sevilla tapas bar experience.

Cesar's menu doesn't list either dish, but they have marinated anchovies and jamon serrano, both of which I order in addition to a classic potato omelet and roasted peppers.

While we wait for our drinks and tapas, Nathan stares at me for an interminable minute, head tilted a little and eyes alight with a smile. I fidget on my seat and look away.

He has sensed my discomfort and he asks if I've made progress on my proposal. I utter a peremptory "Not yet." I'm still clinging to the hope that I can submit a medieval illuminated manuscript as my thesis.

I forestall further talk about my thesis by asking Nathan the unanswered question often at the tip of my tongue the few occasions we've relaxed into "small talk." I do so with some trepidation, remembering his evasiveness at our first meeting at the Emeryville coffeehouse. But that was a while back and we've become more comfortable in each other's presence.

He meets my gaze with squinting eyes. But instead of being evasive, or worse, offended, he's amused. "You won't let this question rest until I give you an answer that will satisfy you, will you?"

I'm disconcerted. He lifts an eyebrow and his steady gaze twinkles in amusement. But I catch a note of sarcasm in his voice. Is he trying to disguise his reluctance to share anything personal? Have I treaded into forbidden territory?

"I'm sorry. I shouldn't have asked. It's none of my business,"

"No, it's okay. I can understand why you're curious. I don't mind answering. But I won't guarantee it will satisfy your curiosity. If I were Kurt, I might be able to inject some drama into how I tell my story. It's actually boring."

I wanted to protest that he needn't answer. But he's right. I'm curious and boring will be as good an answer as exciting.

"My parents are both doctors, as you probably know. And I'm an only child. So, naturally—well, you know. Anyway, I went along for the first year or so, but it didn't take long for me to realize this noble profession—my parents' words— wasn't where my heart was. Without informing them, I started taking art classes. Kind of an antidote. Also, for me, more fun. I loved it."

At this unexpected disclosure of an early love for art, I was moved. Moved so deeply that I'd never forget how his eyes shone at that moment. I don't interrupt his confession.

"I knew my parents would never let me switch majors. So, I stuck it out in medicine for as long as I could. Maybe too long. That is, until I finished my course work. I tell myself it's because I like to finish what I've started, but maybe I couldn't take my parents' disappointment.

"But I could endure my unhappiness only for so long. When it was time to do my residency, I balked. Long story short, my parents disowned me."

"No," I say, shaking my head.

He stares at me, amused. "You look shocked. But that's how it was. I couldn't believe it myself at the time. I thought we'd sit down and talk, and I could make them understand I had my own unique interests. But they refused to talk to me except to say they felt betrayed. They stopped paying for my apartment, closed my credit card, changed their locks, and ignored my calls. To be disowned at the ripe old age of 25—I felt a sense of shame. Why? I didn't know at the time. I wasn't that self-aware.

"But I learned quickly. How was I to survive on my own? I had written some papers for my art classes that my professors praised. I thought—why not submit them to an online art magazine? I had nothing to lose. To my surprise, they published two, maybe because art reporters don't usually write about illuminated manuscripts. They paid me. Not much, but it helped. I believed I found my calling."

"But you're back working for a clinic."

He chuckles, uneasily. "We all say nothing is ever black or white. But until you find yourself in a dilemma, you don't know what that aphorism means. My rebellion didn't last that long.

"I'm going to confess something I'm a bit ashamed of. As you may have guessed, I was a spoiled brat, used to a life of comfort, of getting what I wanted sometimes before I even asked for it. Writing occasional pieces for magazines couldn't support the lifestyle I was used to. And to my surprise, I missed medicine—the prospect of helping people heal and feel better. Yeah, there might be a bit of messianic complex in that mindset.

"Anyway, I did finish a medical residency in internal medicine. Not the specialty in neurology or brain surgery my parents envisioned for me. But I like being a part-time internist. It's given me time to feed that part of me who loves art and write about my experience of it. And still go for an occasional fancy dinner."

"Have you reconciled with your parents?"

"We're back on speaking terms. They're still disappointed I didn't turn out to be the ideal son." He smiles wryly and I detect a wistful tone in his voice.

"That's sad."

He shrugs, "Doesn't bother me anymore. In retrospect, everything that happened was for the best. I moved on. I learned to be independent a little later than I should have and would have wanted, but I am where I want to be. There are many facets to every person, but sometimes a couple of those facets clash and the person must choose between them. Or he could look for ways to reconcile them in himself."

"I understand. You work as a doctor, and still find time to write about art."

"Yes. I've had to compromise, taking part-time work to accommodate my interest in art. I have other interests, dormant passions I could cultivate further, and I'll find time for those at some future time."

"Breaking away from family is tough, though, isn't it? Especially when you genuinely care for each other."

"It is. But it's your life. Your choice. You're going through something like that now, aren't you?"

"You could say that. I went through a breaking-away phase from my family more than a year ago. And I was grateful and happy Arthur decided to join me months later. So, really, what I'm striving for now is some permanence. Finding a place I can call home."

"Which I assume you haven't found yet."

"No. I still haven't much of a clue what it takes. Do you have to have lived in a place long enough to really know it, establish lasting connections with people in it? Build up a store of memories you can associate with the place? I'm waiting for that 'Aha' moment when I can say, 'This is home.'"

"Oh Clarissa, maybe a place is not really what defines a home."

"Maybe not. I'll have to keep searching."

I find the turn of our conversation intriguing and would have wanted to keep probing into Nathan's last remark, but the waiter has arrived, two wine glasses secured between the fingers of one hand and a bottle of white wine in the other.

He places glasses and bottle on the table, opens the bottle, and fills our glasses halfway. While we're sipping our wine, he returns carrying a tray. He unloads marinated anchovies, jamon serrano, tortilla de patatas, and skewers of grilled pork pieces redolent with spices, a dish Nathan ordered. Minutes later, the waiter brings another tray on which are stacked plates of roasted peppers, roasted white asparagus, fried calamari, and an assortment of three Spanish cheeses.

Chapter Thirty-Eight

A Break

It may be inevitable that our conversation would segue back to my thesis proposal. After all, Nathan did say we could devote time over dinner for me to ask questions and for him to clarify his comments and suggestions. Presumably in a rational and intelligent manner.

As we ate, we talked about the tapas we've sampled. We've declared our favorites and ordered more of those. I've also recounted my tapas soiree in Spain with my parents. We're waiting for dessert and coffee, and our evening is nearing its end. Back of my mind, we're within seconds of the inevitable. But when it comes, I'm unprepared.

The waiter has taken away the empty plates and we're still waiting for him to bring our dessert. Objective and back on task, Nathan says, "Shall we talk about my comments to your thesis proposal?"

His gaze is fixed on me, his brow knitted and his eyes questioning, waiting for an answer. I return his look with a blank one. And I shrug, still reluctant to talk about his comments, and dreading to dig deeper into what they mean.

In the minute or so of muteness that follows, I recall how his comments sent me into a kind of funk. But now, returning his steady gaze, I realize I was hurt. And it puzzles me. I've received enough critical comments on papers I've written for classes and on artwork I've done that are presented for oral critiques in front of a class. I have developed a thick hide for them. Often the papers have been graded and couldn't be resubmitted for a better grade, but I wanted to understand what I did wrong or didn't do well enough, and research ways to correct or revise them. For the future, I told myself.

I'm less inclined to revise an artwork based on critiques by teachers and classmates. An artwork is too personal both for the artist and the viewer who may see different things in the same artwork. But I'd evaluate my work anyway, and based on my original intent for the piece, I'd rework it or ignore the critique and set the piece aside if I'm at a loss about what else I can do to satisfy my standards of good art.

I haven't reviewed Nathan's feedback since the first time I read it a few days ago. It's only now as I fidget, ill at ease, and eventually avert my gaze from his, that the pain caused by reading those comments hits my gut.

I tried to forget his comments by losing myself in sketching a pastel still life. As I sketched, and with the help of my inner voice, I reasoned myself out of my funk: A thesis is a lot weightier than a term paper. Therefore, for everyone, including me, ego gets inexorably tangled up in it. After all, a thesis could determine whether you're awarded your Master's or not, which, in turn, could affect your future.

Now, while Nathan is waiting for me to say something, I'm speechless. Not only is my bad humor back. I'm also hurting and confused.

I shrug once more.

Nathan says, "Nothing to say? I can't believe you're just accepting what I wrote on your proposal."

I'm tempted to shrug again, but his unflinching gaze is searching deeper.

This time I conjure up a response that I hope will end Nathan's probing. "Frankly, I haven't had time to think about your comments. I've been busy searching the internet for ways to create a medieval-style illuminated manuscript with modern materials."

"I see. That's equally important, or more so, since you must submit an artwork. In any case, don't hesitate to call me when you're ready to talk about the written content of your proposal."

Nathan must know my response is evasive, but he's letting it pass for now. He turns to the almond cake that has been waiting for us. The waiter brought it in the middle of what might have looked to him like an argument. Me balking like a spoiled child, and Nathan frowning and serious. I watch Nathan turn his full attention on eating his cake. He's disappointed in me, I'm sure.

I pick up my dessert fork and slice a thin piece of my almond cake. I've lost my appetite for it, but I eat it anyway. Isn't that what everyone does at dinner when you've run out of things to say? I finish my cake, not knowing whether I like it or not.

The wall between Nathan and me is up once again, and it doesn't bode well for the comfortable atmosphere I've begun to expect co-authoring a book with him. It saddens me, but I console myself: Writing is best done in solitary peace, anyway.

Shortly after dessert, and having nothing more we could think of to talk about, we leave the restaurant and drive quietly back to my apartment building. All I could think of to say before getting out of his car is, "Thank you for a nice dinner."

I smile as sincere a smile as I could muster and hope he can tell that I did find much of the evening rather nice.

"My pleasure," he says, pursing his lips in a failed attempt to smile. "Do you need me to see you up to your apartment?"

"No, I'll be fine."

"Call me when you're ready to discuss your thesis."

Chapter Thirty-Nine

I'm Here, Sis

In the elevator up to my apartment, I glance at my watch. A little over half-past eight. I have time to do more research on the internet to find a substitute for parchment.

Conflict can be motivating. I'm wound up and I need to channel brain energy into something constructive. I march straight into the bedroom, toss my purse on to the bed, peel off my clothes and let them drop to the floor. Usually, I hang them on hooks in my closet. Tonight, I step over them and continue to the bathroom.

I turn the shower on a little warmer and a little gentler than usual. I close my eyes as the water falls on my head and flows down my body, its warmth soothing and sensuous. For a minute or so, I luxuriate in the soft caress of its liquid warmth and imagine the tension in my muscles and my mind seeping out of every pore in my body. Minutes later, I open my eyes like someone reborn. I could indulge myself longer. But ... I have work to do, and I heed the constant public message that California is in a perennial state of drought.

Ten minutes later, I step out of the shower and into my bath robe, and blow my hair with a dryer until it's almost dry. Mellow and rejuvenated. I change into my most comfortable nightgown, one I've owned for years. It's molded itself to the contours of my body and feels like a second skin.

I gather all the articles and books I have on illuminated manuscripts, dump them at the foot of the bed and climb in to join them. I turn on my laptop. On impulse, I open my email app. And send Arthur a message: "Can you come and keep me company tomorrow?"

I stare at the text, my finger poised to hit the send icon. The text is direct and clear. But it sounds like a plea. A pathetic plea. I plop my hand to my side. Will Arthur sense the plea behind this message?

Why bother him? He's busy and has his own life. And his new relationship with Jeffrey must claim his leisure hours as well. We see each other now less than we used to. I've never bothered my little brother with my problems, and I don't intend to do so now. I click the "Delete" key. But my inner voice shouts: *Stop.*

Never before has my inner voice sounded strident. You need a friend. Today. Now. Someone who would listen and care, and maybe help you understand what's going on with you. There's Mom, but she asked to be left alone until she contacts us. Arthur is your only friend. Apart from me, of course. And I'm telling you—send that message.

I retype the deleted letters, and without further thought, click "Send."

Arthur is unlikely to see my email tonight, but I'll be thankful if he shows up in the afternoon, or even in the evening.

I spend the next three hours in a more thorough study of the many elements involved in my thesis project. Conflict has been good for my productivity. I end up making definite decisions. Parchment is out and hanji is in. Hanji is a Korean paper made of mulberry bark that a website claims has origins traceable to the third century. Some extant historical documents using it had been written eight hundred years ago. It's stronger and more durable than rice paper, and it doesn't cost a fortune.

I go to bed in better spirits. Not only have I found a viable alternative to parchment, I've learned about binding a book, and dug deeper into the history of manuscripts. I have a few more things to research, but I've advanced. I know I'll complete my thesis art project by the end of the school year. At least, I'm determined to do so.

Snug in bed, all the lights off, my eyes closed, and counting old books marching into my mind's visual field, I chase sleep. But we're not always in total control of our brain. My mind wanders away from the parading books and hits the nebula of my delayed reaction to Nathan's feedback on my thesis proposal.

It's unlike you to wilt under professional criticism, my inner voice reminds me. You're mature enough not to take it personally. I protest. Maybe, I don't know myself as well as I thought. But I don't want to go there. Too much soul searching.

Thankfully, my body is tired enough that my mind eventually succumbs to sleep, though at way past midnight.

*****

Sunday morning, the buzzing of the doorbell jolts me out of a dream. A quick, blurry glance at the alarm clock on my nightstand tells me it's nearly a quarter to eleven in the morning. I jump out of bed. I'm up four hours later than usual, and Arthur must be here early.

I don't bother to look in the mirror to see how disheveled I must look. I don't put a robe on top of my short cotton night gown, either. That's how comfortable I've become in my brother's presence.

When I open the door, I'm surprised to see Arthur and Jeffrey. It's the first time I see the two of them together since Arthur told me about their intimate relationship.

"Come in," I say in a voice weak with the residues of sleep.

"Sexy," Jeffrey says.

"Shut up," I say.

"Why do you always hide under those loose black shirts hanging over your jeans?" Jeffrey is being too familiar. Is that what I can expect from his intimacy with my brother?

"Jeffrey, I just woke up. Go easy on me," I say, somewhat irked.

"Sorry. Why don't I make you some coffee?"

"Yes, please. Thank you. Arthur, can you help him please? Jeffrey might not know how to operate my Moka pot."

"How late did you stay up last night?" Arthur says.

"I don't know. Late. Didn't look at the time. I wasn't expecting you until this afternoon at the earliest."

"We've come to take you out for some fun. I know you've been working on your thesis proposal, so you must be stressed-out. And whatever happened to that thing you were doing with Nathan?"

I ignore his questions and insinuations, "Where are we going?"

"We'll drive to the coast. Stop when we feel like it. As often or as little as we like. Take in the fresh ocean air to clear our lungs. Our minds, too. Hopefully." He watches me with concern in his eyes. "Sis, what's going on?"

"I'll tell you later. I need a shower and some coffee before I can even think."

After showering and changing into fresh jeans, and a loose black shirt with long sleeves rolled up to my elbows, I join Arthur and Jeffrey at the kitchen counter for some coffee.

They glance at me, smile, but say nothing to me as I pour coffee into a cup they put out for me. They're talking to each other, not addressing me, but not completely ignoring me, either. I suspect they're waiting for me to get into a more sociable mood.

After a few sips of coffee, I say, "I'm hungry and it's past noon. We should have something to eat before driving to the coast"

"We're hungry, too," Arthur says. "But we don't want to eat with someone in a sour mood. Are you feeling better? Ready for a bit of fun?"

I am feeling better. I grin. "You know I am. Let's go before hunger makes me cranky again."

An hour later, after a quick lunch of hamburger and fish sandwiches at a fast-food restaurant, I'm hemmed in between Arthur and Jeffrey in the front seat of Jeffrey's car. We're driving north toward Petaluma. We've done the Golden Gate Bridge walk and strolled the main streets of Sausalito on a tour Arthur and I took when we first arrived. This time, we agree to go farther north towards Petaluma, and from there, to Highway One for a leisurely cruise along the coast.

Jeffrey slips a cassette into his radio. He says it's a playlist of songs he likes, both old and new.

To my relief, the music has replaced any need for conversation. I don't want to mar this coastal drive with talk about my problems.

The guys are both enjoying the music. They sing along with a few of the songs. Jeffrey has a nice voice and can hold a tune well, but Arthur is often a little out of tune. I can't imagine a more carefree afternoon than being with my brother and his lover. Before long, I find myself humming along with them, although I'm not too familiar with many of the songs on Jeffrey's playlist.

Arthur puts an arm around my shoulder and kisses my cheek. "Louder, Sis."

I sing louder.

We stop at various points on the coast, usually designated state parks where we find free parking. A few have walking paths that invite us for a stroll. The coastline on this stretch of California is spectacular. At certain vantage points, as you look out to the infinite ocean—sometimes a shimmering silver, sometimes a dark and impenetrable blue—you see a small peninsula farther south. Point Reyes national seashore, according to our map. We resolve to visit it sometime.

The beauty around us is enough to free my mind of bothersome thoughts. But the coast is too generous to leave it at that. The gentle ocean breezes of summer, waves swooshing against rocks, and seagulls hooting and flying overhead— soon, my body yields to them and lets go.

Before we know it, hours have passed. Arthur suggests going for oysters at one of the two or three restaurants we drove by.

I'm more cheerful and in a better frame of mind as we approach my apartment building that evening, Arthur tells Jeffrey to let us off at the entrance to the building. He's staying the night with me.

Unlike previous times, Jeffrey does not object. Arthur leans in front of me towards Jeffrey, and they kiss. I thank Jeffrey for a pleasant afternoon, kiss him on the cheek, and descend from the car after Arthur.

"Thank you for keeping me company this evening, little brother." I say as I slide my sandals off my feet and plop my body down on the couch.

"You looked like you could use it. I'm still here, ready to listen to your tales of woe. Have you made progress on your illuminated manuscript?"

I ignore Arthur's question. "I don't know why I'm exhausted. I don't think we walked more than a couple of miles on those trails."

"Why do I get the feeling you're evading my question? Remember your promise to answer when I ask you about your thesis."

"There's nothing to tell."

"But something is bothering you. I can see it and I can feel it. But you ... you don't want to face it."

He's right. Though I agonized over it, I asked him to come. No, I pleaded for him to come. I owe it to him to be more forthcoming.

Chapter Forty

The Reckoning

"Sis, you were there when I opened my heart, confessing to you about Jeffrey. Telling you that sad episode with Nathan. Admitting my unhappiness and resentment about Mom and Dad leaving me in the care of our grandparents. Give me a chance to reciprocate. I can see something is bothering you."

"A lot of things bother me. Big things and little things."

"Well, today, you're acting like you're the one who has an itch to scratch. A big itch."

I shrug and try to change the subject. "Have you heard from Dad lately?"

"He sends me regular emails, but all of them have to do with how I'm doing. How's school? What's the weather like? Oh, and he does ask when I'm coming home to visit. He misses me, he says."

"I've sent him emails. You know he's never answered any of them."

"I know. He blames you for my coming here to live near you."

"You knew."

"Remember, I grew up in his country. I know the mindset. He and grandpa are alike in so many ways."

"Are you going back to assume your predestined role when the time comes?"

"'Predestined?' Really? Are you being sarcastic? Anyway, I don't know. It's too far into the future to worry about. But if I do, I'll change a lot of things. And Dad will have to accept me for what I am."

"I'm impressed, Arthur. You have it all figured out."

He shrugs. "I'm studying to be a lawyer, and out in this bigger world, I'm learning about bargaining chips."

"I sent Dad an email recently about my progress at school, how I'm doing an illuminated manuscript."

"And he hasn't answered your email. Is that what's bothering you?"

"It is." I wanted to add "but that's not all," but I don't. And it's at this moment that I experience a kind of epiphany. Some truth I'm struggling to accept. Truth that needs solitary reflection. That I hesitate to confront and won't talk to Arthur about. Not now.

Arthur says, "Is that your big itch? Dad ignoring your attempts to reconnect? Don't worry. He'll come around. I should have told you earlier. He asked me how you were. What you've been doing. Not in his last email, the one before."

Incredulous, I stare at Arthur. "Did he say anything else?"

"I'm afraid that was it. But that means he is thinking about you."

"Yes, I guess he is. Well, then, I'll keep up my emails to him, wear him down until he answers."

"Don't talk too much about your illuminated manuscript. Dad is an intelligent, astute man, but he's ignorant about art. To him, art is either a painting or a sculpture you use to fill up space because you can't stand to see it bare. Your kind of art is alien to him."

A little miffed, I say, "Well, that's unfortunate. If he wants to know how I'm doing, he'll be hearing about illuminated manuscripts. I won't inundate him with it, though."

"The best news you could give him is that some guy, rich and handsome, has asked you to marry him," Arthur says, laughing.

"He can't be that old-fashioned. No, don't answer that. I know. I've already accused him once of being sexist."

"You didn't."

"I did. He got mad but apologized later for his temper."

"Good for him. He's not a hopeless case. I'm sure he'll answer your email one of these days."

Arthur fixes his gaze on me. "Have we scratched your itch enough, Sis?"

"I'll be okay."

Chapter Forty-One

August 2001

The Fog Is Lifting

I wake up at my usual hour to the darkness of my windowless bedroom. I welcome the dark on weekends when I can indulge in the luxury of falling back to sleep, recovering from the stress of the past week, and doing things on my schedule, my pace, and in my own way.

Today is not a weekend. It's Monday, but I'm still on vacation for two more weeks. My time is mine to use without worrying about pleasing anyone but myself. And yet, I'm restless. My room is more claustrophobic than usual. I crave the reassurance of a world outside my little room. A world bathed in light, awash in the clatter of everyday life., and suffused with the varied scented cuisines of my neighbors in the apartment building.

I sense a change from all the days that have gone by, a change triggered by Arthur's well-meaning intent to scratch my pestering itch. I sit up, yawn and stretch, climb out of bed, and drag my bare feet into the living area.

A thick blanket of fog greets me from the one window in my apartment. But if today is like the past August days we've had this year, the sun will soon assert its presence. Though much of California sweats out August, the Bay Area lives through cool, misty summers. It's worse in San Francisco where fog lingers till nightfall most summer days. Visitors to this area like to quote a line they attribute to Mark Twain: the coldest winter I've ever spent is a summer in San Francisco. But that attribution is doubtful.

I walk the three steps into my kitchen, twisting my hair into a bun on top of my head. I brew my wake-up coffee in the Moka pot, pour the strong coffee into a deep bowl and top it off with milk. My usual breakfast. On weekends and holidays, I treat myself to a piece of toast with melted cheese. But not this morning.

I sit on a stool at the kitchen counter, sipping café au lait. I have a year to work on my master's thesis art project. But it requires skills I have yet to learn—painting and writing on unfamiliar paper including fancy initial letters I have to decorate and gild, applying gold leaf to paintings, creating a cover and binding the manuscript. I have decided to use the Carolingian miniscule, a medieval script that, in this modern internet age, can be downloaded as a font. I found a few articles on it, including a YouTube demonstration on how to write it.

While I sip the rest of my coffee, I search the internet for journal articles or books on the process of creating illuminated manuscripts. An hour later, I've found a couple of books that I order online—one that covers manuscript production, from parchment making to binding, and the other on how to paint illuminations. Gold leaf apparently must be stuck on and burnished before colors can be applied. The books should arrive by the end of the week.

The fog has lifted and the sun casts filtered sunlight into the living area, inviting me for an invigorating stroll at the university campus. But I have neglected my café au lait and I'm still in my nightgown.

I reheat my bowl of coffee in the microwave, and while sipping the last drops, my landline rings.

I've given this phone number to exactly four people—Arthur, Mom, Dad, and Professor Fischl—but only Arthur calls me. He must have something more to say after our talk last night.

"Hello, Arthur," I say in a bright voice.

"Clarissa, it's Nathan. I got your number from Arthur. I hope you don't mind."

It takes me a couple of long breaths to answer. "No, not at all. How are you, Nathan?"

"As well as can be expected. I have some good news."

"What about?" I perk up. I'm starved for good news.

"The German church manuscripts"

"The ones Joe Junior stole."

"How would you like to go to that church to examine them?"

"You mean the originals, not facsimiles?" This time, I hold my breath.

"Yes, the originals."

"But how? I mean ... that kind of privilege is granted only to experts and a select few. Either way, you ask or apply for permission to see them, hold and smell them, open their pages, and be entranced by the illuminations." My incredulity is expanding every few seconds. And so is my imagination.

"Well, thanks to Kurt, you and I belong to the select few who can have a face-to-face audience with these manuscripts." I can almost hear the mirth in Nathan's voice. He's enjoying my reaction.

"But how ...?" I can't continue. Too excited for words and suppressing an urge to shout in delight.

"I called Kurt. He contacted the church official who manages the museum. The church might feel they owe him something for his work and the fact that they disregarded his advice not to pay to have the treasures repatriated. So, they granted him an expedited okay for the three of us. They've had protocols in place for people who examine these manuscripts, so all we need to tell them is when we can come."

"This is unbelievable. I have to hug myself, or I'll be flailing my arms around, dancing for joy. My living room isn't big enough for that."

This time, I hear Nathan laughing over the phone. "Are you ready to fly to Germany three days from now?"

"I'd fly right now if I had wings."

He laughs more heartily. "I'll call you when I have the flight details. I'll set up the appointment to see the manuscripts for Wednesday afternoon. Kurt might be there, too."

"I can't wait. And Nathan, I don't know how to thank you. And Kurt, of course."

After that most unexpected call—an exhilarating one, in fact—I gulp the rest of my coffee drink and change into jeans and t-shirt. I must rush into open air and sunshine to celebrate my good luck.

Before I go out, I pick up the unicorn standing on the living-area chair. It has taken up residence there since I tossed it carelessly nearly a year ago. I kiss its horn and its mouth, and marvel at how a five-minute phone call has changed my mood and my day.

Chapter Forty-Two

The Golden Manuscripts: An Audience #1

Kurt is at the Berlin airport when we arrive via an overnight flight. He has visited the church several times. But this is his first chance to see the treasures that he devoted many months, much legwork, endless hours of poring over archives, persistence and frustration to search for and recover.

His coming is welcome. Navigating this unfamiliar town will be easier, and because the church knows him, they may not bother with certain protocols. Asking us for passports to prove our identities, for instance. And to be truthful, I've dreaded seeing Nathan, and Kurt's easy, engaging demeanor will alleviate my discomfort in refusing to deal with Nathan's critique of my thesis proposal. Kurt never ran out of interesting facts and anecdotes to share, or quirky stories to make us laugh.

He leads us to a Volkswagen bug he has rented for this trip. He stares at me a moment and grins. "You're looking good, Clarissa."

I've exchanged denim jeans, loose shirt, and sneakers for black creaseless polyester pants, purple short-sleeved shirt tucked into my pants, and leather flats. I thought a less casual outfit more appropriate for a meeting with medieval treasures.

I smile and say "I would like to doze off a bit." And without waiting for either to answer, I climb into the back seat. Long flights leave me with a disorienting illusion of swaying that gets worse with a subsequent car or train ride. I'm hoping closing my eyes and sliding into partial oblivion would restore my equilibrium. I want to be at my best getting to know the manuscripts as well as I could in the few hours we're together.

Four hours later, I wake up to Kurt's voice. "We're here. You okay back there, Clarissa?"

"Okay," I say, shaking the cobwebs out of my head as he drives more slowly through the town. My sporadic slumber has revived me enough to listen to Kurt's brief incredible history lesson. The town, designated a World Heritage site in the mid-1990s, is about a thousand years old, with a royal pedigree conferred on it by the first Saxon king and his heirs, and the royal abbesses who lived in an abbey attached to the church. These abbesses, starting with the widow of the Saxon king, ruled the town for two centuries. How cool, I think, to have women ruling a town for all that time.

Spared from the extensive bombing that leveled big German cities during the second world war, the town has also, unfortunately, acquired infamy: the "castle" on its famed hill—a church, in fact—had been a Nazi hangout. One proudly proclaimed to the world by the Nazi eagle and swastika glued outside the church's clerestory.

A well-preserved medieval town of cobblestone streets and half-timbered buildings a few short miles from the Harz mountain range, it's one of those towns tourists tag "charming and quaint." But, the inner me retorts, adding, *tainted by its past pro-Nazi sentiments.*

The timbered buildings remind me a little of the Grand Ile in Strasbourg, a city of blended French and German culture. But this town's structures pale against Strasbourg's much grander gothic cathedral. The Grand Ile was also declared a World Heritage site.

Kurt doesn't take us on a tour of the town. He's pressed for time. He's scheduled to meet friends and relatives in Munich in the evening and must leave as soon as our museum visit is over.

He parks the car in a designated lot, and we go for a quick lunch at a restaurant where he's eaten once or twice. He orders a flammkuchen for the three of us. An Alsatian style pizza— tarte flambée to the French—I've had it in Strasbourg. Its thin crust is topped with fromage blanc, lots of caramelized onions, and bacon. Kurt tucks into it with gusto. Nathan finishes three pieces while casting quick glances at me. I force mouthfuls of a piece into my gullet, still off-kilter, maybe from my disrupted routines of sleep and mealtime, as much as my excitement from our forthcoming meeting with the manuscripts.

After lunch, we hike on cobblestone alleys to the church's hillside location. The climb up the hill is steep and protected with a three-foot stone wall wherever it strays to the edge of the hill, down a cliff. On the way, Kurt tells us the church, like the town, has a long and illustrious imperial past. It was founded in the tenth century by the widow of the Saxon king, Henry, who had been the first king of East Francia, a state that had ties to Charlemagne.

This piece of information is nearly as exciting to me as discovering a year ago that this German church had reported the loss of the manuscripts we've been trailing. I've found the one missing piece of the puzzle I needed to situate the older manuscript in the Carolingian renaissance.

We've reached the top of the hill, and at some distance from the church, I can see it spreads across much of the hill's plateau. Sadly though, Kurt says, the hill has been eroding. So soon after recovering its looted treasures and undergoing renovations to safeguard them—installing secure, light-modulated display cases, and climate and humidity controls—the German Cultural Foundation has been forced to focus on a funding campaign. They need to be ready for the future when the church would require reconstruction because of its age and the erosion problem.

Kurt leads us a few steps, to a curvy, gently rising path. More cobblestones, of course. "It'll take us directly to the abbey and its museum," he says.

My foot slides off a shiny stone, but I manage to keep my balance. Cobblestones burrow in place a long, long time, but they're not easy to walk on.

I look up at the building, its lower section hidden behind trees growing on the cliff. I can see its semicircular arched windows on what I presume is the church's clerestory. "It's Romanesque," I say.

"Hmmm," is all the response my companions humor me with.

I learned little about architecture from art history classes. But I remember that semicircular arches in doors, windows and ceilings, and massive walls and columns to support stone rooves, distinguish Romanesque from the subsequent Gothic style. Sensitive to the power of light even then, the English and the French innovated with pointed arches and ribbed vault ceilings, as well as flying buttresses, to build taller buildings and thinner walls pierceable for more windows. Medieval Christians glorified light before the impressionists mined it for ways to revolutionize art. The famous Cathédrale Notre-Dame de Paris is in the gothic style.

By the time we reach the massive arched door to the church, I wish I had eaten more flammkuchen. I'm warm and my gut gurgles. Kurt is panting a little, but Nathan appears not to have broken more sweat than is usual on a breezy summer walk.

I scan the old wooden door, searching for a human-sized entryway built into the massive one. It's not uncommon in ancient churches. Before I see it, Kurt has pushed it open, and gestures for me to enter. He and Nathan walk in after me.

The interior of the church is plain—austere, in fact—unembellished with sculptural reliefs and wall paintings. Entering a church never fails to hush people up. None of us utters a single word as Nathan and I follow Kurt through a narrow hallway north of the choir to a room, its door open.

The room is an office, with a desk, a printer, a bookshelf and a few filing cabinets. An attractive blonde woman of about fifty, seated behind the desk, smiles and gets up to greet us.

Kurt goes through the requisite introductions. Ms. Brühl shakes my hand, and then Nathan's. She shakes Kurt's hand, too, with a reserve I wouldn't have expected. Kurt has known her for at least five years.

Although a soupçon of a smile lingers on her lips, she doesn't bother with pleasantries. She says, "Welcome. I'll take you to the conference room, where you can examine the manuscripts in comfort and quiet. It's yours for the rest of the afternoon. The pages are rather fragile, as you might expect, so we're furnishing you with gloves. Made of silk, by the way. Keep them as souvenirs. Come, the manuscripts are waiting for you."

Kurt says, "I'll take them to the conference room."

"Fine. But maybe you should show them the other treasures first. The museum space is on the way to the conference room. I will see you there." Chin up, she marches away.

More than fifty treasures are on display in the church museum, a few steps up from the chancel. The treasures Joe Junior stole are here, displayed in separate glassed-in cases: the ivory comb, the reliquary box, and the small crystal and gold containers of fragments of fabric, bones, hair, and teeth. I recognize them from the pictures Nathan and I saw at the art dealer in Switzerland. I see an empty rectangular case, maybe the home of the illuminated manuscripts. Except for the comb, I'm somewhat disappointed. Maybe I'm too impatient to commune with the manuscripts. I imagine them laid out on the conference table, waiting.

I walk over to Kurt who's looking at objects in another display case. "Kurt ..." A muffled echo bounces off the walls of the cave-like space.

He turns his head. "Yes, Clarissa," he answers, a tad above a whisper.

I tone my voice down to match his. "Do you mind showing me where the conference room is?"

"Are you done looking at this exhibit?"

"I went through them quickly. I'm here mainly for the manuscripts and I'm afraid I may not have enough time to examine them. We only have three hours left."

"Okay, let's ask if Nathan wants to come now, too."

We approach Nathan who is peering into another reliquary box, decorated with carved leaves and flowers and encrusted with stones.

Kurt says, "I'm taking Clarissa to the conference room. Would you like to stay here a little longer? I can come back for you."

"I'll come with you. These treasures are interesting, but we came for the manuscripts."

Chapter Forty-Three

The Golden Manuscripts: An Audience #2

The conference room is on the other side of the chancel. We go through the ambulatory behind the altar to reach it.

Ms. Brühl is waiting in the room, seated at the table, reading a magazine. A ledger is on the table in front of her. She has laid the manuscripts on opposite ends of the long table.

She closes the magazine, rises and stands behind the chairs. "Maybe you already know something about these manuscripts, but I can tell you more about them, if you like."

Kurt says, "We're fine for now, Ms. Brühl. We'll come to you if we have questions."

"Fine," she says. She points to the manuscript to her left— "the tenth-century gospel," then, to her right—"the fifteenth-century psalter."

She opens the ledger to a page and flattens it. "But first, I need your signatures, the current date, an address, and the institution you work for. There are columns to indicate the reason you're examining the manuscripts, and how you learned of their existence, but they're optional. We'd appreciate it, of course, if you filled those out, too. "

While we sign the ledger, Ms. Brühl enlightens us a little more about the manuscripts. "The tenth century Gospel, as well as a few of the treasures in the exhibit—notably the spectacular ivory comb—have been endowed to the church by the heirs of King Henry, the first Saxon king. We're not as certain about the fifteenth-century Psalter which was produced during the early Hapsburg years. The church has owned and safeguarded these treasures for centuries, about a thousand years for the oldest ones. We had to hide them during the last world war. But some of the most precious treasures were lost for about half a century."

She's clearly proud of these treasures and the honor and distinction of their having been gifted to the church by imperial families. She's also being a bit too delicate in omitting the fact that an American soldier had stolen them and kept them for that half century.

As she exits the conference room, she says, wiggling a hand, "Remember ... the gloves."

Minutes later, I'm perusing the psalter while Nathan and Kurt are at the opposite end, engrossed with the gospel. It's our first time to come in direct contact with illuminated manuscripts. We know the content of these manuscripts only to the extent that we know the gospels and the psalter. For me, that's not much. Neither Mom nor Dad participated in religious rituals, though they were both baptized Catholics.

None of us three examining the manuscripts can read medieval scripts, though Nathan and Kurt seem to know some Latin.

We've all brought cameras to take pictures of the illuminated pages. I photograph every page of the psalter, including the colophon at the end of the manuscript that states when and where it was produced.

The gospel has four illuminations only, one of each of the gospel writers, the evangelists Mark, Matthew, Luke and John. Each illumination marks the beginning of the version of the gospel according to that writer. Apart from gilding on the illustrations, the text pages shine from the gold ink the scribe used, proclaiming the wealth and importance of the personage who has commissioned this gospel. It's also inscribed on vellum, the highest quality parchment. Apart from some browning of the vellum, the manuscript is intact and free of tears or fraying. It must have helped that it has had only one owner, and Joe Junior must have taken reasonably good care of it.

In so far as content is concerned, the fifteenth-century reproduction of *The Utrecht Psalter* is faithful to the original. However, the ink illustrations of lively figures—sketches as in the original—are larger, outlined in black ink, and embellished with pure watercolors.

Two things make this reproduction different: The text is printed, not handwritten, on parchment. Gilding is applied to large, decorated beginning letters of the psalms and on illustrations of vines and flowers at the bottom of the page. Psalms are rubricated; that is, their headings are inscribed in red—rubric is the Latin word for red.

Technically, this psalter is not a manuscript, but it's still one of a kind. Artists must have worked on gilding letters and illustrations, after the text was printed. Possibly among the earliest printed versions of the psalter, the colophon shows it was produced in 1462 in a German scriptorium.

It's past five in the afternoon when we leave the church and descend back to the town. Kurt proceeds to the parking lot for his rental car. Nathan and I check in to a small bed and breakfast inn Kurt has recommended. We're flying home the following day.

Nathan and I agree to meet back in the common living room at half-past seven, and walk to one of the nearby restaurants for dinner.

The light is still bright, and the weather warm and windy, when we venture out to find a restaurant. We're too tired from a long day and not enough sleep to search far or linger over dinner. The place we choose offers outside seating, fast service, and standard German fare. We go al fresco and order bratwurst and sauerkraut. Nathan takes his order with beer and I ask for freshly-squeezed carrot juice.

The tension between us has evaporated into a sense of easy togetherness much like the time Nathan came to give me a stuffed unicorn and plane tickets to London. How could it not after sharing extraordinary experiences in a new place? Who could forget handling and studying manuscripts that spoke to us from across hundreds of years? We're aware it's a once-in-a-lifetime experience we'll both treasure. A gift for a privileged few. We'll talk about it for a long time—a conversation that begins as we eat.

Nathan says, "What was it like, touching these manuscripts, turning their pages, gazing for as long as you liked at the illuminations, even smelling them?"

"Nothing like I've experienced before. One of my most memorable experiences looking at artworks was seeing

Edouard Manet's two wall-sized paintings on the same day at the d'Orsay."

"*Dejeuner sur l'herbe* and *Olympia*, you mean."

"I stood in front of each one for nearly an hour. I'm sure part of it had to do with knowing how they started a revolution in art and ushered in the modern period. You can't help regarding them with some reverence. But I also felt like I was drawn into the painting, that I was really there, part of the whole tableau.

"I was also in awe of these manuscripts and regarded them with reverence. But it was more like confronting royalty. You're outside looking in, grateful to them for granting you the rare privilege of a private audience. Maybe the reverence also comes from their being so old, as well as their narrative content being inaccessible to me. The illustrations are vivid and beautiful, but I can't get it out of my head that they're religious. I'm not free to imbue it with a personal meaning. All the while, I'm also wandering if my handling the manuscripts might damage them somehow. They're so fragile and ancient. And mysterious."

"But you said earlier that they meant a lot to you."

"I did, because I perceived them as ancestors of picture books. I continue to regard them that way, but really, they transcend personal meanings. They continue to have something to teach us—the images of a period forever gone, the colors and techniques they used, if not their content."

"Did seeing the psalter give you ideas on how to do your thesis project?'

"Yes, as a matter of fact. It freed me. You were right. Artists and scribes of medieval manuscripts felt free to revise and add. Adapt to the times. Be whimsical even. *The Utrecht*

Psalter doesn't have colorful vines and flowers at the bottom of the page. This one does and it uses red ink for the psalm titles. Those are techniques that we can apply regardless of content."

"Oh, Clarissa, that's wonderful." Nathan gazes at me with a look I've seen before. A muted intensity I've ignored or turned away from. This time I meet his gaze.

A half hour later, he sees me to the door of my room at the inn, I turn around to face him after I've unlocked it.

"Thank you for this day. For everything you've done for me this past year."

"I'm your friend, Clarissa. I've been your friend since Paris. I'll be here for you for as long as you want me to be."

I don't answer. I pull his face down and press my lips to his.

Epilogue

Spring 2010

Life, in its infinite possibilities for realizing it, prevented or interfered with my intentions of spending most of my time with paints, brushes and the message of old manuscripts to preserve the union between words and images.

My deep dive into illuminated manuscripts started as a quest for a home, a concept I couldn't define. Art—or, more specifically, picture books—had been the only constant in my life while growing-up. Naturally, I tried to capitalize on it to find a place I can call home. That is, until Nathan taught me passion has meanings beyond art, passions that might outweigh the need to define a home. And until my brother Arthur showed me that a family is what a home can be, and that family doesn't have to be in one permanent place, or always together.

These days, I only see Arthur on Thanksgiving, Christmas, and my birthday. He moved to Los Angeles three years ago where he's working to establish a law practice. And to my initial surprise, he has a girlfriend, an artist. He met Kayoko years after living unattached, a choice he made after he and Jeffrey parted the year before he went to law school. She's the reason he moved to Los Angeles.

My surprise at this new pairing lasted only until I met Kayoko. She came to San Francisco to exhibit at an art show and Arthur brought her over for dinner. She's a beautiful and talented Japanese American whose Zen-like presence can either intimidate or attract, as it has attracted Arthur. She charmed both Nathan and me. We watched Arthur closely. His devotion and caring for her was obvious. He has matured in ways I have yet to articulate. Nathan and I bet on them staying together a long time.

*****

The absorption and seemingly insatiable passion of our first years of marriage both hindered and helped Nathan and I finish writing our book after I submitted my thesis. The book made lists for a month or so. It still brings in modest royalties. Writing the book also convinced Nathan to unite his interests in science and art. He's gone back to the university part time to learn and do research in neuroaesthetics, a new field that studies the intersection between neurological processes and our response to art.

I intended to embark on another project when the book was finished. I wanted to adapt my thesis into a picture book for young readers about illuminated manuscripts. But three babies started coming every two years. And our days were gradually eaten up caring for a family. My thesis project, touted and exhibited by Professor Fischl as a unique, imaginative master's thesis, has been lying in hibernation for eight years.

That part of me as a mother has also left seeds of doubts in my mind that I could do what my mother had done for me. I wanted to be a mother like my own, inspiring a love of art in my children that could grow into a passion they would pursue. Or at least an interest keen enough for them to find meaning and pleasure in it. But encouraging them to do art in their free time and exposing them to all kinds of art in museums can only do so much. Their histories can never be like mine. They would never have to grapple with the question of what a home is. A question I was only able to answer in my mid-twenties.

The past years have left me little time for reflection. And acting on my plan to create a children's picture book on illuminated manuscripts has seemed like a far-fetched dream.

But dreams can come true. With help from someone who cares enough. A couple of weeks ago, Nathan came home, greeting me with a mischievous smile. He pulled me into his arms and whirled me around the room. He said he had a surprise for me. "I talked to the publisher of our book and pitched your children's picture book to him."

"You didn't."

"I did, and he was intrigued. He asked to see your illuminated manuscript. I know where you keep it, so I took it when you were in the shower and showed it to him the following day."

"And?"

"He wants to publish it."

*****

A few days ago, I met with the publisher in his office. I signed a contract to produce an illuminated book geared for children on the making of illuminated manuscripts. The books would be printed, but I also agreed to produce three manuscripts, their texts, illustrations and gilding to be done by my hand. Manuscript copies that he hoped would attract collectors and bring in more money. He promised to set aside funds for advertising them.

Before the publisher's offer to produce my book, I had already been devoting serious hours on art after our youngest,

Maddie, now four, began preschool. This year, we also decided to let the children stay for the after-school program. Nathan would pick them up on his way home from the university, so I could have more uninterrupted time in my studio.

My studio at the back of the house used to be a garage. A conversion that only required Nathan and me agreeing it would be a studio from that time on. It preserves the convenience of a garage door I can open with a remote control. Its main attraction is the natural light coming through the wall-to-wall door, left open for as long as I'm in the studio.

Privacy is usually not a problem. Houses on our block back up to a narrow street, built for residents to drive through to their garages. From this back street, the terrain drops into a shallow ravine and slopes up a hill to a row of bluish-green pine trees.

In my studio, I put on a stained but clean artist's smock hanging on a hook at the back of the easel. The smock, bought in my second year of college, has seen years of use. But to me, it's a talisman. One day, it would bring me unusual inspiration. And much-needed luck to produce a piece of art which the art world—when they see it—would say, "Oh, yes, that's an Issy Martinez."

No, I don't aspire to the wonder with which the art world exclaims, "That's a Matisse. That's a Manet, ... a Monet ... a Cezanne ... Van Gogh ... Rembrandt." I'll be content with fifteen minutes of fame in my lifetime.

To limber up for creating the illustrations my children's picture book would need, I've been drawing and painting small pictures, mostly of people going about their business. Writing or painting at their desk. Sitting and thinking. Eating. Walking. Buying supplies. Talking to another person.

I sit on a swivel chair in front of my easel. Behind the easel, a large rough-hewn table sags a little down the middle. Nathan built it for me half a year into our marriage. It took weekend work of several months, and though the table is clearly the work of a dabbler, he felt good building it. He was touched when he saw my eyes watering as he presented it to me: "An art table built especially for you." He had budgeted time and sweated a bucket on a table that marks this large room as a place of my own. A sanctuary where I can unleash my imagination and let it fly.

Today, I reach for a pad of drawing paper at one end of the table where I have piled reams of drawing and pastel papers and stretched canvases. Next to the papers and canvases are boxes and cans crammed with tubes of paints, pastels, pencils and charcoal sticks, brushes, rags, and bottles of medium and paint thinners. Remnants of my life as an art student. I make a mental note to look into shopping for a tall deep shelf for storing paper and canvas supports, as well as finished sketches. Someday, I might need room on the table to paint a large canvas.

Only a few papers in the pad are blank. The rest are filled with drawings, a few of them recent, but most are from my college days.

I choose a fat charcoal stick and from several swift strokes, emerge a sketchy portrait of Susie, our oldest. Wide-eyed, watching, and serious. Her arms are crossed, resting on her chest as if she's challenging her viewer. I rise and step a few paces back from the easel, scrutinizing the sketch. The physical likeness to Susie isn't strong. What I've captured is the expression she assumes when she thinks someone may be watching her surreptitiously.

Back to the easel again, I add shading with the side of the charcoal, some areas darker than others, until the expression on Susie's face becomes more pronounced. I step back once more and shake my head. It's a skillfully done sketch, a realistic portrait that would appeal to many people, but it does not satisfy me. Something is missing.

I swipe the next blank page over the finished sketch, pick up the chair, and a box of fat charcoal sticks. Positioning the chair at the entrance to the studio, I sit and sketch the landscape in front of me. I've done this many times before. Landscapes have never been my forte, but I have refined my craft well enough to produce landscapes and still life people like to buy. I had sold a few such pieces on an online art marketplace. Landscapes and still life would keep me from starving, if I were living on my own. Today, they help relieve my frustration when my people sketches fail me.

*****

You have talent, Professor Fischl said, when I submitted my master's thesis. He had not seen many of my artworks before. But what does it mean—talent? How much does it count towards the value of a piece of art? Nowadays, art is a commodity and its monetary value—the only value that seems to matter in our modern world—may owe less to its intrinsic qualities than what it will fetch in the art market. A well-known art critic may like your work and write about it, giving it exposure that translates into currency. An obsessed collector, who considers an art piece as investment, may pay a huge amount of money, particularly when an artwork's provenance is unquestionable.

I shake my head and scrunch my lids. I'm getting teary-eyed. Frustrated and angry at the same time. "What am I?" I say out loud. A mother, a wife. Not very good at the first, but a shining example at the second in Nathan's eye. And yes, I'm an artist, although I have hardly any outstanding artwork to show for it. Only that art project I submitted for my master's thesis.

Such was the extent of my short-lived, artistic fame. I wanted to be an artist, first and foremost. Before I was a wife. Before I was a mother. But life has not followed the pattern I envisioned when I first decided to go my own way. I don't regret the past years and all the detours I took from my imagined path. I have known moments of ecstasy, and moments of despair. My world has expanded, and with it, my concept of home. But doubts have never ceased to haunt me.

I'm a few years from forty, and I have achieved more than my mother, who wanted to be a practicing artist, but never managed to earn her degree. I thought that when she left my father at 46 years old, she would return to school. For whatever reason, she didn't. I don't think it was for lack of money. She was receiving generous alimony.

She did take up painting again, though she insisted it was "just a hobby," to fill her time when she's not helping her brother run the farm in Illinois. She does landscapes and on one of her yearly visits to us, she gifted me one of them. She's a better landscape painter than I have ever been, and I told her about online marketplaces for art where she can sell her work. Then, I helped her set up an account in one of those sites.

We do what we can. And we learn to accept what we achieve. I will struggle on until I've forged an enduring path for myself in the art world. For now, that path includes picture books.

That night, I bring up a suggestion Nathan made a few weeks before. I had rejected it then as unnecessary. I insisted I could cope well enough taking care of the house and the family and still have time to spend on my art. But I was wrong.

In the bathroom, Nathan has finished his shower and is drying himself with a thick white towel. "Are you going in?" he says. "I've warmed up the water for you."

"No, not tonight. I want to talk about your suggestion some time back about hiring someone once a week to help in the house."

"Are you finally agreeing we need one? I never expected you to be a superwoman, you know. You have this passion seething beneath the surface. You need time, time alone to nurture it. Express it. You have a lot of work to do on that children's picture book. So, get going, woman. Make your dream come true. The kids and I will thrive along with you."

I wind my arms around his waist. He's warm from his shower and smells of lavender soap. "How can you see so clearly into me? And how did I find a treasure like you?"

He tosses the towel into the laundry bin and returns my embrace. "You didn't find me. I found you."

"We found each other. What if I were to ask you to leave this place and find a home in another country?"

"If you had asked before we had kids, I wouldn't hesitate for a second."

"I know. Anyway, I wouldn't want to inflict my history on my children."

"When will you get it into your head that your home is in here?" He kisses my forehead. Then, he kisses my chest next to my heart, "and here, and not necessarily a place?"

The Golden Manuscripts

Author's Notes

Many individuals in this country feel they'll always be in the margins of the dominant society because they look different, and they grew up either in an alien or multicultural context. There are those like Clarissa who can't just pass herself off as either Asian or White. She's preoccupied with defining and asserting her individuality and place in the world (partly expressed in a search for home) as someone of mixed race through her passion for art, particularly picture books.

The story is inspired by a real World War II case on two illuminated manuscripts stolen by an American soldier. It becomes the vehicle for illustrating what's wrong with today's art world. Though I present this case as I imagined the incident happened, the narrative is factual on what was stolen—except for the second stolen manuscript which I change into a copy of *The Utrecht Psalter*—how the treasures were later returned, and how the family of the thief made several million dollars.

The case never attracted the same level of publicity as the theft of paintings from the Isabella Stewart Gardner Museum. We're much more familiar with Monet (maybe Manet too and his nudes) and Rembrandt than with *The Utrecht Psalter* or even *The Canterbury Tales*, also an illuminated manuscript.

One final note: in case you're wondering what Carolingian means, it's derived from the Latin version of Charlemagne—Carolus Magnus.

More Books by Evy Journey

Between Two Worlds

A series of six standalone tales about negotiating separate, sometimes clashing, realities

Set 1

A family saga.

Three tales of loss, love, second chances, and finding one's way.

Laced with a twist of mystery, the healing power of music, and international political intrigue.

Hello, My Love (Book 1)

A modern-day pastiche of Jane Austen's Pride and Prejudice with a twist of whodunit.

Hello, Agnieszka (Book 2)

A seventies story of love, betrayal, and the healing power of music.

Welcome Reluctant Stranger (Book 3)

Can she run away from a mysterious past in the Pacific Island she was forced to flee as a child?

Set 2

Three multicultural, multiracial women.
Their passion for cooking, travel, and art.
And their adventures navigating an unfamiliar, sometimes menacing world.

Sugar and Spice and All Those Lies (Book 4)

Chanterelles garnished with cream and mayhem.

The Shade Under the Mango Tree (Book 5)

Can she emerge unscathed from a world steeped in ancient culture and the ravages of a deadly history. An award-winning tale.

The Golden Manuscripts: A Novel (Book 6)

In her quest for stolen art, she discovers a passion and a home.

Margaret of the North

Can a Victorian feminist tame her man? A North and South sequel.

Brief Encounters with Solitary Souls

"Life is for each man a solitary cell whose walls are mirrors"—Eugene O'Neill

About The Author

Evy Journey is a writer, a wannabe artist, and a flâneuse. Her pretensions to being a flâneuse means she wishes she lives in Paris where people have perfected the art of aimless roaming.

She's a writer because existential angst continues to plague her despite such preoccupations having gone out of fashion. She takes occasional refuge by invoking the spirit of Jane Austen and spinning tales of multicultural characters finding their own way. Tales sometimes set in foreign locales into which she weaves mystery or intrigue.

In a previous life, fascinated by the psyche and armed with a Ph.D., she researched and shepherded the development of mental health programs. Now, she writes blogs and mostly happy fiction.

Author Site: I see, I listen, I think. Therefore, I write.
Evy Writes
Book review blog:
Escape Into Reality
Musings on art, travel, food:
Artsy Rambler